NO BEACH LIKE NANTUCKET

A SWEET ISLAND INN NOVEL (BOOK TWO)

GRACE PALMER

JOIN MY MAILING LIST!

Click the link below to join my mailing list and receive updates, freebies, release announcements, and more!

JOIN HERE:

https://readerlinks.com/l/1060002

ALSO BY GRACE PALMER

Sweet Island Inn

No Home Like Nantucket (Book 1)

No Beach Like Nantucket (Book 2)

No Wedding Like Nantucket (Book 3)

No Love Like Nantucket (Book 4)

Willow Beach Inn

Just South of Paradise (Book 1)

Just South of Perfect (Book 2)

Just South of Sunrise (Book 3)

NO BEACH LIKE NANTUCKET

SWEET ISLAND INN SERIES (BOOK TWO)

Mae Benson needs a fresh start. Can she find peace and happiness on the beaches of Nantucket?

Last summer, a storm blew Mae's life to bits.

It's been almost a year since that fateful day.

Since she learned that life at the beach isn't all sunshine and rainbows.

She and her children are doing their best to pick up the pieces.

While Mae is running the Sweet Island Inn,

Eliza is learning what it means to be a mother.

Sara is rediscovering her passion in the wake of heartbreak.

Holly is searching for stability in her marriage.

And Brent is—well, Brent isn't doing so great.

Despite these challenges, the Bensons just might make it—if they can stick together.

But right when it seems like they're going to be okay, terrible news strikes.

A call from Aunt Toni changes everything.

And suddenly, Nantucket doesn't feel quite like home anymore.

Come book your stay at Nantucket's Sweet Island Inn—where the water is warm, the sun is shining, and everyone welcomes you like family—in this heartwarming, inspirational women's fiction beach read from author Grace Palmer.

PART I

ONE YEAR LATER

1

MAE

A warm Friday morning in April.

"More coffee?"

"That would be lovely, thank you." Dominic looked up at Mae and gave her a broad smile.

It had become a morning ritual between the two of them—sitting on the first-floor wraparound porch of the Sweet Island Inn and sharing the first cup of coffee of the day. Half the time, they didn't even say much of anything. Instead, they just sat there, soaking up the sunrise and each other's presence. The company was nice, as was the stillness, before the hustle and bustle of an innkeeper's never-ending work began.

It was strange to Mae to start her days so peacefully. After all, she'd spent most of her six decades on this earth hitting the ground running. Maybe this was a "growing older" thing. A new chapter of her life, so to speak. She still felt young at heart, but she couldn't deny that her knees and wrists tended to get a little cranky if she got them going too abruptly first thing in the morning. Slipping into the day, like going one toe at a time into the first ocean dip of spring, felt right.

Eventually, though, the time came when the rest of the inn's guests would start to stir and she'd have to get going. She always felt just the slightest pang of annoyance when she heard a noise from upstairs. She still loved running the inn, but she loved these quiet morning moments with Dominic, too.

"Is today the day?" Dominic asked with a wry grin as he took a sip of the fresh coffee she poured him.

She settled into the rocking chair next to his. "Perhaps tomorrow," she said with a teasing smile of her own.

That little exchange was a ritual, too. A running joke that had started some time ago and never really stopped. He'd asked her suddenly on one of their first mornings sharing coffee on the porch if today was the day she kicked him out of the inn. Just like she'd done on that first morning and every morning since, she had said, "Perhaps tomorrow." She didn't mean a word of it.

It was true that he'd been here for quite some time now. Nearly a year, actually. He'd extended his stay in Room 1 indefinitely. Mae was hardly upset about it. She liked his company, his politeness, how he knew when to ask a question or make a joke, and when to just smile and enjoy the sunshine or the snowfall.

"Can you believe it's been nearly a year?" she said suddenly.

He nodded slowly. "Time certainly passes with haste. More so, the older I get, despite my protests."

"What a year it has been," she murmured.

"That it has. That it has."

What had happened? So much and so little at the same time. Her old life had been irretrievably shattered by the tragic loss of her husband, but she had found a new and beautiful one inside of that, like a Russian nesting doll breaking open to reveal something equally as gorgeous within. The inn was a blessing she had never anticipated. She was newly a grandmother once more, and it gave her such pleasure to see Eliza blossoming into the motherhood that she knew her eldest daughter had given up hopes of long ago. There was happiness in so many places in her world.

There was a little corner of happiness seated with her on the porch just now. Dominic was a source of happiness in her life; there was no denying that. Theirs was a comfortable and pleasant friendship. She had come to rely on it whenever sadness reared its ugly head.

They heard a big yawn come from upstairs. It was a warm morning, so the Robinson couple in Room 4 must have opened their window to greet the dawn. "I should get hustling," Mae said with a tinge of sadness. Again, she felt that little irritation at having to spoil this nice, quiet moment. But such was her life and her duty to her guests. Once she was in the thick of her errands, she didn't mind. The hummingbird side of her personality that so loved flitting from task to task to task wouldn't ever leave her.

"And so begins another morning." Dominic smiled. "Time for me to go back to sleep then, I believe."

Mae chuckled at that. She knew that Dominic only got up so early for her sake. He worked late into the night six or seven days a week, tapping out the beautiful words of his novel into his laptop. So, once they'd shared their coffee, he went back to bed for a few hours before getting back up and beginning his day properly. Sara had made one or two sly comments about it. *"He wakes up that early just to hang out with you? Oooh lala!"* Mae had just swatted her youngest daughter with a dish towel and told her to hush.

They bid each other goodbye and went their separate ways. Mae went into the kitchen to pop her blueberry muffin mix into the oven in time to serve breakfast once the Robinsons came down and put a fresh pot of coffee on to brew.

The rest of the day went by in a hazy blur. A trip to the grocery store to restock the inn's pantry, a long overdue deep clean of the bathrooms in Rooms 3 and 6, and then hanging up some new pieces of art in the living room. It was a pair of paintings she'd purchased at Winter Stroll last Christmas and had been meaning to take care of ever since. She particularly liked one of them, a blurred watercolor of a Nantucket lighthouse. The color palette was soft and muted and the scene it depicted was a frigid beach in the dead of a harsh winter, but there was something indescribably beautiful about it anyway. If Nantucket could be pretty in the midst of a blizzard, then it could be pretty any time at all.

Before she knew it, the late afternoon rays were slanting through the kitchen window, and it was time for the other event on today's calendar. She'd been ignoring it all day long, trying not to expend too much mental energy on it. But now, here it was, up close and personal, and there was no avoiding it any longer.

One year since the accident aboard Henry's boat, *Pour Decisions*.

One year since everything had changed forever for the Benson family.

It had gone so fast. The year had been full of many moments both happy and sad.

But try as she might, she couldn't remember many of them off the top of her head. Only a few stood out: the return to Nantucket of her daughters, one by one, each for their own challenging reasons. The birth of her granddaughter. The inn, of course. The journey of her youngest son, which had been full of switchbacks and turnarounds. She hadn't spent much time looking backwards. Onwards and upwards, as the saying went. Mae was particularly good at keeping her eyes rooted on the future.

But today, a year to the day since the accident that took her husband, it was time to reflect. This night, at sunset, she and her children would be honoring Henry.

Mae took a deep breath. She felt tears brewing deep down inside, but it wasn't time for that yet. First, she would get ready. Then, she was going to meet her children at Henry's favorite beach and remember him.

2

HOLLY

Life had a funny way of coming full circle.

Seven months had passed in the blink of an eye. It was April now in Plymouth, Massachusetts. The winter had been brief but brutally cold, and only now was Holly beginning to feel like she could actually thaw out and resume life as she'd once known it. Or, more accurately, as she'd wished it had always been.

After last summer in Nantucket, she'd been on a high. Things were going to be different. Better. The way they were supposed to be. Pete was going to love her and her kids were going to listen to her and the whole world was going to fall into order around her.

For a little while, that had actually seemed plausible.

But not anymore. Now, it seemed like her control over her surroundings was fading away bit by bit. She was trying to grab after it, but like sand at the beach, there was just no way to keep it from slipping through her grasp.

Which wasn't to say that Pete didn't love her. He'd been extra careful since their quote-unquote trial separation to make sure he told her all his Pete Things. They'd implemented new rules in their relationship: ten kisses a day at a minimum, no going to sleep angry, and the first and last thing they said each day was, "I love you."

That was nice. For a while, that had worked, too.

But not anymore. Lately, the words felt hollow. The kisses felt emotionless. And while Holly wouldn't exactly say she was going to sleep angry, she also wouldn't say she was totally pleased when her head hit the pillow each night. She wasn't miserable, per se. Just a little unhappy. The kind of insidious, creeping unhappiness that had blossomed into an ugly flower of discontent last summer.

More than anything else, she was mostly worried that the whole debacle was going to happen again. And then again, and again, like a bad luck merry-go-round.

Not unlike the mess she was currently dealing with.

"Mrs. Goodwin?" came a serene, high-pitched voice from the other side of the secretary's desk. "Principal O'Shaughnessy will see you now."

Holly sighed, picked up her purse, and walked into the principal's office. The secretary, Marsha, gave her a sad smile as Holly passed. Marsha was a nice woman and had a son of her own in Grady's class. She and Holly volunteered at PTA events together sometimes. Holly didn't have the energy to return it.

Inside Principal O'Shaughnessy's office, she saw her son, Grady, fidgeting in a chair that was much too tall for him despite his recent growth spurt. He'd turned eight the month prior, and he was in the early stages of that transition from chubby little boy to the leanness of a tween. But whatever forces of nature were stretching him out had also conspired to unlock a hidden reservoir of god-awful behavior in him. The kiddo had been an absolute nightmare since January 1st, as if he'd decided that this year was going to test Holly's patience like never before.

Holly paused for a second and looked at him. He glanced up at her sheepishly, then back down. That was good. Any eight-year-old who wasn't at least a little bit scared of being sent to the principal's office and having his mother called in would probably need a psychological evaluation. He still respected her enough to fear her. That was a good thing, even if the rest of this ordeal was going to stink.

She looked back at him and tried to summon the appropriate seriousness. Principal O'Shaughnessy hadn't been too clear over the phone, saying he'd prefer to discuss the details in his office. Whatever Grady had done, it was fairly bad. Holly needed to be stern here.

But she wasn't sure which direction to go in, emotionally speaking.

Part of her was simply sad. Where had her angelic little boy gone? Grady had been such a happy baby, once upon a time. Happier than Alice, even. Happier than her sister Eliza's little girl, Winter, who was scarcely three months old but already had her mother's trademark seriousness in her gaze. Grady had loved cuddling with his momma, and he'd laughed like crazy when she tickled the insides of his thighs, and he'd slept through at least one night out of every two for the first six months of his life, which Holly knew was an absurdly rare blessing.

Now, though, that all seemed like a distant memory, and she half wondered if she'd just made it all up. This was the second time this year that Holly had been called down here to account for Grady's behavior. The first time, he'd pulled Cindy Mason's pigtails so hard she cried. She still didn't know what today's crime du jour was. She wasn't sure she wanted to know, either.

Holly hated this part of motherhood. All her fantasies while playing "House" during her own childhood had starred children who adored her, who wanted to bake cookies with her and let her read them bedtime stories before she tucked them in each and every night.

But Grady wanted none of that. He wanted to jump out of trees and throw mud pies at passing cars when it rained in the park. He despised bedtime stories, and if Holly pushed him on the nightly question of whether or not he had actually brushed his teeth—with toothpaste and everything—he threw fits that could bring the roof down. He delighted in mayhem and little boy filth, a kind of filth all its own. Holly found it harder and harder each day to communicate with him.

That all made her sad, in a deep and profound way that she knew she'd one day have to accept. He couldn't be her darling little boy forever.

But, as much as she sometimes wanted to throw herself melodramatically on her bed and sob about all of it, the truth was that, right here and now, she was actually having trouble stifling a giggle. Something about the way Grady was sitting—morosely swinging his feet back and forth in that chair that was much too big for him—seemed hilarious.

This was her little tornado, her little four-foot-eight inch nightmare on wheels? This was the cause of sleepless nights and restless days? When life was up close in your face all the time, she realized, stuff just got thrown out of proportion.

Holly took a deep breath, stifled both her laughter and her sadness, and turned to look at Thomas behind his desk.

"Good afternoon, Principal O'Shaughnessy," she said gravely, inclining her head in greeting. She turned back to Grady. "Grady, do you want to tell me what I'm doing here?"

Good start, she congratulated herself. She was mad, make no mistake about it, but she also knew that she had a role to play here. So, even if she didn't exactly feel the way she was acting, she had to keep it up anyway. For Grady's sake, if nothing else. Pulling pigtails today turned into stealing cars and dealing drugs a few years down the line. She needed to nip this in the bud, like a good mother should. She fixed him with her sternest Momma Bear glare, crossed her arms, and waited for him to respond.

"I'm—I'm sorry—it wasn't my fault—it was Danny, he—"

"Grady Carl Goodwin!" she interrupted. "Tell me the truth right now. Lying or blaming others is not going to help you." Out of the corner of her eye, she saw the principal steeple his fingers together and watch mother and son act out their respective parts over the rim of his eyeglasses.

Grady's head fell and he gnawed at his bottom lip. That was his telltale giveaway. The lip preceded tears, ten times out of ten. Holly felt a pang in her chest. She wanted to sweep him up and hold him tight, tell him everything was going to be okay.

But she couldn't, not yet. She had a role to play first.

"I'm sorry," he whimpered, this time in a soft, sad voice that wrenched her heart out of place. "I shouldn't have put glue in Sally Bryant's hair. It wasn't nice of me."

It took every ounce of willpower for Holly not to burst out laughing. As exhausting as the last three or four months had been since Grady's behavior had taken a turn for the worse, this was an unforeseen development. He put glue in a little girl's hair?

She managed to squelch the laughter as she sighed, rubbed her temples, and took a seat in the other chair in the office. *This is important,* she counseled herself. *Remember Kathy Swanson's kid, Jeremy? He used to color on the walls with permanent marker, and now he's tending bar at a strip club in Southie. Nip this in the bud before it's too late.*

"If I may ..." Principal O'Shaughnessy began. He arched an eyebrow at Holly as if to ask for her permission. She glared at Grady once more, then nodded and let him continue. "Young Mr. Goodwin here has been on a bad run, shall we call it?" he said.

Holly did her best not to roll her eyes. The principal, Thomas, was a reasonably good guy. He was married to Holly's dentist, so she and his wife chitchatted about school stuff every now and then when she went in for cleanings. But he was an insufferably long-winded speaker. Holly could swear that he lapsed into a nonsensical British accent from time to time, though he was born and raised in Plymouth, as far as Holly knew.

"That seems like a fair way to describe things," Holly replied.

"He and I have spoken at length about this, and I'm sure you'd like to do the same. But, if you don't mind, I'd like to let you do that at your leisure at home, and instead take this time for you and me to talk, Mrs. Goodwin. Is that suitable for you?"

Holly nodded. She looked at Grady. "Go. Wait for me outside. Do not even think about moving from that waiting room, am I understood?"

Grady nodded back, bottom lip still trembling. She could tell that he was fighting tears. It hurt her heart. He slid from the seat, dropped down to his feet, and pushed through the door.

They both watched him go. When it clicked shut, she looked back to Thomas.

"It's been a tough semester for him," Holly began. Her stern Mom face had left with Grady, and in its place was the mask of sheer exhaustion. Life had come full circle indeed. Returning from Nantucket in September, she'd felt alive in a way she hadn't felt for a long time. But that energy, like Grady's baby giggles, seemed like nothing more than a distant and possibly invented memory.

"That it has," Thomas agreed.

"It's just that his dad has been working a lot, and Grady's going through kind of a stage or whatever where it's been hard to get through to him, and Alice is well, I don't even know, she's doing her own thing, like opposite but equal, and it's just that—"

Thomas held up a hand. "I understand, Mrs. Goodwin."

"It's Holly, please."

"If I may, it appears to me as a long-standing professional in the educational field that what Grady needs is a firm hand at the reins, so to speak. He needs a father figure. A mother is good for love and care, but a father must set the lines to be followed."

Holly had to bite her lip to stop from saying something rude. Thomas had just crossed the line from windbag to jerk. How dare he? She was every bit as capable of being as "firm a hand at the reins" as Pete was. Being a woman had not a thing to do with that. She wanted very much to be insulted.

But there was also the fact that, all stereotypical concepts of gender roles aside, Holly herself just wasn't that good at being an authority figure. Her thoughts since stepping into the principal's office confirmed that, didn't they? It had nothing to do with being a woman or a man or a mother or a father. It had to do with the fact that Holly herself wanted unconditional love from her kids and she wanted to love them unconditionally in return, and she had an awfully hard time doing anything but that.

So, as she wrestled with those thoughts in her head, she just nodded curtly to Thomas. It was all the cueing he needed to launch into a long spiel about the importance of the father in the home, and how a young boy is wild at heart but needs strict boundaries, and blah blah blah. *Whatever,* Holly thought. *Let the man babble.* Her own train of thought was taking her far away from this cramped, overly colorful principal's office.

Truth be told, she was thinking about Pete. She didn't want to lose him again. She'd lost him once before, or had come very, very near to it, and the thought of going through that roller coaster of emotions a second time filled her stomach with acid. She wondered what he was doing right now. He was probably in his cubicle at the firm's office, hunched over a laptop and churning through case files on some horribly boring corporate merger or debt issuance. She wondered if he was thinking about her.

More than likely, he wasn't. He was a one-track kind of guy, her Petey. Never much good at multitasking. She loved that about him. Well, mostly. It was cute to see him utterly engaged in something, even if it was something as simple as a crossword puzzle. When he used to bathe Grady and Alice during their bedtime routines, he was so careful and thorough about it. He'd shampoo and rinse out their hair with careful, thorough hands, and wrap a careful, thorough towel around them, making sure not to spill a drop of water on the bathroom tile. She used to sit on the bathroom counter and just watch him do it, scared to say a word in case it broke his concentration.

Pete hadn't handled the bedtime routine himself in over a year now.

"Holly?"

She glanced up at Thomas. Apparently, he was done. She nodded again, said, "You're one hundred percent right. I'll talk to Pete once we get home." That was a shot-in-the-dark reply because she sure as heck hadn't been listening to a word that this misogynistic, old-fashioned buffoon was lecturing about. But it did the trick, because he gave her a toothy smile—had he gotten veneers?—and walked her to the door.

Holly collected her miserable-looking son from the waiting room, and they went home.

3

ELIZA

As it turned out, motherhood was hard.

Not all of it, of course. Parts of it were downright blissful. Like, the question that Eliza asked herself each and every day: Would looking at her daughter ever get old?

If the last three months were any indication, then the answer was "definitely not." Eliza had spent God only knows how many hours since January just staring at her baby since the day she was born. Sleeping, eating, tummy time—Eliza could watch all of it over and over and over. It was like Winter was the first baby to ever be born. Since Eliza was the one who'd been blessed enough to deliver her into this world, it had become her responsibility just to gaze at her daughter around the clock.

It didn't hurt that Winter was beautiful—not just by her mother's standards, but by anyone and everyone's. Eliza had lost track of how many people stopped her on the sidewalks and streets of Nantucket to grab her by the arm and gush over how jaw-droppingly gorgeous her little girl was.

It was true. Winter was Gerber baby material. Diaper commercial material. A future pageant queen, runway model, an A-list celebrity. Who could deny it? Who could stop her? No one. Her daughter would conquer the world.

"My angel," Eliza murmured over and over in that sing-song mommy voice. She'd sworn she would never use it but had nevertheless busted it out the second she was given Winter to hold in the hospital on the day she was born.

As a matter of fact, Eliza had gone back on a lot of things she'd sworn she would never do. Motherhood thus far had been full of ironies like that. It was hard to wrap your head around things when it was just other moms telling you about their experience. "You won't sleep through the night for the first year"—*yeah, right, get real.* "You'll be so tired that you'd sell anything but the baby just to get a full night's rest"—*c'mon, that's a little melodramatic, don't you think?*

Wrong on both counts. Eliza was tired in a way that she didn't know was humanly possible. Every time she heard Winter crying in the middle of the night, she sat bolt upright in bed, heart racing a million miles an hour. It took a long time to unwind and go back to sleep after that. Especially when she knew that, in just a few hours, she'd have to do it all over again.

Thankfully, Winter was in an unusually good mood this morning. She'd only woken up twice last night, which was a new personal record.

Eliza walked over to Winter's crib and gazed adoringly down at her daughter. Sure, she didn't smile much, and she didn't giggle like Eliza's niece and nephew had done when they were Winter's age. But she was utterly beautiful, and she was *hers.*

Winter held her little fist towards to her mother and gave her a look. That was all she needed to say.

"Come here, baby," Eliza said to her, reaching into her crib and pulling her out. They walked out into the living room and took a seat on the couch across from Oliver.

Her daughter was cool to the touch in her arms. Eliza had asked the doctor about that. Actually, she'd asked the doctor about everything, arriving in his office for each appointment precisely on time, carrying yellow legal pads bearing line after line of questions written in neat cursive.

But he'd said it was nothing to worry about. "She runs cool, that's all. No biggie." That had been his reply. Eliza was of the opinion that medical advice shouldn't ever be couched under the phrasing of "No biggie," but Dr. Davidson, the best pediatrician on Nantucket, was infamously laid-back, much to Eliza's chagrin.

In some ways—though not many—Eliza found herself missing the buttoned-up professionalism of the life she'd left behind. On Wall Street, at Goldman Sachs, in the finance world, *everything* was "biggie." There were no small fish, no unimportant details. People did their job and they did it well or they didn't get a chance to do it anymore. They cared—way, way too much. Eliza had developed a hunger for caring about stuff. Not in an emotional way, though. God forbid anyone try to be vulnerable or have a heart while working in the business she'd once been in. But she'd cared in the way that alpha wolves care about the well-being of their pack. Ruthlessly but passionately.

Now, though, she was living in a "no biggie" world. Everyone on Nantucket might as well get that phrase tattooed on their forehead. Late delivery? No biggie. Missed reservation? No biggie. Anything and everything that went wrong was met with "no biggie" or something similar. It had been tough at first to let go of her frustrations, but she was getting better at it with each passing day.

That didn't mean she didn't bring some of her Wall Street attitude towards her new job at the Sweet Island Inn. She'd more or less taken over the business side of things: advertising, reservations, and so forth. Mae had been more than happy to let those tasks go. Same with Toni. They both recognized that Eliza had an aptitude for those affairs. And it was true—she did. Reservations were increasing, new systems were in place for garnering customer reviews, and so on and so forth. It pleased Eliza to have things humming along efficiently.

And when she came home at night, back to the little bungalow that she now shared with Oliver and Winter, things were humming along there as well. She looked over now, from where she sat on one end of the couch with Winter at her breast, to where Oliver was sitting on the other end. He was reading the newspaper, just like he did every morning—an old-school quirk that she loved in him.

"You know, all that stuff is online way before it gets printed and arrives on our doorstep," she teased, poking him with a bare foot.

He peered at her over the top edge of the paper with a faux-serious expression. "A citizen of the world reads the *New York Times* every day," he intoned.

"Yeah, an *old* citizen of the world, maybe."

He poked her back. He was wearing plaid pajama bottoms, the ones she'd gotten him for Christmas. "Bite me, Benson."

She chuckled. "Don't start with me today." Winter cooed in Eliza's arms, and she looked down.

"How's the little princess doing this morning?" Oliver asked.

Eliza tilted her head to get a better look at Winter's facial expression. "Stern, I'd say."

"Just like her momma."

Eliza glared playfully at her boyfriend. It was still weird calling him that. She wasn't sure why. High school girls had boyfriends. A woman of Eliza's age and stature had ... well, also boyfriends, she supposed. But there was a different feeling to it.

Boyfriend just sounded too impermanent. Since the night he'd spilled a beer on her in the bar—which he'd later admitted had been only ninety-five percent accidental—Oliver had been a fixture in her life. She couldn't remember a time when he wasn't there.

What she loved most about their life together was all the little stuff. It felt like she'd gone thirty-plus years without ever really taking the time to smell the roses. Oliver made her slow down. She wondered how much goodness she'd let pass her by when she wasn't paying attention.

There were so many good things ripe for the noticing. There was the smell of clean bedsheets mingling with the beach breeze whenever it was warm enough to crack open the window of the laundry room. There was the Nantucket sunset that she could see from her bedroom each night. The sight of her mother, bustling around the kitchen of the Sweet Island Inn with an apron tied around her waist and her hair frizzy from the heat of the cooking, happy as a clam, firmly in her element.

There was all that and a million things more that Eliza couldn't remember right now and didn't want to. If she was busy remembering all the things she'd loved recently, she wouldn't have enough brain space to recognize the things that she could be loving right this very second. Like how Oliver was trying to sneak his cold toes up the hem of Eliza's sweatpants to warm them up on her calf. And how cute he looked with bedhead. Like how their little home was always warm and smelled good and was filled up with laughter. She chose to focus on those things. She was learning to let go of the relentless thrum of ambition that she'd spent three decades attending to, along with the bitterness that accompanied the end of her tenure at Goldman Sachs. For the most part, she was pretty successful at it.

Life was good.

"What are your thoughts on the topic of pancakes?" Oliver asked, one eyebrow arched.

"Strongly in favor," Eliza said with a smile.

"I motion to commence pancake proceedings."

"Seconded."

"Let us put it to a general vote, then. Winter?"

The baby cooed, right on cue.

"Let it be so. Motion passed. Pancakes incoming." He stood up, folded the paper neatly and set it on the coffee table, then strode into the kitchen to get breakfast going. Eliza watched him go, with a permanent smile on her face. Her calf was cold where Oliver's toes had touched her. But, like everything else about her life on Nantucket, that too was no biggie.

4

HOLLY

The drive back to their house was silent. Grady, who lately thought it was hilarious to shout out the color of the vehicle every time he saw a punch buggy—and usually slug his sister in the shoulder while doing so—didn't utter a peep. Again, Holly had an almost overpowering motherly urge to reach over and touch his forehead, to reassure him. He hadn't cried—he was fighting it very hard—but he was awfully close to it.

She was just about to give into that urge when her phone rang. She glanced down at it in the cupholder. Pete's name was lighting up the screen, and his ringtone—"Mambo No. 5," for which he had a goofy little dance he'd concocted and surprised her with on their wedding night way back when—echoed tinnily.

"Hey," she answered.

"Bad news."

She sighed. "I really wish it wasn't. Grady got sent to the principal's office today."

"Sorry. Can't avoid this one. What'd he do?"

"Put glue in Sally Bryant's hair. They had to cut it out." She could tell Pete was holding the phone away from his mouth as he tried not to laugh audibly. She bit her lip. She wanted to laugh with him. Not necessarily about this and not necessarily right here and now—she wasn't *that* lax of a mom—but she just missed the feeling of laughing with Pete. When he really got going, he'd alternate between snorting and whistling through his front teeth. It always made her laugh that much harder. They'd fall all over each other laughing. Well, they used to. Not in a while, though. Not since ... when was the last time? Maybe when Grady got a bucket stuck on his head last fall while trying to goof off during yard-work chores. That had been priceless.

"What's your bad news?" she asked.

"The usual, unfortunately. Will be here for a while. I'm sorry, Hollz."

She let out a sad breath. She'd been hoping it was something else—a flat tire, a mustard stain on his favorite dress shirt. She'd been hoping he was just calling to bemoan the terrible—but really not so terrible —fate the world had inflicted on him, just to make her smile.

But no, it was actual, for-real bad news. He wasn't calling to make her smile. He was just calling to let her know.

"It's okay," she said, trying to mask her sadness. "When do you think you'll—"

"What? Yes, SMZ Inc. IPO paperwork is here. The Barclays forms are over there. They need it by seven p.m. Sorry, Hollz, someone just walked into my office. I gotta go. Everything okay on your end?"

"It's ... yeah, it's fine. I'll see you tonight."

"Love ya. I'll text you later."

"I love you."

Grady retreated to his room, sans Gameboy and television privileges, as soon as they got home. Holly busied herself packing everybody's lunches for the next day until Alice got dropped off after gymnastics practice by Mrs. Chandler, who had carpool duty on Fridays. She heard the Chandlers' minivan pull into the driveway, heard the doors slide open, then slam closed. Little footsteps pitter-pattered up to the front door.

She was hoping for a big hug and kiss from her little girl to take some of the edge off this miserable day. But Alice beelined for her room right away with scarcely a word, leaving a trail of four barrettes, three scrunchies, two bags, and one sad mother behind her.

Holly sighed and checked her phone. No text from Pete.

She went into their bedroom, ironed Pete's dress shirt and slacks for the next day, and took care of some other odds and ends around the house. Then, dinner time—pork tenderloin and green beans—which was eaten in silence. Pete's chair was conspicuously empty.

Still no text.

After dinner came bedtime showers and teeth brushing for both her kids and a story for Alice, who tolerated that much at least, thank goodness. They'd just embarked on the first installment of *Harry Potter* together. Holly wasn't much of a reader herself, nor was she particularly good at narrating. Pete, on the other hand, used to do different voices for all the characters. Sometimes he'd even get up and act out a scene, which never failed to make Alice giggle.

But Holly just read the words straight. Alice was asleep in five minutes flat. When she was snoring softly, Holly stood up and walked out of her room as quietly as possible, leaving the door cracked open just a sliver behind her so she could peek in on her daughter later.

When she got out to the kitchen and checked her phone where it was plugged into the charger ... still no text.

She sighed again and fell into the brown leather loveseat in the living room. She looked around for someone to talk to—literally anybody —and settled on a Frankenstein'd G.I. Joe/Barbie monstrosity that Grady had doctored. She held it up in front of her face.

"My husband loves me, right?" she asked. She knew she was being melodramatic, but she also knew that she wasn't being too overly ridiculous. There was real doubt there, back for the first time since last summer. Heck, maybe it had never left.

"Of course he does," she replied back to herself in a silly, husky voice. "He loves you very much. You're his Hollyday."

"So why does it feel like he doesn't?"

"You're just tired," said the action figure. "Go take a long bath, light candles, put a face mask on, have a little you time. The kids are asleep. Your husband isn't home. Treat yourself. You deserve twenty minutes of peace and quiet."

"That's a fantastic suggestion, G.I. Barbie."

She started to sit up, but then spied her phone still sitting on the marble kitchen countertop and decided to try calling Pete first. She didn't want to bother him too much at work—he didn't want to be there late either, she knew—but she had a burning desire to hear his voice. If she could just hear a couple little words, that would go a long way towards pushing back the tide of ugly thoughts brewing in her head. She found his number in her favorites, dialed, and waited.

But she didn't have to wait long at all, because it went straight to voice mail. She hung up and tried again. Same deal. Was his phone off? Dead? Busy? She wasn't sure.

Then another thought occurred to her. Surely, it was a crazy one. Surely, it was an unnecessary one.

But was there a chance that Pete wasn't telling her something?

He'd been the first one when they returned home from their Nantucket sojourn to suggest stricter limits on his working hours whenever possible. He'd only broken that agreement a handful of times throughout the fall and winter. But now that spring had sprung, it was happening more and more. Third time this week, eleventh or twelfth time in the last month. They were crumbling right back to where they'd started. And where they'd started was a bad place. Holly didn't want to go back. She couldn't handle that heartache again. If there was a risk of it happening, she needed to find out sooner rather than later.

Nip it in the bud.

Whether she truly believed that or whether she just desperately wanted a valid-sounding reason for her next action, she wasn't sure. Either way, the result was the same: she dialed the number for the firm's office.

An exhausted-sounding secretary answered on the first ring. "Zucker, Schultz, and—"

"Hi, Annette, this is Holly Goodwin." She bit her lip. Her voice had come out sounding far clingier and whinier than she'd intended.

"Oh hi, Mrs. Goodwin," Annette said, sounding surprised. "Is everything okay?"

"Yes. I was just wondering if you could put me through to my husband? His phone must be dead, because—"

"Your husband? I'm sorry, I'm a little confused. Pete left hours ago. Early today, actually. Maybe around four p.m.? I assumed you knew."

The blood drained from her face. "Oh yes, yes, of course," Holly stammered. "I just, uh, thought he might've gone back to, um, back to the office for his, his—his things. He must've—okay, thanks, bye." She hung up hurriedly even though she knew it was rude. Her heart was pounding in her chest so loud that she couldn't hear anything else. She felt faint. Like the walls were collapsing inward.

One question ran through her head over and over: Was Pete cheating on her?

5

MAE

"A year," said Eliza.

"A whole year," whispered Sara.

"I miss him."

That last one was Brent. No one looked at him, but Mae and Sara both put a gentle hand on his shoulder. He hadn't cried yet, and Mae doubted he was going to, but they all knew that Brent had perhaps been hit hardest of all by their father's loss.

"Well," Eliza said, clasping her hands together. "Let's get started."

The four of them were seated in a semicircle around a thick white candle they'd stuck in the sand. The sun was setting off in the distance, and the ocean was unusually calm, calm enough to reflect the oranges and purples of the evening like watercolors come to life.

Eliza struck a match and lit the candle. There was a slight breeze, but with their bodies blocking the worst of it, the flame only flickered and didn't go out. "Do you want to say something, Mom?" Eliza asked once the wick was going.

Mae thought about it. To be terribly honest, she didn't quite trust her voice right now. But she knew that, even if this was for her own grieving, it was also for her children's sakes. Henry had been her husband, and that was special, of course. But he had been a father to each of them, too. Those relationships were every bit as unique. So, even if she didn't particularly want to speak out loud to offer up a remembrance for her departed husband, she decided she would. For Brent. For Eliza. For Sara. For Holly, who was present via video chat on Sara's cell phone.

"I loved your father very much," she began hesitantly. "I ..."

She felt her kids' eyes on her. She hesitated. What was the right thing to say? No words were going to erase the grief that still snuck over her children's faces during idle moments. She knew that the sorrow left in Henry's wake would be with them forever. That much was obvious. But, if tonight was to be a night of remembering, perhaps it would be best to remember everything, all the way back in the very beginning of their family. Yes, that seemed like a good idea indeed.

"Well, maybe I should start with our story." She cleared her throat. "I was a shy girl in college. Still lots to learn about the world. My own mother and father had done a good job keeping me safe and protected from everything that's out there, but sooner or later, every man and woman has to face those things. So, when I went from our little farm in Tennessee to college at Boston University, it was my time to face 'em.

"I wasn't much for partying or for drinking like some of the other kids. But I got dragged out one night anyway. Rebecca Milton was the instigator. She loved to dance, that girl. She was interested in a Harvard fellow at the time, so off we went to a Harvard bar. This would've been about 1968, I believe. The very early days of disco. Not that this was a disco club. Anyway, I'm losing the thread ... where was I?"

"Harvard bar," Sara offered. "Rebecca Milton."

"Ah yes. So, we went to this bar, and Rebecca might've gotten me out of the dorms, but she sure as heck couldn't get me to talk to boys. Not even with a drink or two in me. But there was one boy there—one man, rather—who didn't mind my shyness. He was an ex-Marine, and Lord, he was handsome. Had that blond hair and that deep tan and he was so muscular! Why, you could've eaten caviar off those abs."

"Mom!" Holly squealed from her end of the video chat, half laughing and half mortified.

Mae blushed, but kept going. "Well, that was your father. He kept sending drink after drink my way, though I hadn't touched any of them and I refused to look up at him after that first guilty glance. Finally, he came over and asked how many drinks he'd have to buy before I talked to him. I asked him, *'How much money do you have in your wallet? Because I am awfully shy by nature.'* He seemed to think that was very funny.

"We got to talking. He was visiting his sister in town—your aunt Toni. Though, when I asked why he was at a Harvard bar in particular, he insisted that he'd come to make fun of the nerds. I laughed at that. *Hank* was how he introduced himself. Henry Benson. He was nice, your father was, and he was a talker. Goodness gracious, was he a talker! I could've listened to him for a long, long time. But Rebecca got upset because the boy she'd come to flirt with didn't seem much interested in her, so she made me leave a little sooner than I might have otherwise. *Pity*, I remember thinking. *Hank was a nice man. I would've liked to have spent a while longer talking to him.*

"But little did I know, that wasn't the last I'd see of him. I woke up that night to something hitting my dorm room window. Imagine how I laughed when I looked out and saw your father, standing in the quad two stories down! He had a pile of pebbles at his feet, but that wasn't what was making the noise. Apparently, he'd tried throwing pebbles at the window, but I hadn't woken up after the first two or three dozen. So he'd resorted to breaking off a few tree branches, tying them together with his belt and socks, and tapping on my window with this long contraption from thirty feet below! I laughed and laughed and laughed."

"Only Dad," Sara said, shaking her head and chuckling.

Mae nodded and continued. "Now, we weren't allowed to have boys in the dorm back then. So I went downstairs and we snuck out and went to an all-night coffee shop. I told him off for being so cheesy. And do you know what he told me? He said, '*Well, I made this for you, and I just couldn't rest until I'd made a proper gift of it.*' And then he showed me what he made—a flower whittled out of a block of wood. It was beautiful. I darn near tried to smell it, that's how lifelike it looked. You children know your father. He was gifted with his hands."

"I remember," murmured Eliza.

"We started going steady—very slowly, of course, because I was still a shy girl from Tennessee, and as nice as he was to me, I was still a little bit wary of this handsome Marine who'd seen the world and had such a smooth way about him. So, that's how things went for a while. Learning about each other and getting to like each other quite a bit.

"Eventually, he brought me back to Nantucket for a weekend, back to where he'd grown up, and he took me on a sunset sail one night. And do you know what happened on that sail?"

"Here it comes ..." Sara groaned.

"Be nice!" Holly interrupted. "This is my favorite part."

"We got stuck!" Mae yelped. "That darn fool got us stuck on a sandbar, miles away from help! Can you believe that? I thought we were gonna have to spend the night on that godforsaken boat, eating sardines out of the can. Oh, I was steaming mad. Didn't last long, though, because he said to me, '*I guess this is as good a time as any,*' and he dropped to one knee and pulled a diamond ring out of his pocket and asked me to be his wife. I couldn't be too mad after that now, could I?"

These memories were decades old, and yet, as Mae told the story, she could close her eyes and still see Henry kneeling on that sandbar, the sun lighting up his blue eyes, and that warm, mischievous smile, the one that could get a laugh out of her whenever he pleased, no matter how irate he'd made her. She could still see how the ring looked in the sunset. She could still remember the feeling of his embrace and his kiss after she'd said yes, she would spend the rest of her life with him.

Her heart throbbed.

It had been a struggle over the last year to honor Henry and yet keep living her own life at the same time. She couldn't very well put the world on hold to mourn him, even if that's all she wanted to do sometimes. She had to keep moving forward. But it was an awfully hard balance to strike. Some days were better than others.

Having her children around her, as they were now, was helpful. After all, there were pieces of him in each of them. It was like seeing broken shards of mirror reflecting a little of Henry's soul from different angles. In that way, he was still very much alive. In her. In them.

She looked around the circle and met each of her children's gazes.

Eliza was first. She had fled New York with her heart frozen in place by a bad relationship and a job that drained the soul out of her, even if she didn't know that's what it was doing. And look at her now—thawing in the warmth of the love she shared with her beautiful baby, and with Oliver, who seemed like such a good man.

After Eliza, she looked at Sara. She, too, had come running from the big city with pain in her wake. That restauranteur she'd been so smitten with, Gavin something-or-other, had been no good at all for her. Mae knew how easy it was for a young woman to fall in with a man like that. Sometimes, one had to succumb to a bad temptation in order to learn from it. Sara had certainly done that. It was still too soon to say that she had found her place in the world yet, but Mae felt confident that she was on her way. Her headstrong daughter just had to do things in her own time. Like Henry, not a soul on this planet could rush her or change her mind.

Then came Holly. Now, *there* was love. She and Pete had something special, the kind of fragile-seeming love that was in reality made of tougher stuff. The two of them had made it through good times and bad, and they'd become parents to two beautiful children of their own. Mae loved seeing Holly embrace motherhood. It had brought them closer together than ever before.

She saved Brent for last. When she looked at him, she saw the sadness that still cloaked his eyes. Henry's death had done a number on his soul. She knew there were still rivers of guilt in him. Enough to consume and blind him. Mae held his gaze longest. As she looked at his face, drawn tight with the effort not to cry, she tried to say with her own eyes what she'd told him so many times over the last year.

I love you. Your father loves you. And this world is filled with love for you, too. Sooner or later, you're bound to find it.

She believed that with all her heart. The question was ... did he?

6

BRENT

Brent stared at the fat white candle, sitting there stuck in the sand in the middle of their semicircle. He could swear he saw his last twelve months play out like a movie in the flickering flame.

He saw the day of The Accident, as he'd come to think of it. Waiting for Dad at the dock. Going out in the boat, catching that dead shark, then feeling bummed out. Parting ways angrily. The storm that came rolling in once he'd gone back to shore. The call from Roger, the marina owner, after Brent had grown sick of waiting for his father and returned home. *You need to get back here, right now. Something's happened.*

He saw his dad's gravestone. He had missed the funeral on purpose—he knew that had broken his mom's heart, but he just couldn't bring himself to be there. It was too much then. But he had gone back by himself at night a day or two later to sit in front of his father's final resting place and apologize.

He saw in the flame the downward spiral that had followed. Eleven months of sobriety, drowned suddenly and irrevocably in so much stinking booze. And the fighting he'd done—so much fighting.

Fighting with friends and strangers alike. Getting drunk and angry and beat-up and then passing out in his crummy apartment, only to wake up and do it all again.

He saw his own rock bottom—getting arrested by Sheriff Mike. Then the resurrection, the come-up. All those long days spent slaving over the guesthouse renovation at the inn. The pride on Mom's face at the big reveal. Finding his dog, Henrietta, rooting around hungrily in that dumpster. She was his only friend who could look at him without judgment in her eyes.

He saw Rose, and—*no*. He closed off his gaze to her. He didn't want to see Rose. Not at all.

He saw the months that had come after that. The final fight, the straw that broke the camel's back and landed him in jail. He'd avoided jail time, thanks to a sympathetic judge. Gotten off with just probation and lots of community service. He was lucky in that regard; he knew it. But he didn't feel very lucky at all.

And what had happened since that "stroke of luck"? Not much of anything, really. Mostly just the daily struggle of looking at alcohol and forcing himself to stay far away from it. Of trying to bury his emotions in work and failing. He'd been picking up odd handyman jobs based largely on the strength of his father's reputation. And though he did good work and kept his head down, it wasn't headed anywhere long-term. The other general contractors on the island had a kind of fragile, unspoken accord between them as to how customer territory should be carved up and business should be conducted. The intrusion of a rogue element like Brent didn't sit well with them, so they froze him out whenever possible. That made it hard to get steady work. So there were hours—way too many—that yawned wide open with nothing to fill them. During those times, he ran on the beach with Henrietta and he helped his mother at the inn and he tried not to think too much of the past.

After Mom finished her story about meeting Dad, Brent was the first to stand up to leave.

"Going so soon?" Eliza asked carefully as he dusted the sand from his hands.

"Yeah," Brent muttered. He eyed the ocean warily. It looked dark and foreboding. He didn't like being near the water anymore. Even when he ran with Henrietta, he stayed high up on the beach, in the soft sand at the foot of the dunes, though it slowed him down and made his calves ache after a few miles. Better to have sore legs than to wander too close to the waves.

"You sure, honey?" Mae asked. She had a lone tear hanging on for dear life at the corner of her eye.

"Yeah. Gotta take care of some stuff." That was a lie and they all knew it, but he stuck to it anyway, even if he felt the bloom of shame in his cheeks as soon as the words had left his mouth. "I'll be at the inn for dinner."

"Good," Sara said. "Lobster tonight. Don't be late."

"I won't." He turned and left before he had to say anything else. Holly waved goodbye from Sara's phone screen.

He took the long way driving back to his apartment. It was a warm day for April. That was a relief, after the harsh winter they'd had. The cold had come in suddenly and exhausted itself just as fast. Good riddance, as far as Brent was concerned. He'd never much liked the wintertime.

He got back to his place, mounted the stairs, and unlocked the door. Henrietta jumped at him as soon as he entered.

"Hey, girl," he cooed softly. He knelt and rubbed her ears as she lapped at his face. "I missed you too. Easy now, you're gonna knock me over."

She whined in response.

"Hungry already?" he said. "Let's see what we can rustle up." He got to his feet again and surveyed his apartment. It was small and cramped and ugly. Brent felt like that was a pretty good reflection of how he felt internally.

When he'd come home after the fight that landed him in jail, he'd poured all the beer and liquor out in the sink immediately. It took a little bit of his soul down the drain with him. Good riddance to that, too. But without alcohol, there wasn't much left in his kitchen. He walked over and pulled open the rusted door of the refrigerator. It groaned as it gave way to reveal a stick of butter, a gallon of milk flirting recklessly with its expiration date, and leftover steak in a Styrofoam takeout box. He grabbed the steak and the milk and set both on the counter. Turning to the pantry, he retrieved a box of stale cereal. He heated up the steak and made a bowl of cereal. Once the steak was hot, he sliced it up and put it into Henrietta's bowl. He took the cereal for himself.

"Dinnertime, girl," he said.

She came over and wolfed the steak down, then looked at him balefully the second it was gone.

"Yeah, yeah, yeah. Don't give me those eyes. I already gave you the steak instead of keeping it for myself. What, you want my cereal too?" He offered it towards her jokingly. She came over, took a sniff, and backed away. He chuckled. "Didn't think so."

He wound his way into what passed for a living room and sat down on the couch. Henrietta followed him and curled into a ball on the threadbare carpet at his feet. She started snoring immediately.

He ought to get out of this dump, he knew that. With money as tight as it was, he was having enough trouble coming up with the rent payment each month. But he had no desire to move back home to Howard Street. That place was chock-full of memories he didn't much feel like confronting. And besides, going back home was admitting defeat. He wasn't ready to give up yet. Soon, maybe. But not yet. Not now.

As he drank the last dregs of milk from his bowl, he thought suddenly about Rose. It was like she kicked down the door of his mind and demanded to be acknowledged.

"What do you want?" he asked out loud. He knew he sounded like a crazy person, conversing with his own thoughts. But his apartment was empty, so he figured it was all right for now, as long as Henrietta didn't tell anybody about him losing his mind.

Just wanted to say hi, said Imaginary Rose.

"I don't really wanna talk to you," he replied.

You oughta.

"Why's that?"

Because you're headed back the way you came. The way you were when you found me.

"Maybe. Maybe not."

Who're you kidding, Brent? Asked the ghost in his head. *Look around. Just 'cause you're not drinking doesn't mean you've conquered your demons.*

He looked around. Imaginary Rose had a point. Trading out the devil of his alcohol problems for the devil of depression wasn't an improvement. It just meant he'd removed the Band-Aid over the open wound and done nothing about the wound itself.

As to what should be done about that wound ... he wasn't quite sure. Eliza had mentioned therapy a few times in a roundabout way. He knew she didn't want to bring it up directly for fear of pissing him off. She also knew that he wasn't likely to take to the idea. She was right on both counts. Some PhD psycho-shrink wouldn't know him or his dad. So he didn't see what good it would do.

But what else was there? Drinking had worked for a little bit, but that was no longer on the menu. Going out on the water had been a mental salve once upon a time, but that was similarly scratched nowadays. Rose had broken his heart. He still had Marshall, his best friend since he could crawl, but Marshall had a business to run, a sick mother with Alzheimer's to care for, and a life to devote himself to. Brent had none of that. It had thrown a wedge between them, though neither man wanted to admit it. They were hanging out less and less often these days.

So without those things, what was he supposed to do about his problems? Heck, he barely even had a job anymore. All he had was time.

Way, way too much of it.

7

SARA

What on God's green earth was better than the first buttery, delicious bite of fresh Maine lobster? As far as Sara was concerned, not a dang thing. And she wasn't talking about just plain old fresh lobster, but rather the kind that you'd bought off the brother or uncle of a kid you went to high school with, or your old neighbor who had a few traps out that he checked on the weekend. Real *local* stuff. The kind of fresh lobster that came to you still dripping the saltwater of the ocean. The kind of fresh lobster that grew up near where you grew up. It was like there was a little Nantucket magic sprinkled on top of each bite. In all her months in New York, hunting for the best seafood that the Big Apple had to offer, Sara hadn't found anything as good as what her mother used to cook up once or twice a month for Benson family dinners.

Sara thought back on the family dinners of her childhood as she prepped that evening's meal in the kitchen of the Sweet Island Inn. Growing up, her mother and father had been adamant that dinnertime was family time. At least four nights a week, and usually five or six, the whole family sat down at the dining room table together and shared a meal. No cell phones, no laptops, no books, no

TV, no headphones allowed. Sara had a vivid memory of defiantly arriving at her seat with her Walkman headphones on blaring some music—she was pretty sure it was during her U2 fixation phase—and Mom snatching them right off her head. Rules were rules. Family dinners were sacred.

Back then, Sara had hated that, just like she'd hated pretty much all her mother's rules. But now, she could appreciate that there was a special kind of beauty in a bunch of people gathering to break bread and laugh with each other.

Did this mean she was getting old? Lord, she hoped not.

"How's it coming, hon?" Mom asked as she swooped into the kitchen. She was holding the huge plate they sometimes used to serve big meals on. It was a piece of pottery that Dad had gotten Mom as a gift one birthday long ago. The artwork on it was done in a million different shades of blue. It depicted a Nantucket beach at sunset, complete with a lighthouse, swimmers amongst the waves, houses lining the shore. Mom loved that plate more than life itself.

"Speak of the devil," Sara said with a smile. "I was just thinking about you. It's coming. We're on schedule. Fifteen, twenty minutes out, max."

Mom moved around the island and set the plate carefully on the dead center of the dining room table. She gave it one final polish with a dish towel before stepping back and smiling softly at it. When she was satisfied with the placement, she turned back to Sara. "Good thoughts, I hope?"

"Only the best for you, mother dearest."

"That's right. And don't you forget it." Mom smiled and swatted at Sara's bottom playfully with the dish towel.

"I was just thinking about family dinners. Remember how serious you were about those?"

"With good reason!" Mom crowed. "Dinnertime is family time. You kids don't even realize how important it is."

"I think I'm starting to. Maybe."

"Blossoming before our very eyes, aren't you, my little rose?" Mom tweaked Sara's nose between her thumb and forefinger. Sara still hated that habit of Mom's as much as she always had.

"Back off before I drench you with the faucet," Sara warned, aiming the sink hose at her mom with a ready finger on the trigger.

"Don't threaten your mother!" interrupted a new voice. It was Mom's friend Lola, who had just arrived at the inn and was wiping her feet on the welcome mat by the kitchen entrance. "Knock knock, by the way," she added. "I brought wine."

"Hi, love!" Mom crooned as she went over and gave Lola a hug and a kiss on each cheek.

"Hi, Aunt Lola," Sara said. Lola wasn't really her aunt, just a friend of her mom's, but she'd been a family friend for so long that Sara had taken to calling her that years ago. "Don't worry. She deserved it."

"I highly doubt that. Your mother is a saint," Lola tutted, coming over to give Sara a kiss on the cheek in turn.

"I sure hope so," Sara retorted, "because we're gonna need a miracle to make this lobster feed all the people who are likely to be showing up tonight."

That was the truth and then some. Sara's "Friday Night Feasts," as they'd come to be called, had been growing by leaps and bounds over the last few months. It was no understatement to say that the Sweet Island Inn was the place to be on Friday nights in Nantucket if you were hungry and liked good food.

It had started as a little thing. Sara was bored and lonely on Friday nights after last year's Russell-Gavin love triangle debacle, so she'd started hanging around the inn and helping her mother cook dinner for the guests. It didn't take long before she was also helping out with the shopping and prep, then scheduling meals ahead of time. And then, before anyone knew it, the inn on Friday nights had become her laboratory. She found herself spending days testing new dishes and bringing them to the table to see what people thought. Like clockwork, each dish was met with rave reviews.

Tonight's menu would start with a light chilled salad of fresh local produce, topped with a beet reduction that Sara had made and remade in over a hundred different formulations until she was satisfied with the final product. After that was butternut squash macaroni with melted gruyere cheese. Then, the star of the evening: handmade ravioli stuffed with lobster, shrimp, and ricotta cheese, tossed in a brown butter crab sauce. There were some traditional cheese biscuits, coleslaw, and corn on the cob for sides—couldn't stray *too* far from people's expectations of a real Nantucket dinner— and dessert was a homemade vanilla bean ice cream with espresso- chocolate sauce to drizzle on top.

The food was to die for, in Sara's humble opinion and the opinion of everyone else who'd been lucky enough to wrangle invitations since she'd taken over. She was, after all, a classically trained chef who'd worked in some of New York's most cutting-edge kitchens. She did it all, she did it artistically, she did it creatively, and she did it really freaking well.

Which was why attendance at these Friday Night Feasts had gone through the roof—almost literally. Neighbors had begun swinging by unannounced. Sheriff Mike "happened to be in the neighborhood on patrol" and stopped by to see if there were any leftovers. Old friends who'd "heard she was in town" would text her on Friday mornings to see if they could "catch up" that night. Sara would just laugh, shake her head, and get more food. As long as people brought a few bucks to cover the cost of groceries, she had no problem opening up the kitchen to more and more folks.

Maybe she had a little bit of her mom's hospitable spirit in her after all. It felt good to serve good food and see people satisfied. And it felt really, really good to hear people say the one thing they said every single time they sat down at her table, without fail: "You *have* to open your own restaurant."

If she had a nickel for every time someone said that, she'd be able to bankroll her own restaurant right this very second. But no matter how many times she heard it, it never got old. Really, it became like a tiny little seed, and every time the mantra was repeated, it was like that seed got watered a little bit more. In her idle moments, she'd started to wonder: was that possible? Her own restaurant? Could she do it?

Tonight, though, there weren't many idle moments to be had. She'd gotten a late start on prep, since they'd gone down to the beach at sunset for Dad's memorial. So now, she was cooking in a frenzy. The salad was already prepped and chilling in the refrigerator, but there were so many other things left to be done. As soon as she'd said her hellos and how are you to Aunt Lola, she put both her mother and Lola to work.

"Yes, chef!" Lola said with a cackle. She'd had a glass or two of Chardonnay before she'd come over, so she was a little giggly already.

But the joke just made Sara's heart throb unexpectedly. She thought of Russell and his *"Yes, chef!"* on the night of their flour-fight-slash-date-night. That felt like so long ago—or did it actually feel like it had just happened? She couldn't decide. She looked over at her phone as she'd done so many times over the last few months. Every time she looked, she was hoping that there would be a text from Russell lighting up her screen. It didn't have to be a big manifesto of forgiveness, not by any means. She knew that the window for him forgiving her for what she had done had slammed shut a long time ago. And she couldn't blame him for that, as much as she wanted to. Everything that had happened was her fault. She'd been the one to hurt him, not the other way around. She deserved this radio silence.

But it didn't change the fact that she herself was hurting. She ached for what they'd had—a fragile, blossoming relationship—and for the way she'd trampled all over that with one stupid decision.

She would've loved to hear from him. A classic Russell *Whazzupppp!?* text.

But her phone didn't light up. So she went back to cooking.

"Bon appetit!" she said with a flourish a little while later, setting down the first course of chilled salad. Mom and Aunt Lola were walking around the table pouring wine for everybody. There wasn't much in the way of elbow room, but nobody seemed to mind too much. Sara put the salad bowl down and stepped back to watch the meal begin.

She looked around the room. There was the main wooden table that Aunt Toni had picked up from an antiques shop on the mainland years ago. Jammed alongside that were two more plastic card tables, and a big white tablecloth draped on top of everything. Mom had arranged as many chairs as she could fit on all sides. Every single one of them was occupied.

Guests of the property had first priority, and not a single one of them would dare miss a Friday Night Feast at the Sweet Island Inn. Mom had three couples vacationing here ahead of the tourist deluge that would come after Easter and Memorial Day weekend, along with a family of four, the DeVrys, who were taking a year to travel the world and homeschool their kids. Nestled amongst them were friends and neighbors of the Benson family, as many as could squeeze an invitation out of Mom. Every single one of them was licking their chops in anticipation. As soon as the salad hit the table, it was on.

By the time Sara had gone to the kitchen to fill her wineglass with some pinot grigio and come back, the salad was pretty much devoured.

"Welp, that didn't take long," Sara muttered under her breath.

"This red stuff is good!" chirped Sandy DeVry, a seven-year old girl with long red pigtails like Pippi Longstocking.

"That's beets," Sara replied with a laugh. "I'm surprised you like them, actually."

"Oh, Sandy eats everything," said her mother with a smile. "We have a standing family policy to try anything at least once. Makes traveling more fun."

"I'm sure it does!" Mom chimed in. "Tell me, where all have you been since you began your travels?"

"Oh, here, there, and everywhere," joked Robbie DeVry, the father of the family. "We sold our home in Florida and went to Australia, Japan, Greece, France, and now back here for a wedding before we go back overseas. The kids have loved it. Right, kiddos?"

Michael, their oldest, an eleven-year-old bookworm, nodded fervently. He had the redness of the beet salad dressing smeared all over his lips like a hungry vampire. His mother caught his eye and tapped on her own lips to tell him to clear it up. He blushed as red as the beets, and Sara laughed. They were a cute family.

But she still had three more courses to serve, so she reluctantly pulled herself off her little perch on the windowsill where she liked to sit and watch her guests eat. Walking back to the kitchen, she plated everything for the mac-and-cheese course. She looked at her phone again. It was a stupid habit, she knew. Russell wasn't going to text her. She ought to just move on. Focus on something else.

For now, the food would do.

An hour and a half later, the dining room was filled with the groans of people who'd eaten far too much.

"I swear, one more bite and I'll explode," said David Higgins, another of the inn's guests. Sara smiled. She was in the kitchen, starting to wash some of the mountain of dishes that had accumulated before her. "Sara, you have a gift."

She demurred. "Aw, thank you."

"No, I'm serious," he continued. "A *gift*. When are you opening up a restaurant? You could charge two hundred bucks a head for a dinner like this, easy."

"Easy!" agreed his wife, a petite brunette named Jillian. They'd both been at the inn long enough to have two of Sara's Friday Night Feasts. "I'm just upset we have to leave in the morning!"

"Definitely. But we'll be back, guaranteed. Maybe you'll have a restaurant by then and we can eat your food every single night of our next trip."

"Now you're just trying to blow my ego up," Sara teased.

David raised a hand like he was swearing into court. "The truth, the whole truth, and nothing but the truth, so help me God. You're an artist. I've never had lobster that good in my whole life."

"Me neither," said another of the guests, Robert, who'd only arrived that morning. "And I used to work on a lobster fishing boat."

"Well, I appreciate it," Sara said shyly. She tried not to let her smile get too big. She didn't want to come off as egotistical. And she genuinely appreciated the praise.

But what they were suggesting—a whole restaurant—just seemed so daunting. She didn't have any experience with outfitting a kitchen, or running a waitstaff, or any of the million and one things that being a successful restauranteur required. And the one person who was in the best position to help her out—her old boss, Gavin Crawford—was the last person on this planet she wanted to talk to. Not to mention the question of where she would find enough money to get started.

Still, for just a moment, it was nice to close her eyes and dream. *My own restaurant,* she thought. *Could I do it?*

8

ELIZA

"Sorry we're late," Eliza said as she muscled open the front door with one elbow and swung Winter's car seat in behind her.

"All good," Sara replied, wiping some sweat off her forehead with one sleeve.

"Save some food for us?"

"Well, you're gonna break Sheriff Mike's heart if you take the last of the lobster, but family first, you know?"

Eliza smiled. "Family first. Hi, Mom." Mae had come swooping over and picked up Winter from her seat before even saying hi to her eldest daughter. Eliza just laughed and rolled her eyes. Grandmotherly behavior at its finest.

"How's my little angel?" Mae cooed. Winter reached out and touched her grandma on the nose.

Sara leaned over to Eliza and stage-whispered behind an upheld hand, "You know, I think you can physically see her heart melting when she does that."

The women laughed. It was true. Mom turned into the world's biggest softie whenever any of her grandchildren were around, and Winter was no exception.

"I can hear you, girls," Mom chided. "Am I not allowed to love on my beautiful little granddaughter? Is that such a crime?"

"No, Mom, not a crime," Eliza said. She leaned over and gave her mom a kiss on the cheek. "But the level of hunger I'm currently experiencing ought to be illegal. Sara, show me to the grub." The sisters walked into the kitchen as Grandma brought Winter over into the dining room to show off her granddaughter to anyone who would listen.

Sara stopped a few steps into the kitchen and turned to look at Eliza. "You look ... radiant."

"Radiant? That's a five-dollar word, especially for you, sis."

"Yeah, well, *bite me* is two words."

Eliza chuckled. "You're right, you're right. I'll be nice. My stomach is at your mercy, anyway."

Sara smiled back. "For real, though. You look good, Lizzy. Like, happy. Glowing."

"Radiant."

"Radiant," she agreed.

Eliza knew what Sara was talking about, even if she wanted to give her younger sister a hard time. The truth was that the sheer goodness of her life was leaving a physical mark on her. Or maybe it was just erasing the physical marks that her old life had left on her. Her hair was longer and blonder than it ever had been before. Whether it was the smog of the city getting washed out or something else, Eliza wasn't sure, but she saw the same thing Sara was seeing whenever she looked in the mirror: like she was beaming, a source of light in her own right. She knew why—she had her family and her Oliver and her daughter with her. And the Nantucket magic in the air that just seemed to settle deeper and deeper into her skin the longer she stayed here.

"So, can you direct me to this food, or am I going to have to beg you?"

Sara tilted her head with a wry grin on her face. "I wouldn't mind seeing a little begging and pleading first."

"Not even in your wildest dreams, sis," Eliza shot back. "I'll help myself, thank you very much." She laughed and grabbed a plate from the cabinet, loading it up with what remained of the ravioli and a few cheese biscuits. She didn't hesitate to finagle a fork and shovel a bite into her mouth. She could feel Sara's eyes on her, but that didn't stop her from offering up the most honest reaction she could: "Oh my God, Sara, this is incredible. Your best yet."

"You're just buttering me up."

"Nope. Dead serious. It's—mmphf—jeez, what's in there? Crab?"

"Crab, lobster, shrimp. The works."

"I want to bathe in this sauce."

Sara wrinkled her nose. "Gross. I mean, thanks, but gross. Please don't."

Eliza was too busy letting her taste buds zoom up to heaven to keep bantering with her sister. The food was honestly that good.

"Girls?" came Mom's voice from the dining table. "Come here for a sec! Mr. Higgins used to work on Wall Street. He wanted to see if you knew someone or other."

Sara chuckled. "You're on, sister dearest."

Eliza sighed and set down her plate, scraped clean already. "And so it begins—the social hour."

"All good things come with a price," Sara agreed.

Eyeing her empty plate mournfully as she went, Eliza walked into the dining room and put a smile on her face. She wasn't the social butterfly that her mother liked to be, but she knew that she ought to be pleasant and host-like regardless. She was an employee of this inn too, after all. The least she could do was chitchat with guests for a little while.

The house was dark when Eliza got back after another successful Friday Night Feast at the inn. Oliver was working tonight—playing piano at a private event in 'Sconset—so he probably wouldn't be home for a little while longer. She got Winter changed into pajamas and set her down in her crib. Eliza wasn't tired yet, so she decided to pour herself a small nightcap and sit down next to her sleeping daughter for a little while. She turned on the baby monitor, went into the kitchen, and plucked a half-empty bottle of chardonnay from the refrigerator. Then she returned to her bedroom, settled onto her side of the bed, and sipped slowly from her drink as she watched Winter slumber. Every time her baby's chest fell with an exhale, she held her own breath with a tingle of fear until Winter inhaled again.

She wasn't sure how much time had passed like that before she heard Oliver's keys scraping in the door. He was quiet when he came into the bedroom, as always. When his eyes landed on Eliza's, she held a finger up to her lips and pointed at Winter. Oliver smiled. He slipped off his shoes and walked over to the side of the crib to peer in carefully.

Eliza loved watching Oliver with Winter. Their whole situation was weird and delicate—Winter was not his biological daughter, after all —but Oliver had never paid an ounce of attention to all that. He loved Winter like she was his. Eliza wasn't quite sure how she'd gotten so lucky.

Oliver straightened and looked at her. He jerked his head towards the living room. Reluctantly, Eliza slid out of bed, put her feet in her slippers, and followed him out. He was waiting for her on the couch when she emerged. He patted the seat next to him.

"I have news."

Eliza's heart leaped into her throat. When he saw that, he smiled. "It's good news. No need to worry."

She sat down on the couch, but stayed perched on the very edge, like she was ready to flee at any moment. What news could he have? He'd been working all evening, right?

"Are you gonna tell me, or are we playing Charades?"

Oliver laughed and ran a hand through his hair. His green eyes shimmered in the light from the lamp on the end table. "I got an offer."

"What kind of offer?"

"A big one."

"Okay, now you're really gonna bug me. Can you just come out with it already?" Oliver loved these guessing games sometimes. He was like a cat with a ball of yarn when he had a story to share or a secret to reveal, swatting at it endlessly. It drove Eliza up the wall.

"You remember my buddy Slick Eddie, right?"

Eliza rolled her eyes. "Do you really think I could forget about someone who voluntarily goes by 'Slick Eddie'?"

"You're right. Unforgettable kind of guy. Anyway, he called me."

"Oliver, if you don't get to the point, I'm locking you in the backyard for the night."

He laughed again and grabbed Eliza's hands in his. He had such beautiful hands. Pianist's fingers, long and soft and supple.

Sometimes, when they were falling asleep cuddled together, he'd tap softly on her back, pretending to play her spine like a set of keys. It was oddly calming.

"He has a friend who has a friend who knows a guy, and, long story short, this band wants me to open for them. The Fever Dreams."

Eliza's mouth fell open. The Fever Dreams were a popular rock band based out of the Boston area. They weren't huge yet, but their buzz had grown and grown over the last few years. Everyone kept saying they were on the verge of making it big. In fact, they'd just dropped a new album recently that had garnered some really positive early reviews and media attention. Eliza didn't have to know much about the music industry to know that Oliver hitching his wagon to their train could be huge for him.

"By 'open for them,' you mean go on tour."

Oliver wrinkled his nose. "Well, yeah. A tour, of course."

"Away from Nantucket."

He smiled. "I mean, they aren't exactly gonna tour to 'Sconset and back for the next eight months, obviously. It's nationwide, plus a few dates in Canada."

Eliza didn't know what to say to that. Eight months? Nationwide? Her heart ached suddenly. Life had seemed so good, not so long ago. In fact, just a few minutes ago, it had been pretty close to perfect. And now, she felt like someone had thrown a rock through her window.

"I ... I, uh. I don't know what I'm supposed to say next. See you in eight months, I guess? Congratulations? I don't know. What's my line?"

Oliver squeezed her hands tighter. "No, you clown, you're supposed to say yes!"

Eliza was confused. "Yes? Yes to what?"

"To coming with me."

She sat back on the couch. "You want me ... to come with you. On tour. For eight months. With the Fever Dreams. Nationwide."

"Plus Canada."

"Plus Canada," she echoed.

This couldn't possibly be real life. In real life, she had escaped from the cold clutches of a bad relationship and a soulless job in New York City and was just now getting comfortable in her happily-ever-after. Her happily-ever-after most certainly did *not* include an eight-month tour with a rock band. That wasn't a thing that happened in real life.

"So what d'ya think?" Oliver said. He was bristling with energy, and now that she was paying a little more attention, she thought he might be a little drunk, too. It must've been a raucous party.

"I think that you forgot I have a three-month old daughter, is what I think."

He frowned. "You're not excited about this."

"Excited about what? About running away from home on a joyride? About living out of hotels for eight months? Tell me, Oliver, which part am I supposed to be excited about?"

He let her hands go. "I thought you'd be happy for me, at least."

"I'm thrilled for you! Go ahead, have a grand old time! Send a postcard! Winter and I will miss you!" The more she talked, the angrier she got. This wasn't *fair*. This wasn't how things were supposed to go. Her boyfriend wasn't supposed to just take off gallivanting on an eight-month bacchanalia of drugs and drinking and rock 'n roll shows! Who knew how many groupies would be there, throwing themselves at the members of the band? Who knew what kind of parties burgeoning rock stars got invited to? Was she supposed to just walk in to some crazy party, holding Winter in one arm and Oliver's hand in the other? Had he lost his mind completely?

"This is huge for my career. You should be happy for me."

She threw her hands in the air. "I am happy for you. It is huge. You're right. Have fun out there. We'll be here when you get back. *If* you get back."

"What's that supposed to mean?"

"It means whatever you want it to mean, Oliver. I'm tired. I want to go to sleep now." She started to stand up, but he grabbed her hand and pulled her back down to the couch.

"Eliza, come on. Just sit and talk with me about this. I can tell you're upset, but this is a good thing."

"I'd really love to hear you explain how this is a good thing. I have a three-month-old daughter, Oliver. Maybe a year ago, this would have sounded like a good thing. Now, it sounds like a nightmare."

"Eliza, please. Just hear me out."

She tried to pull her hand out of his, but he wouldn't let her go. She sighed and rubbed the bridge of her nose. She had a headache all of a sudden. "I'm listening," she said.

"Look at me. Liza, look at me."

Sighing again, she looked up and met his eyes. Her head felt so heavy, and she was so tired. But his gaze was steady and sincere. She felt the tide of her anger start to ebb just the tiniest bit.

"I want you to come with me—both of you—because I love you both. You're my family. My girls. And I can't do this without you."

"Oliver ..."

"Just hear me out, babe. This is big for me, yeah. We've talked about this kind of thing before, remember? You know I don't want to spend the rest of my life playing bars and rich-guy parties. I'm so sick of that. But I'd do it if I had to. For you. For Winter. If I had to spend every day until I'm dead and gone performing at company Christmas parties—but I got to come home to you two every night—then I'd do it without ever regretting it. Do you believe me?"

She didn't want to keep looking into his eyes because she felt like she might cry. But Oliver had reached out to lightly grab her chin and keep her face trained on his. So she bit her lip to hold back the tears. The craziest thing was that she believed everything he was saying. When he turned on the power of his eyes full blast like he was doing right now, he was like a star, up close and personal. There was such a powerful, radiating intensity to him. Even now, months since she'd first come into his orbit, that intensity made her shiver.

"I believe you," she whispered.

"I'd do it and I'd love it. Because of you. Okay? Because of you."

"I believe you," she repeated.

"But this is a chance for all of us to do something special together. We can chase our dreams, together. You and me and Winter. Our little family. I want you with me, Eliza. I want you to come. I can't do it without you. I *won't* do it without you. So if you say the word, I'll call Eddie right now and tell him no. Just say the word."

She hesitated. She wanted so badly to believe what he was saying. Almost all of her did, like ninety-nine percent of her heart had already packed her bags and boarded the plane. But there was one percent left that just couldn't quite commit yet.

Oliver searched her eyes, saw the hesitation there, and reached for his phone.

"No," she said suddenly, leaning forward to snatch his cell phone out of his hand. "Don't call. Just ... give me the night to think it over, okay?"

He smiled softly. "Of course. I love you, Eliza."

She rested her forehead on his chest. "I love you too, Oliver. Can you just hold me for a little while?"

In response, he pulled her into his embrace. He smelled so good. As always, she couldn't quite pick out exactly what it was that made his scent so powerfully attractive to her. It was a mix of his cologne, the whiskey fumes soaked into the fibers of his clothes, and the faint edge of his musk beneath all that. She closed her eyes and snuggled into him as thoughts ran rampant through her head.

She was a brand-new mother. She had her family here in Nantucket, and something akin to a job.

But those things would always be here. She had a chance to go on an adventure. She had enough money saved up to go comfortably. And maybe the goodness of her life wasn't a factor of being on Nantucket, but just being with Oliver. Maybe she could take that goodness on the road. See the world and show it to Winter at the same time.

Maybe she could make this work.

Her thoughts ran in circles like that, like a carousel spinning faster and faster, as she eventually extricated herself from Oliver's arms and went to brush her teeth and get ready for bed. She could feel his eyes on her the whole time. He was trying to suss out what she was thinking, she could tell. But he didn't say anything. He just gave her space. She appreciated him for that.

A few minutes later, they were curled up together in bed. He nestled her from behind, one arm draped over her midsection. It didn't take long before he was snoring very softly in her ear. But Eliza couldn't sleep. Again and again, she pored over the same set of facts.

An eight-month-long tour versus a three-month-old baby.

"Take a chance" versus "Stay in place."

Nantucket versus who knows where.

Oliver versus who knows what.

It was so wrong and so right, so unexpected and so perfect all at once. This was his big break, the stroke of luck he deserved. She wanted so badly to see him share his talent with the world. She wanted so badly to see him lose himself in music he loved, music he played for his own sake, not for the benefit of some rich old guys murmuring about stocks and real estate over expensive martinis in an expensive beachside house they used once a year at best. She wanted to support Oliver like he'd supported her when she needed it most.

But was bringing her baby on tour a wise thing to do? Babies needed so much—milk and clothes and diapers and a crib and on and on and on. A mountain of things wildly out of proportion to their size. Was it irresponsible to take Winter around the country? She knew Oliver wouldn't even be considering this plan if he hadn't already thought all this through. He wouldn't have invited her along if he didn't truly mean it. He was a careful thinker, an inveterate planner. She trusted his judgment ninety-nine times out of one hundred. But was there a chance that his excitement was overruling his decision-making? Was feeding into that the smart thing for her daughter?

She didn't know. The man she loved wanted to take her and her daughter on an adventure. Nantucket would always be here for them to return to. Life here was good. Life out there could be even better.

In the end, what made up her mind was this: Old Eliza would never, ever have gone.

So she rolled over and brushed Oliver's face with her fingers. "Oliver," she whispered. His eyelids fluttered open.

"Mmf?" he said sleepily.

"I want to come," she said.

He smiled and kissed her forehead.

9

SARA

Friday night.

The dishes were washed, the kitchen was empty, and Sara was finally alone.

That sucked.

Every Friday went like this. She'd wake up thinking of food. Dreaming of it, almost. She'd see recipes taking shape behind her eyelids, she'd taste the food on her tongue, sense the flavors mingling and transforming one another. For all her hard-eyed cynicism, Sara knew she was a romantic at heart. She wasn't pretentious enough to call herself an "artist," like some of her classmates at the Culinary Institute of America had done, but there was no denying that there was absolutely an element of art in what she did for her passion and profession. You could write out all the steps of a recipe in as much detail as you wanted, but every chef would make it differently. The steps might be the same, but the rhythm, the flow—that was unique, that was hers and hers alone.

So when she opened her eyes every morning, she'd hear—or feel, taste, sense—that flow already building up inside of her. Her fingers would be tap-dancing on the bedsheets, eager to get started. She'd spent her whole life fighting the alarm clock—Sara Benson had never, ever been a morning person—but on the dawn of a Friday Night Feast, she inevitably popped out of bed with fire in her footsteps.

The day would rage like that. Hotter and hotter the fire would grow. She began the mornings by prepping, maybe with a little foot tap here and there to the jazz music her mother liked to play on the inn's record player. By noon she was humming. By the early evenings, she'd be singing under her breath, and by the time dinner drew within an hour, she was in full force, pirouetting from fridge to sink to cutting board and back, inhaling deeply the pearls of steam rising from pots boiling on the stove, dipping tasting spoons into this and that to get the balance just right. She loved it. She immersed herself in it.

But then came the crash.

After the crescendo of the dinner itself, after the compliments came pouring in like a tidal wave, there was only a bitter, empty silence waiting for her. It kind of took her by surprise every time, how bad she felt after another Friday Night Feast had ended. Like she'd hoped —without ever consciously realizing that she was hoping for it—that this time would be different. This night, maybe she would return to the kitchen once all the food was gone and the guests had left and she wouldn't feel sad. This night, maybe the glow of pride would sustain her. Maybe the satisfaction of a job well done would carry her off to bed, happy and fulfilled.

Tonight was not that night.

Tonight, she felt hollow. The glow of compliments faded as quickly as it started. By the time she'd finished scrubbing the pans and loading the dishwasher to the bursting point, she felt worse than ever.

She checked her phone. There was no text from Russell, as expected. There was, however, a text from Gavin.

What's up, sport?

"Sport?" she scoffed out loud into the empty kitchen. "Does he think he's my dad or something?" She ought to text him back, *Not much, slugger.* Or *Just had dinner, champ.* Maybe throw in a "bud" or "pal" or "kiddo." She started to type it out, then stopped. Started again, then stopped once more. That was childish. She wasn't going to do that. Gavin already occupied far too much real estate in her mind, and she was determined not to let him annex anymore. She'd spent nearly a year trying to evict him as it was. Somewhat successfully, she had to say. But the man had an infuriating knack for texting her just when she was starting to feel like she'd finally turned a page in her life and was ready for whatever was coming her way next. It had only happened sporadically over the last seven or eight months, but the timing was exquisite every time.

They hadn't talked much after the night he surprised her. Russell had come in, seen Sara and Gavin kissing, and then he was gone, taking her hopes of happiness with him. Gavin had tried to hang around, but Sara had been resolute in kicking him out. He'd hung around the island for another couple of days after that, cajoling her via text message to come see him, but she steadfastly refused again and again until he'd given up and gone back to New York. She hadn't heard from Russell even once.

Funny how that worked. It was always the guy you wanted so badly to hear from who stayed silent, while the one you couldn't get away from fast enough kept blowing up your phone.

Except, "funny" might not be the right word. "Depressing" would be a little more accurate. Sara didn't really want to consider herself depressed, but she certainly was checking off a lot of the boxes. Outside of Friday Night Feasts, she wandered aimlessly around the island all day every day. She'd helped out at a few catering events with a friend's family that she knew from back in high school, and she worked shifts at the Club Car whenever they had a chef call in sick. But when she wasn't doing those things, she mostly just lounged at the beach and wondered what had happened to her life.

Now, sitting in the empty kitchen, with soap suds still clinging to her forearms, she wondered the same thing. This wasn't real life. It couldn't be. This was more like a holding pattern, like purgatory. She was stuck waiting for what would happen next to her. Should she go travel? Get a job? Start online dating? None of those options sounded appealing in the slightest. That was another reason she knew she was depressed: she hated everything she was doing, and yet she didn't have the slightest desire to do anything different.

"Hon?" interrupted a familiar voice. "You okay?"

"Yeah, Mom," Sara said, sighing and standing up straight. "I'm fine. Just finished up."

Mae put a pot of water on boil to make her regular nighttime tea. When it was going, she turned to look at Sara. "You look tired, darling," she commented.

"I just said I'm fine."

She reached out a hand towards Sara, saying, "Look at these bags under your eyes. You should get a good night's sleep, maybe sleep in a little tomorrow, and—"

Sara slapped her mother's hands away. It was harder than she meant to, and the sound of skin hitting skin seemed to echo forever in the kitchen. Mae froze. Sara felt bad immediately. She might as well have slapped her mother in the face. She knew that she had gone too far, been too cruel, too cold. Her mom just pushed her buttons sometimes. She hated the way Mae Benson seemed to have this incredible gift for getting Sara to go from zero to one hundred at a moment's notice. This was one of those moments.

It was a shame, too, because they'd been getting along so well lately. Better than ever, actually. Throughout her whole life, Sara had relied on her father to be the mediator between her and her mother. Now, without Henry there to play the role of peacekeeper, she'd had to watch her words and actions more carefully. She owed her mom that much. The woman was a grieving widow, after all. The least she could do was be nice to her, especially since Mom had been so kind to Sara when she needed it.

But with everything else swirling through her head, she just hadn't wanted to be touched. So she'd slapped her hands away. That was wrong, though. It didn't take a genius to look at Mom's face and see that she was on the verge of tears.

The two women stood there in silence for a few long moments. "Well, I'll ... I'm sorry, dear. Have a good night." Mom turned off the burner and left the kitchen without her tea.

Sara didn't budge. She stared at the floor. A few drops of water had flown off her hands when she'd slapped at her mother's touch. She looked at where they'd pooled on the tile like little translucent beads.

Maybe the peace between them had been a sham. Just a truce in the aftermath of tragedy. Now that time had begun to take some of the sting out of Dad's loss, maybe they'd just go back to where they had been before. Not enemies, not adversaries, but something like that. As diametrically opposed as a mother and her daughter could be.

That sucked, too.

Brent came by a little while later. Sara was seated at the kitchen counter nursing two fingers of bourbon poured in a glass tumbler. She was still staring at the floor like there might be answers written there.

"Hey, Sara," Brent mumbled. "I just came to get some stuff I left here. Mom around?"

Sara shook her head.

"You all right?"

Sara shook her head.

"Wanna talk about it?"

Sara shook her head.

"Wanna drink about it?"

Sara looked up at that. Brent was standing in the kitchen doorway, wringing his hands in front of him. He looked exhausted. She wondered if he was sleeping as badly as she was these days.

"Not me, I mean. Still sober. But I'll come sit with you. If you want."

She thought about it for a second. "Yeah, let's do it."

They got into his car and drove to the local bar down the street. It was quiet inside, not many patrons tonight. Still too early for tourists, so it was mostly just a handful of locals who wanted to get out of their house for a few hours and pretend to be functional members of society. Sara could certainly understand that desire.

Brent ordered an iced tea and Sara got a shot of tequila and a beer. She regretted it as soon as she placed the order. Tequila was what Russell had ordered the night of their date, way back when. The memory made her nauseous. As soon as the bartender put the shot glass down in front of her, she threw it back and chased it with the beer. Better to get it over with sooner rather than later.

Brent raised an eyebrow. "That bad, huh?"

"Like I said, I don't wanna talk about it."

"Fair enough. Me neither, I was just being nice. You're always a crab about your problems."

Sara laughed cynically and elbowed him in the ribs. "Look who's talking. Pot, kettle, black."

"It's Sara's world. We're all just living in it."

"Whatever you say, li'l bro. What about your problems?"

"Let's just enjoy our drinks in silence, how 'bout that?"

Sara groaned. "Not if it means I have to listen to this Bruce Springsteen garbage. You got a dollar? I'm gonna go change the jukebox." Brent handed her a crumpled dollar bill. Sara took it and slid off her stool, headed for the back.

This bar was shaped like a long rectangle, with the bar at one end and a bunch of booths lining the wall all the way down to where the jukebox sat at the other end. Sara sidled her way down, subtly eyeing each of the booth's occupants as she passed. Mostly single older men, a few couples. A family. And then, in the second-to-last booth on the left-hand side ...

Sat Russell Bridges and a petite blonde.

They were seated on the same side of the booth, laughing together, a few empty bottles of beer and upside-down tequila glasses in front of them.

Tequila. Beer. Laughter. A pretty girl, who had her hand on Russell's thigh. Sara's throat tightened. She swallowed hard, turned around, and walked back to Brent before Russell could see her.

When she got back to the stool, she slapped the dollar onto the bar in front of him. "Bartender?" she called. "Tequila, please. Make it a double."

10

BRENT

His sister's sour mood was somehow even more sour when she got back from the jukebox. "You all right?" he ventured. "Music didn't change ..."

"Machine was broken. Keep the buck." She threw back the tequila double she'd just ordered, then followed it with a very long chug of beer.

"Uh, okay. You sure you're all right?"

Sara whirled to face him. "I thought I was very clear that I didn't wanna talk about my problems."

He held his hands up. "You did. We'll let it go."

They both turned to their drinks. Neither one said a word for a long time.

Brent knew that he was doing the worst of all the Benson children. But he also knew that Sara wasn't far behind him. Maybe it was kindred spirits recognizing each other, but it seemed to him like Sara had been seeking him out more and more over the last few months. Like tonight, she never wanted to talk about her issues or the things weighing on her heart. She mostly just wanted to wallow with him in silence.

Fine. So be it. Talking about his problems wasn't gonna solve them, so why would talking about Sara's problems solve hers? As far as he was concerned, they could sit at this bar until closing time and not utter a peep. That was as good a form of therapy as anything else. Sometimes you just had to sit with something for a while until you found a way around or through it.

Though, to be fair, he'd been sitting with guilt for his father's death for a year to the day now, and he didn't feel much nearer to a way around or through it than he had since the moment it had happened. Maybe his theory sucked after all. At least Sara could drink to ignore the things troubling her. He didn't even have the luxury of masking his problems with alcohol.

Brent felt a hand clap on his shoulder. He looked up to see the grinning face of the one and only Marshall Cook. He just sighed.

"There he is!" Marshall declared loudly. He'd always been loud, even when they were little first-graders playing dodgeball on the playground at Nantucket Elementary School, where they'd met. "The man, the myth, the legend. Brent 'Triple B' Benson!" Marshall looked around like he expected the bar to burst into a standing ovation. Brent wouldn't have been too surprised if they had. Marshall had a way of connecting with people immediately. He just had this natural warmth to him. It made you want to be his best friend from the second you met him. It was a big part of the reason why he was so good at his job.

"Just what we needed," Brent remarked to Sara. "The Marshall Show."

"Now now, that's no way to greet your best friend," Marshall tutted. He pulled up the barstool next to Brent. Leaning over, he greeted Sara. "Hello, Dinosara."

"Not the night, Marsh-head."

Brent just shook his head and laughed. Marshall gave everybody he encountered a nickname. Sara was Dinosara, Eliza was Frizzy Lizzy, Holly was Showstopper. "Holly" had become "Hollywood," which eventually evolved into "Showstopper" ... Brent had always rolled his eyes at that one. Brent wasn't aware of a single living person who actually liked the nickname Marshall bestowed on them, but that didn't stop the guy from doing it anyway. And once you received a Marshall Cook nickname, you were stuck with it for life. Like, for instance, his nickname for Brent—"Triple B"—which made no sense, because Brent's middle initial was E. for Evan. Logic wasn't necessarily Marshall's strong suit, though. At least Triple B was better than Booger, which was what Marshall called their mutual friend Freddy Lopez for reasons Brent thought were best left unexplored.

Marshall looked back and forth between Brent and Sara. "Boy, you two are a real fun time tonight. What's got y'all down?"

"'Y'all'? Where'd you stumble across the redneck accent, sport? Someone's been watching too many cowboy movies." Sara's tone was sharper than necessary, but Marshall didn't seem to notice or care.

"Just embracing my family heritage." He shrugged.

"You took a family vacation to Georgia one time!" Brent retorted. "That doesn't exactly make you a Southerner."

"Farther south than you've ever been, my culturally challenged compadre."

"'Compadre' is even farther south, Marsh-head, and I'm darn sure you've never been to Mexico."

"Woof, tough crowd tonight." Marshall sighed, shaking his head sadly. Then a thought apparently occurred to him, and he perked up right away. Brent could only laugh. Marshall was interminably happy. Nothing in the world could keep him down. Not even the bitter moods of the two youngest Benson kids. "Say, you know what the best cure is for a bad attitude, Triple B?"

"Don't start," Brent warned. "We've been down this road before." He knew exactly where Marshall was headed. But Marshall must've taken some lessons out of the Henry Benson book of stubbornness way back when, because he had a head of steam and he wasn't anywhere close to stopping.

"Getting out on the water! Yessir, can't be upset on the ocean. Physically impossible. A trip on the boat will fix both of you right up."

"Sounds more like Brent's cup of tea than mine," Sara grumbled.

"It does indeed sound like it's right up Triple B's lane, don't you think? C'mon, man, when's the last time you went out?"

"Doesn't matter. Not going again."

"Ever?"

"Ever." Brent meant it, too. Ever since the night he'd gone out rip-roaring drunk to the Garden of Eden and screamed at his dad's ghost or memory or whatever he'd been screaming at, he'd sworn off the water forever. No more. Not again. It held only pain for him.

"Not even for forty bucks an hour plus tips?"

Brent sighed for the umpteenth time since Marshall had first burst onto the scene of his and Sara's pity party. There it was, the question he'd been ducking away from forever now.

Marshall had been bugging Brent in one form or another for the last five years to start coming out with him as first mate on some of the charter fishing trips he ran for tourists to Nantucket. It had started as a small side gig and quickly blossomed into a lucrative business. Marshall complained all the time about how he often had to turn away paying customers because he just didn't have time to handle everything by himself. He'd tried hiring other guys from the island to help him, but none of them worked out for one reason or another. He saw Brent as the answer to his problems. Best friend, first mate. Perfect fit.

Brent, however, didn't agree. He hadn't been anywhere near the water in months now, and he didn't want to break that streak. Not for Marshall, not for anyone.

But he couldn't deny that he needed the money.

"Forty bucks an hour plus tips is pretty good, Brent," Sara said casually. She was on her third beer already. She must really be feeling sorry for herself this evening.

She wasn't wrong, though. Forty bucks an hour plus tips over a six-hour trip could work out to over five hundred dollars if he did a good job and had some clients with loose wallets. Contracting jobs had been slow lately, so that money would really help him out. He'd be able to put up rent money, prolong his independence, stay away from the nightmare show of bad memories that was the Benson family home on 114 Howard Street.

But it would also mean facing something he'd been trying very, very hard not to face. Brent wasn't exactly superstitious, but he was maybe a little "'stitious," as the joke went. And going back on the water was bad news. It wasn't quite ghosts or anything like that he was afraid of. Lord knew he had enough ghosts in his head. But the thought of going back onto the ocean felt like—well, like trampling on his father's grave. Intruding on a dead man's resting place. It felt utterly, creepily wrong. He wanted nothing to do with it.

But he needed the money. Gosh, did he need the money.

What else could he do? Beg on the docks? This at least was good work, honest work, work that he knew he could do well. The only thing stopping him was himself. Too bad that was one heck of an obstacle.

"I just don't think so, pal," he said. He couldn't quite bear to look at Marshall in the face as he said it. He'd turned down his friend's offer a thousand times before. What made this time any different?

As it turned out, Sara made it different when she leaned over to him and whispered, "Henrietta deserves some treats every once in a while, you know?"

"Oh, c'mon now," Brent growled. "That's a low blow."

Sara shrugged. "I've gotta go get some fresh air. You boys have fun gossiping." She stood, a little unsteadily, and headed for the front door.

Brent took in a long, slow breath. Henrietta. Why, of all things, was that the straw that broke the camel's back? He pictured her. She had been his sidekick for over eight months now, ever since he found her rooting around in a dumpster, looking dirty and disheveled. He'd brought her home, cleaned her up, fed her real food. Didn't she deserve nice things? Didn't Brent himself deserve nice things?

He wasn't so sure about the latter question. But he knew for darn sure that he was the kind of man who took care of his dog. So he sighed, drained the last of his iced tea, and looked up at Marshall, who had stayed uncharacteristically silent while Brent had wrestled with his thoughts.

"All right," he said. "I'll do it."

"Excellent!" Marshall cried. "Ladies and gentlemen, he's doing it!" He held up his glass and looked around the bar. The bartender rolled his eyes. Nobody else paid him any attention.

11

HOLLY

Just past midnight on Friday night.

Holly slept like a rock, but she had nightmares that grabbed her in their claws and refused to let her go. Violent, gnashing, ugly nightmares. She was running and tripping and then she had a pain in her shoulder, a jabbing, sharp pain that struck her again and again until ...

"Holly!"

She sat bolt upright. It took her a moment to get her bearings. It was dark outside. The house was silent. She must've fallen asleep on the couch in the living room, waiting for Pete.

Pete.

All the thoughts that had borne her off to sleep came rushing back in at once. Pete was cheating on her. Pete had lied about where he was. Pete was hiding secrets, and he was going to come tell her that he wanted a divorce because he was going to run off with some other, younger woman, and, and, and ...

She realized suddenly that he was standing over her. The pain in her shoulder during her nightmare had just been Pete grabbing her to wake her up.

"You were whimpering," he explained. He looked worried. Worried that he'd been caught, she wondered? That his little lie was up? She honestly couldn't believe it had come to this. Never in a million years did she think Pete would cheat on her. Pete Goodwin was a lot of things, but cheater never seemed like one of them. Then again, no one really expected their partner to fool around on them, much less someone who'd married her high school sweetheart. It was always the nice guys who did you the dirtiest.

"I had a nightmare. Turns out it might've been true."

He furrowed his brow deeper. "What? Wait, let me go first. I have news. Big news. Are you sitting down?"

She swallowed back the words that were fighting to rip from her throat. Let him try to explain himself, she figured. Then she'd bring down the sword of justice and give him the tongue-lashing he deserved. "Yes, Pete," she drawled, her voice dripping with sarcasm. "I'm sitting down."

"Okay, but are you ready?" He was grinning wildly. He looked way, way too excited. Holly looked at the clock over his shoulder. It was one-thirty in the morning.

None of this was making any sense. What kind of cheater comes home at one-thirty a.m. and wakes up his wife to deliver news of an impending divorce? Had she jumped to a really nasty conclusion?

No. He'd lied. His secretary had confirmed it. There was no other plausible explanation, as far as Holly could tell. Why else would a man leave work early and lie about it? Why else would Pete not answer his phone when she'd called after arriving home?

"Tell me what's going on, Pete."

He wrung his hands in front of him like a little kid who couldn't decide which candy he wanted at the movie theater. Holly felt nauseous. This was all so wrong. So messed up. Finally, he dropped onto the couch next to her, grabbed her hands in his, and launched into a speech he'd clearly been practicing.

"I know I've been working a lot, which is explicitly against the rules we made together. But the truth is that I have a secret."

Here it comes. Holly closed her eyes. She didn't want to see his face when he said the words. *I'm leaving you. It's over. There's someone else.*

Impact was coming in three, two, one …

"We're moving to Nantucket."

Holly's eyes flew open. "What?!" she yelped.

Pete's grin grew a notch wider. "That is, if you want to, obviously. But here's the deal. I ran into a college buddy of mine at that conference in Boston a few months ago. We got to talking, one thing led to another, and we're going to open up our own shop. Our own law firm, based in Nantucket. Maritime and property law. The market is huge, it's underserved, we're gonna make a killing, and we get to do it all at home."

"Nantucket. We're moving." Holly knew she sounded dumb, but she was having an awfully hard time just processing the words coming out of Pete's mouth.

"Yes, baby! Back to Nantucket! Beaches and lobster and *home*! I'm ridiculously excited. That is, if you are. You're excited, right? You're on board?"

It took Holly a few long seconds to find her voice again. "We're going to Nantucket. We're moving home."

Pete nodded fervently. He was still holding her hands, and as she repeated herself again and again—"We're going to Nantucket. We're going home."—she founded herself squeezing his hands tighter and tighter, too. "We're going home. We're going home!"

The gnawing dread that had polluted her stomach was gone now, wiped away by pure, sheer thrill. *Home.* Back home to Mom, to her sisters, her niece. Back to Nantucket. *Home. Home. Home.*

"You're on board, right?" Pete asked again. He had finally realized that she was stammering a little, and he looked as concerned as he had when he first woke her up.

She grabbed either side of his face in her hands. "Yes! Yes!" She kissed him, or he kissed her, she wasn't sure which, but either way, they ended up in a sprawl on the couch, kissing one another and taking turns saying, "Yes!" to each other over and over.

They were going back to her family and her home, leaving the dreary confines of Plymouth behind. They were going back to where they'd fallen in love the first time, and then for the second time that previous summer. Pete was starting his own law firm, getting away from the Zucker, Schultz, & Schultz misery factory. Their kids were going to grow up where she'd grown up. It all felt right. She felt horribly guilty for ever thinking that Pete could cheat on her. He was her man, her husband, her love, her Pete. She was his wife, his Hollyday.

And they were going home.

12

BRENT

Pre-dawn, Saturday morning.

Brent sighed. "I don't know if this is a good idea."

Henrietta whined in response.

"Yeah, well, nobody asked your opinion, anyway."

He locked the door to his apartment and made his way downstairs. Ten minutes later, he was at the dock. It was still early, almost forty-five minutes until sunrise proper, so he was alone at the marina. Roger hadn't come to open the store yet. Prior to tourist season—which would be getting started in full force any day now—Roger usually just let Marshall use the dock for his charter trips as needed so he didn't have to get his old behind out of bed at the crack of dawn.

Brent didn't mind the mornings. He liked the silence, the crispness of the pre-dawn hours. It made him feel calm inside—most days. Not today, though. Today, he felt like a stormy ocean was raging in his gut. His fingers had tapped on the steering wheel the whole drive over, and he couldn't stop blinking, like he was just one good blink away from realizing that this was all a big mirage and he was actually still safe in bed, dreaming.

He pinched himself. No dice. This was real.

He stood by his truck for a minute, kicking at gravel. Then, deciding that he was being stupid, he walked down to the dock to get it over with. He hopped over the gate and took the wooden stairs down to the water level. Every step made the ocean in his gut churn more violently. By the time he got to the bottom of the staircase, he thought he might vomit.

He held it together, though, enough to make his way to the very end of the dock and stare down.

The ocean—the real ocean, not the imaginary one suffering from hurricanes inside of him—was calm today. Placid, almost flat enough to see his reflection despite the low light. He could see his silhouette in the water.

"It's just water," he grumbled to himself under his breath. "Just a lot of stupid water."

"Ahoy!"

Brent looked up. Marshall was standing at the top of the stairs. He had a cooler in one hand and a tackle box in the other. "Morning," Brent rasped.

Marshall grinned wide and jerked his head back towards the parking lot. "You're on the clock now, amigo. Come help me get the boat loaded up."

Brent gave the water one last sidelong look—like he was checking to make sure it wasn't gonna pull a fast one on him when he had his back turned—then headed back up the stairs.

Like it or not, he was gonna have to face his fears.

Marshall was waiting for him by the bed of his truck. The tailgate was down and a dozen fishing rods were stacked neatly inside. "Here, grab these," he instructed. Together, they emptied the bed of the supplies they'd need for the day and stocked up Marshall's boat, the *Tripidation II*. They had bottles of water and a few cases of beer for the passengers, along with a whole bevy of fishing gear: bait, rods, gaffs, nets, lures, extra supplies in case something broke or got dropped overboard. Time went by fast as the two men worked together silently to get everything stashed where it belonged. They'd fallen into a working pattern already, as if they'd been doing this for years. Mostly that was because they *had* been doing this for years—some version of it, at least.

Brent's first memory on a boat was with his dad and Marshall. The three of them had spent more hours on the water together than Brent could count, joking and fishing and wiling the weekend hours away. Dad was always "Mr. Hank," until Marshall got old enough to have the cojones to give him a nickname of his own, at which point he became "Mr. Hank the Tank." No points for originality, but the name had made Brent's father laugh every time. He called Marshall "Jitterbug," in return. *"You aren't capable of sitting still for a New York minute, are you, kiddo?"* Dad would joke.

He was right on that count. Marshall was a fidgeter for sure. Even when they were just lazing in the sun, waiting for a rod to hit, Marshall would be tapping a foot or twiddling his thumbs. Some people just had to keep moving at all times, Brent supposed.

It wasn't long before their clients arrived, pulling up in a darkly tinted SUV with Tennessee plates. Brent held his breath, waiting to see what they would be dealing with today. He let out a sigh of relief when a trio of men emerged in well-worn fishing shirts and boat shoes that hardly had any tread left on the soles. That was good. Experienced pros who knew their way around a boat. Brent had been prepared for anything, but this was better than he'd dared hope for.

"Morning, gentlemen!" Marshall hollered from where he was standing on the boat. "Brent, you mind getting the boys situated while I finish up here? Just gonna put her in the water, then we'll all get grooving."

"Sure thing, Cap," Brent said with a wry smile. He went over to greet their clients.

The men turned out to be three brothers from Nashville, up here on a low-key sort of bachelor party for the youngest of them, who was getting married in a month's time. They were all friendly, polite, and easygoing. He could sense them sizing him up as he shook each of their hands and introduced himself. It was a relief to get a firm handshake, a nod, and a smile in return from each of them. He'd passed the first intangible client test, he figured. It oughta be smooth sailing from here.

And it pretty much was. The day went by faster than Brent had expected. The work was mindless, if a little sweaty and grueling at times. He'd practically spent his whole life training for this. He thought about how his mom had said that over and over the last few months whenever anyone asked her about how running the Sweet Island Inn for Aunt Toni was going. *"Why, I feel like I was born for this, I really do! Like my whole life was leading me right here and now. It's a blessing, I'll tell you that much for sure."*

Brent wasn't quite as effusive as his mother, but he was starting to understand the sentiment. All those hours of waking up early, of learning from his father how to prep bait, what to look for in the water, when to wait, when to strike—it all came to bear. The men were impressed with Brent and Marshall's knowledge of the waterways.

But best of all was the fact that Brent didn't think about his fears once. He kept his head down and did the work, nothing more and nothing less. Whenever the ocean in his stomach tried to get too rowdy, he just doubled down on whatever task lay at hand and tried his darnedest not to think about it. He couldn't believe that strategy was working out for him, but working out it was, and he wasn't gonna look a gift horse in the mouth.

So he kept his hands active and his mind occupied. Even when they skirted past the Garden of Eden on their way to a spot a little farther out, Brent didn't panic or vomit like he'd feared he might. He offered up a silent *Thanks, Dad,* and then tried not to bring up the subject in his thoughts again.

It was late afternoon by the time the *Tripidation II* returned home to the marina. All the men were a little sunburned and tired, but they'd brought home a haul of fish: striped bass aplenty, along with a few handsome bluefish and some tasty scup, which were always a crowd pleaser. Best of all, there wasn't a single dead shark. Brent helped to get all the fish tucked away into the ice coolers that Marshall had stowed for that purpose, then escorted the men back to their vehicle to make sure everything else was in order.

"Here you go, man," the oldest brother said just before they all clambered into the car. He held out his hand and offered Brent a shockingly thick roll of cash. Three hundred bucks, it looked like. Brent couldn't quite believe his eyes.

"Aw, you don't gotta go to all that trouble," Brent mumbled.

"Nonsense, brother," the man replied. "You boys are great at what you do, and we all had a good time out there today. Take it and go buy someone pretty a beer, yeah?" He gave Brent a wink, a pat on the back, and then they were gone, kicking up gravel as they went.

"Good crew," Marshall said, coming up from behind Brent. "Nice catch there, too." He nodded towards the cash in Brent's hand. "Keep it all, okay? Call it a signing bonus."

Brent started to protest, but Marshall raised a hand to silence him. "I insist. But we still got a boat to scrub down, so put the cash in your purse and let's go finish the job, all righty?"

He slugged Marshall in the shoulder playfully. The two men went over to attend to the last of the day's tasks. As the sun set over the marina, bathing everything in a creamy orange glow, Brent felt an unexpected smile creep across his face.

Against all odds, he'd actually had a good day.

Who could've seen that coming?

13

SARA

Sunday morning.

Every Sunday for as long as Sara could remember, the Benson family had gotten together in one form or another. When they were growing up, Mom always made banana pancakes—with chocolate chips for Brent—and the kids would all run downstairs to get the first ones hot off the griddle. As they went away to college or the city one by one, Sunday mornings became the time they'd all call one another to check in, chat, catch up on life. But, now that they were pretty much all back on Nantucket, Sunday mornings had once again become banana pancake time.

The kitchen table at the inn was warm in the sunlight, though the air outside was cool this morning. Sara sat with her forehead resting on her forearms, soaking up the sun like a grumpy cat. She had one gnarly hangover that just refused to quit. She supposed she deserved it, after the way she'd been knocking back drinks at the bar with Brent on Friday night. One beer and one shot had turned into four of each very, very quickly. Back in her culinary institute days, that wouldn't have been a problem. Heck, even a year ago, when she was going out regularly with her coworkers at the Lonesome Dove in New York City, she would've been able to drink like a fish and get right back to work the next day.

But now, after a year in Nantucket, her liver had turned on its check engine light. Getting old sucked. A two-day hangover? That seemed unfair. Her body was punishing her.

In some ways, though, she sort of deserved it. Seeing Russell at the bar with that mystery girl had been a blow to the gut. When she closed her eyes and pictured them again—laughing together, her hand on his thigh, his arm around her shoulders—she felt the same grossness in her stomach. It didn't feel good to see him with someone else. Even after everything she'd done or allowed to happen, she still didn't want to see that.

Maybe she'd been hoping that there was a reconciliation in their future. If she just let enough time pass, then he'd relax and forgive her and they could pick up right where they left off—kissing amongst clouds of spilled flour in his kitchen.

But it was clear to her now that that was just a silly fantasy. Russell wasn't going to forgive her, at least not in a way that would lead to getting back together. By kissing Gavin that night at the inn, she'd ruined things permanently.

That realization hurt every bit as bad as the hangover.

"Coffee?" Eliza asked.

"Mmf," was all Sara could muster.

"I'll take that as a 'Yes, lots of it,'" replied her older sister sagely. Sara didn't pick her head up, but she could hear Eliza pour her a steaming mug and set it down on the table at her elbow. She waited to hear the sounds of her footsteps walking away, but instead—much to her dismay—Eliza pulled out a chair and sat down.

"Rough night?"

Sara lifted her head off her hands. It took a gargantuan amount of effort. Hangovers were not meant to last two days. This was cruel and unusual. Some deity had it out for her. Or maybe it was her own brain and body that had it out for her. Whichever way you sliced it, she was on someone's bad list. She was prepared to beg for mercy if she could just find out who was responsible for pulling the levers here. "Very."

"How rough are we talking?"

"Saw Russell."

Eliza winced. "Oof. I take it he wasn't alone."

Sara shook her head sadly and took a sip of her coffee. It was scorching hot and nearly seared her taste buds off. She just sighed. Even the coffee was antagonizing her this morning. "Some little blonde thing."

"To be fair, *you're* a little blonde thing."

Sara fixed her older sister with a glare. "Not the time, Liza."

"You're right, you're right. Do you want some Bailey's in your coffee or something?"

The mere thought of alcohol made Sara shudder in horror. "I'm never drinking again."

Eliza laughed at that. "Famous last words." Her face softened. She laid a hand on Sara's shoulder. "Listen, Sara ... I'm sorry about Russell. I know that hurts."

It was a nice gesture. Eliza had really come so far in terms of being emotional and empathetic. It still took Sara by surprise sometimes when her sister asked how she was feeling about this or that. Old Eliza would've *never* asked about her feelings. This new Eliza was gentle. Still a little weird to see, but not necessarily unwelcome. "Thanks, Liz," Sara murmured. She felt oddly choked up all of a sudden. She could count on two hands the number of times that she and Eliza had ever talked about their love interests at all. Eliza had always kept things private, close to the chest. Maybe they were both doing a lot of growing up in their own ways these days.

Just then, Mom came bustling out of the kitchen, followed by Brent. Each of them was carrying a pair of plates stacked high with banana pancakes and strips of bacon. They set the plates down on the table and took their seats.

Sara's heart did a little twinge when she saw her mother. They hadn't really talked since their argument in the kitchen after this week's Friday Night Feast. Sara felt guilt mixing itself up amongst her nausea. She could still recall the sound of her slapping away her mother's hand and picture the crestfallen look on her mother's face. She knew she ought to apologize, to make things right. But she just didn't know what words to say. It was easier to ignore the problem and hope that it worked itself out in time. That might be the immature route, but it was certainly the easiest. Given the way she was feeling, maybe taking the path of least resistance wasn't so evil. Or maybe it was. She hadn't quite decided.

Apologies could wait until after pancakes, though. Eliza and Mom chitchatted while Brent and Sara dug right in. Brent looked like he had an uncharacteristic amount of pep in his step this morning. He'd lost the bags under his eyes ever since he stopped drinking after getting arrested last year, but there was still a furtive, haunted look in his eyes most days. Not today, though. Today, he had a decisiveness to his movements. He speared a pancake and transferred it over to his own plate. When he caught Sara looking at him, he fixed her with a sidelong look.

"Can I help you?" he asked gruffly.

"Something's different about you."

He cut himself a triangle of pancake, dipped it in his reservoir of maple syrup, and shoveled it into his mouth. "Nope," he mumbled around the bite.

"Yes. Different. You're supposed to be miserable with me. You don't look miserable."

"Oh, I'm miserable," he said. "Or rather, I will be as soon as we're out of pancakes."

"See? That's what I mean. You're joking around. Miserable people don't make jokes."

He shrugged. "What do you want from me, sis? I'm here for breakfast, not the Spanish Inquisition."

Sara frowned. "What on earth do you know about the Spanish Inquisition? I'm pretty sure I remember you cutting social studies in high school to go make out with Carolyn Cunningham in the back stairwell."

Brent stared longingly into the distance while he chewed, as if remembering those days. "Ah yes," he said mournfully. "Carolyn Cunningham. The one that got away."

Eliza butted in. "If I recall, I believe you broke up with her to start dating Rebecca Nelson."

Her brother nodded. "Oh yeah, you're right. Rebecca Nelson. The one that got away."

Sara rolled her eyes. "But if you are still lusting after Carolyn, she and her husband own the gas station downtown. I'm sure she's just dying to elope with you, Prince Charming."

"Gonna stick with pancakes for now, but I appreciate the suggestions, ladies."

"Well, you all are certainly in a chipper mood this morning!" Mom said from her end of the table. "Spring fever?"

"Pancake fever," Brent corrected. "You're doing the Lord's work here, Momma."

Mom laughed and threw a balled-up napkin at his head. It felt so normal for one brief moment; Sara forgot about all the messed-up circumstances that had brought each of them to this table. For one brief moment, life was about pancakes and joking around with her family. It was like how you get that one instant of silence right before your ears pop when an airplane is landing. A sliver of bliss before the sound rushes back in.

"So," Eliza said, "I have some news."

Everyone turned to look at her. "Oh?" Mom asked. "What kind of news?"

"Did Oliver pop the question?" Brent asked teasingly.

"Only if the question is, *When are you moving out of my house?*" Sara added with a wry grin.

"I'll tell you in a second, no, and shut up," Eliza answered in respective order, jabbing her fork at Sara with menace in her eyes.

"Let your sister talk," said Mom.

"Anyway, now that I have the floor ..." continued Eliza. "Oliver got invited to go on tour with the Fever Dreams."

Brent whistled, impressed. "The Fever Dreams? Good for him. That's big. Marshall loves those guys."

"Yeah, it's big," Eliza said. Sara could tell that she was proud of him. Despite herself, she smiled along with her big sister. She ignored the pang of jealousy in her chest. "The other part of that news is ... I'm going with him."

Mom's eyes went round. "You're going with him? On tour? With Winter?"

Eliza nodded. "Yeah, going with him. We talked about it all day yesterday, and I think we can manage it just fine. It'll be hard, of course, but this is the opportunity of a lifetime for him, and he wants us to be there with him."

Sara was a little stunned. As much as she might not want to admit it sometimes, she liked having Eliza around. Her sister had a knack for steering Sara straight when she was about to give into one of her "less productive" impulses, as Eliza would call it. Plus, Winter was cute. It would be a little weird not to see them every day.

She looked across the table and could see that Mom was having a little trouble processing this information, too. "I'm—well, a little surprised, of course—but so happy for you! This will be an exciting adventure, I'm sure."

"Thanks, Mom," Eliza responded, giving her mother's hand a squeeze. "I know it'll be tough, but Oliver deserves this and I want to support him as much as I can. And don't worry, I'll still be able to handle all the inn business from my laptop on the road."

"Oh, I'm not worried about that in the slightest, dear. I just want you to be safe, you know? Those rock stars get up to lots of awful nonsense ..."

Sara laughed. "Have you met Oliver? The only 'rock star nonsense' he gets up to is staying up late to watch *Frozen* with Winter for the billionth time. They'll be fine, Mom." She looked at Eliza. "I'm excited for you, Liz. This'll be really cool."

"Thanks, Sara," Eliza replied with a warm smile. "I think so too."

"Does this make you a groupie?" Brent chimed in. Everybody laughed, and then it was Eliza's turn to throw a balled-up napkin at his head.

After the laughter had settled down, Brent spoke up again. "I've got some news, too, actually."

"Dear, you better not tell us that you're going on tour, too!"

He laughed. "No, no, nothing like that. I'll leave the rock star stuff to Oliver. Mine's not nearly as exciting. I'm working charter trips with Marsh."

Mom clapped her hands excitedly. "Oh, honey, that's fantastic!"

"Yeah, that's really great, Brent," added Eliza.

Sara just smiled. She'd been there at the bar when Marshall had pitched the offer again, and she knew Brent well enough to tell when he was going to say yes to something. She hadn't talked to him since he'd dropped her off at the bar, but judging by his liveliness this morning, his first trip must have gone well. Brent deserved some happiness. He had demons, that much was certain. This could be just the thing he needed to start slaying them.

"And we did our first trip yesterday, and it went pretty well, I'd say."

"I'm so proud of you, dear," Mom said with a huge grin on her face. "I know your father would be, too."

"Yeah," Brent said. The mention of Dad seemed to subdue him a little bit. He looked down at his empty, syrup-smeared plate for a second, then back up with a renewed smile twitching at the corner of his mouth. "Yeah, I bet he would be."

Sara's phone buzzed where it sat on the table. She snatched it up, just like she'd done pretty much every time she'd received a text message or app notification over the last eight months. It had become an empty, silly reflex—*He's not texting you, so stop hoping for it*—but one she was having trouble stopping.

This time, though, it was a text from Holly. *You guys all eating pancakes?*

Yep! Sara texted back.

Good. Calling rly quick. I got something to share.

For some reason, Sara felt another pang of irritation. Everybody else had news to share, great things that were happening to them. Why was she getting left out? She knew it was a stupid, petulant, selfish thought, and yet she was having the hardest time shaking that feeling, like she was the last kid getting picked for a dodgeball team.

She didn't have too much time to reflect on it, though, because her phone started buzzing with Holly's incoming FaceTime call. Sara suppressed a sigh and answered. "Hiya," she said. Holly looked like she was over the moon. Whatever news she had to deliver to the family, it was clearly exciting for her.

"Lemme see everyone!"

Sara rolled her eyes. "What am I, chopped liver?"

"Don't be a drama queen," Holly lectured. "Just spin me around."

Sara did as she was told, turning the phone around so Mom, Eliza, and Brent could all see Holly. They all waved.

"So, guess what?!" Holly squealed without waiting for anyone to ask.

"Don't keep us in suspense," Sara drawled.

"We're coming home!"

"Home?" Brent asked. "Home as in Nantucket?"

"Yes!" She launched into a whole spiel about how Pete had run into somebody-or-other, and they were coming to Nantucket to start their own law firm, so the Goodwin clan was going to make the move back to the island. Sara tuned her out after a while, though her mother and siblings were glued to the screen, listening intently.

Good news after good news, for everyone else—except for her. *Stop being a brat,* she told herself. *You're acting like a spoiled rotten little kid. This is your family. You're supposed to be happy when they're happy.*

But the truth was that she wasn't. And she knew that, the deeper she dug into the black ball of fury nestled in the middle of her heart, the more she'd find that there was guilt in the core of it. She wasn't happy because she herself had done things that ruined that happiness. She had only herself to blame. That was a harsh thing to stomach. She couldn't keep pinning her problems on the world. Other people were neither the source nor the solution of her misery. It was her. It came from her and it ended with her.

What she needed was to do something positive for herself. She needed to pull herself up by her bootstraps and build something she could be proud of. Not for anyone else—not for Gavin or for Russell, not even for her mother or her father—but for *her*. She, Sara Alexandra Benson, was responsible for her own well-being. And it was high time she started doing something about that.

But what could she do? The answer came from deep within her, like she had a disembodied voice shouting from the bottom of a well.

The restaurant.

"You have a gift! When are you opening up a restaurant? You could charge two hundred bucks a head for a dinner like this, easy."

"This is the truth, the whole truth, and nothing but the truth, so help me God. You're an artist. I've never had lobster that good in my whole life."

Those memories and a thousand others just like them flowed through her like water through a broken dam. People believed in her. Perfect strangers took just a bite of food and started offering up hosannas like they were having a transcendent religious experience. It had happened too many times to discount.

Maybe she would never be golden child Eliza, effortlessly good at everything she touched.

Maybe she would never be happy mother Holly, blessed with love and companionship.

Maybe she would never be Brent, who had a hard road of his own but knew what it meant to enjoy the fruits of his own labor.

She would have to be just Sara. Her own person. Her own path. *My little bull,* as her dad had called her.

"I've got news, too," she announced suddenly. She felt guilty for stealing the spotlight from Holly. But then again, everyone else had gotten their turn. Now, she wanted her fifteen minutes of Benson family fame. She felt a swell of pride and defiance in her chest, burning hot. Her face was flushed with excitement.

"What is it, Sara?" asked her mother cautiously.

She felt all eyes on her. At the very last second, she almost changed her mind. Once she said it, there would be no going back, no putting the words back into her mouth. The thought would be out in the universe, and she'd either have to tackle the challenge she was setting herself up, or fail in the face of it. But once it was spoken, those were the only two options.

My little bull. Gavin. Russell. Failure. Effort. The struggle, the reward. *You have a gift.*

She could do this.

"I'm opening a restaurant."

14

MAE

Oh, dear.

A restaurant was a big deal. She knew her youngest daughter was as headstrong as they came, but was this biting off more than she could chew?

Mae had been doubtful when Sara had first announced that she wanted to go to culinary school, nearly a decade ago. It seemed like it had somewhat come out of the blue, like Sara had just seen a magazine article that seemed interesting to her. She'd always been an impulsive thing, quick to glom onto a trend she liked and dive into the deep end head-first. There was a running joke in the family that when Sara learned how to ride a bike and drive a car, no one had ever taught her where the brakes were. She didn't want to brake, she wanted to *go go go*. Sometimes, it made Mae worry an awful lot for her little girl.

But then again, Sara was a woman, full-grown, capable of making her own decisions. And she wouldn't take kindly to anyone telling her no. Mae had wanted to say no when Sara first brought up culinary school, but Henry had convinced her that she needed to let Sara follow her heart, as fickle as it might seem sometimes from a worried mother's perspective. Henry saw a fire in her that Mae often mistook for volatility. *Never afraid of a fight, that one,* he'd say, chuckling, whenever Sara charged headlong into whatever had most recently caught her eye.

Perhaps it was just that she and Sara were so different. Mae was cautious by nature. Henry had had to buy her nearly a half-dozen beers before she'd even *talk* to him that night they first met at the Harvard bar. Sara, were she in Mae's shoes, would have charged over, grabbed him by the shirt collar, and planted a kiss right on his lips. Mae chuckled at the thought. She was a look-before-she-leapt kind of person. Sara would leap without ever checking to see if there was anywhere to land.

Which was exactly how this felt. A *restaurant.* That was a big thing. It was complex, and expensive, and delicate.

But that didn't mean it was impossible.

Mae could swear she felt Henry's hand on her shoulder for just a moment, and something like his whisper in her ear. If anyone could will this thing into existence, it was Sara. She ran through walls because she never even stopped to consider whether or not they could stop her. Wasn't that an admirable quality? Wasn't that worth nurturing whenever she could? Yes, perhaps it was.

They'd chitchatted about Sara's big idea for a little while after she'd first loosed it upon them. Brent had volunteered his services to help her with any of the construction that he could. Eliza said she'd help run the books and the advertising. Mae had wanted to lend a hand of her own, but she decided first to think about how she could be most useful. She also needed a little bit of time to chew on the prospect as a whole.

It felt like a fragile moment in her relationship with Sara. After their conflict in the kitchen on Friday night, Mae had been very wary around Sara, for fear of upsetting her further. It all stemmed from a good place in her heart—she wanted to protect her little girl from having her heart broken again. But as she was only now starting to realize, nearly three decades after she'd brought Sara into this world, living with your heart on your sleeve just meant that it was exposed sometimes. Sara lived a life of dramatic highs and depressing lows. That was her path, her role. It wasn't such a bad thing, necessarily. Hard at times, to be sure, but not a bad thing. It wasn't her role as Sara's mother to make her do things differently. It was her role simply to be there when her daughter needed her.

That was how she landed on the perfect idea for how she could contribute. Eliza had gotten a call from Oliver, saying Winter had woken up from her mid-morning nap and wanted her mother, so she'd said her goodbyes and gone home. Brent needed to go take Henrietta for a run, so he departed as well. Sara and Mae stayed behind to clean up. Mae washed, Sara dried. They worked in silence for a little bit, until the last dishes were done and put away. Then, Mae turned and rested her hand on top of Sara's.

"I want you to know that I support you," she said, staring into Sara's eyes. "In anything. Whatever you do, forever. You and I haven't always seen eye-to-eye—"

"That's an understatement," Sara murmured with a soft smile.

"Yes, maybe it is. But you're a beautiful, proud, intelligent woman, and I'm honored to be your mother. And, if you let me, I'd be honored to be your partner, too."

"My partner?" Sara said, wrinkling her nose. "What does that mean?"

Mae chose her next words carefully. "Your father left some money behind. An insurance policy. I haven't wanted to say anything about it —I haven't wanted to think about it at all, actually. But I'm thinking that now might be a great opportunity to put it to some good use. This is family business, after all. I know that he would love to see his money at work to help you achieve your dreams."

"Oh, Mom!" Sara cried. Mae saw that she had tears pricking the corners of her eyes. They embraced. "I'm sorry, Momma," she whimpered, pressing her face into Mae's shoulder. "I'm so sorry. I love you."

"I love you too, honey," Mae said, squeezing her daughter tight. She kept her eyes shut so that her own tears didn't spill out. It felt like they'd connected for the first time in a long time. Mae hadn't had many moments like this over the years with her daughter, and that only made this one more special.

Eventually, the women separated, but Sara kept her grip on her mother. "I can do this," she said, wiping the last of her tearstains from her face.

"I know you can," Mae said firmly. She wanted to tell Sara with her words, her tone, her body language, her whole heart, that she believed in her. "I never, ever doubted you." Whether that was true or not didn't matter. What mattered was that she meant it now. And she did.

Mae tended to a few small chores after breakfast, but Sundays were generally slow around the inn, especially since almost all the guests had checked out earlier that morning to head back to their lives on the mainland. Her phone rang a little while later.

"Hello?" she answered.

"Hi, love, how are you?" It was Toni.

"Oh hello!" Mae said in delight. She'd been close with her sister-in-law ever since they met, and they'd grown even closer in the wake of losing Henry. They talked once every week or two, whenever Toni found time and cell-phone reception in her travels around the world to give home a ring. "I'm wonderful. How are you? What's the latest exotic locale?"

"That's great to hear. Argentina, at the moment. The wine is to die for."

Mae giggled. "I can only imagine. Save some for us, won't you?"

"No promises. It's just too good!"

"Well, I suppose I can't blame you. How are you getting along?"

"I'm good," Toni answered. "Great, actually. I don't want to be rude, but the reception here has been god-awful, so I wanted to just fill you in on something before the call cuts out."

Mae frowned and took a seat on the edge of the couch. "Oh, of course! What's going on? Is everything all right?"

"Yes, I'm totally fine, nothing like that. The problem is actually that everything is more than all right, if that makes any sense at all. It probably doesn't. It's just ... the world is so big, Mae! I spent almost my whole life in Nantucket, and I think now that I might've been missing out. Every time I think about coming home, I get this awful knot in my chest. So I decided something."

"I must admit, I'm a little bit confused."

"I'm sure. Sorry, I'm explaining this terribly. Let me cut to the chase: I'm not coming back to Nantucket." The words hit Mae like a blow to the chest, but Toni wasn't finished yet. "I'm not coming home, and ... I'm selling the inn."

Mae fell back in her seat. "You're ... selling it?"

Toni was babbling. "I know this must come as a dreadful shock, and I can't thank you enough for all the work you've done in keeping it going. But I found someone who's willing to take it over—a hospitality entrepreneur; he owns some hotels scattered around the northeast and when I mentioned Nantucket, his eyes just lit up and he made such a generous offer that I just can't say no ..."

Mae hardly heard the rest of what her sister-in-law said. Selling the inn ... After a morning of good news from her children, this was the last thing she wanted to hear. It was horrible news, actually. Mae hadn't ever expected to end up quite where her life had taken her over the last year, but she had fallen in love with the inn and everything about it. She liked being useful and welcoming. She liked meeting guests and cooking food for them. She liked being an ambassador for Nantucket and showing people the island that had stolen her heart from the day she first arrived. Without the inn in her world, who knew where she would be? Trapped in her own memories back on Howard Street, probably. Feeling useless and unwanted. That sounded like a nightmare.

But what could she do? She'd just pledged Henry's life insurance payout to Sara for her restaurant, and even if she hadn't, it wouldn't be enough money to cover the cost of the inn. The boom of Nantucket real estate over the last two dozen years meant that property was wildly expensive.

She needed a plan. What that would look like, she wasn't sure. But until she had a plan, she was going to keep this to herself. She would have to take some time to think.

Dominic came into the room a few minutes after Mae hung up the phone with Toni. He'd been on a long walk along the beach and looked tanned and content. "Good morning!" he said brightly. He must've seen something in her face, because his smile turned into a frown. "Is everything okay?"

She forced herself to smile. "Everything is wonderful." Hopefully, sooner rather than later, she would actually mean that.

She just had to figure out how.

PART II

TWO WEEKS LATER

15

MAE

Friday evening.

It had been almost two weeks since Mae's roller coaster of a Sunday morning. She still wasn't quite sure where her head was. There were so many things to take in—Brent was working! Eliza was leaving! Holly was moving! Sara was starting a restaurant! And then there was the bombshell of all bombshells: Toni was selling the inn. It was too much for one person to take in. But for some reason, Mae—who had never been much good at keeping secrets—found herself not wanting to talk to anybody about it. Even now, with two of her best friends standing next to her, she kept trying to find reasons to delay telling them about Toni's news.

Debra, Lola, and Mae were volunteering at a silent auction fundraiser held by the Nantucket Safe Harbor for Animals. It was an annual event, and the ladies were always involved. In the past, Mae had shouldered more of a leadership role—helping to wrangle donations from various businesses and to drum up excitement amongst the island's residents—but this year, she had taken a back seat. With the inn and her granddaughter to attend to, there simply weren't enough hours in the day to devote the proper time and attention to the silent auction. Still, she wouldn't miss it for the world, so she made sure that Debra and Lola signed her up to help moderate the event and assist their guests as needed.

Right now, the three ladies were manning the drinks station, passing out punch to attendees as they wandered from auction item to auction item. It gave them plenty of time to chat. Debra was talking about some upcoming changes to the middle school curriculum that she wasn't pleased with. As a school counselor and psychologist, she was heavily involved with the local public education system. Mae was only half listening, though, as Debra told them about how disconnected and out of touch the state bureaucracy was when it came to ramming curriculum adjustments down the throats of Nantucket teachers. Really, her mind was still on the phone call with Toni.

She'd run through it a million times over the last five days. It still didn't quite seem real. Toni had poured blood, sweat, and tears—not to mention quite a lot of money—into the Sweet Island Inn. She'd transformed it from a ramshackle house that would've likely been bulldozed if it had remained on the market, into a beautiful and thriving business that drew rave reviews from anyone who stayed there. It seemed like such a shame to just let that go. A new owner wouldn't be able to provide the same level of loving care that Toni—and then, in turn, Mae—had shown the property.

And yet, Mae couldn't blame her. If Nantucket was truly the home of painful memories for Toni, then maybe staying abroad and continuing to explore the world actually was the best thing for Toni. Mae cared deeply for her sister-in-law. She knew that Toni needed to mourn in her own way, just like Mae needed to mourn in hers. But what should happen when those ways were diametrically opposed?

The truth was that the inn really had become Mae's way to mourn, to grieve, and—bit by bit as the days went by—to find new meaning and purpose in her life. Without that, she foresaw a sad, empty future.

What would selling the inn mean for her? For her guests? For Dominic most of all? Wasn't the inn his home, too? In a weird way, yes, it was. Mae still wasn't ready to delve into that hornet's nest of emotions. She inevitably landed on the same thoughts every time she thought about him: he was a nice man, a good man, and she was glad he was in her life. With everything else as chaotic as it had become, she just didn't want to go any further than that. Fortunately, he seemed content to just share her company and write his book.

"Earth to Mae?" said Lola. "You're in space, lady."

"Sorry." Mae blushed. "You're right. My head is all over the place today."

"Is something on your mind?" Debra asked.

"No, no, nothing like that." Truth be told, Mae didn't want to talk about any of the things on her mind with her friends right now. It wasn't that she didn't trust them to confide in, or that she had some ulterior motive for keeping things secret. She just felt like she had to crack this particular nut on her own.

"I suspect a little fibbing is taking place," Lola fake-whispered to Debra.

"You might be on to something, detective," Debra murmured back.

"Enough, you two." Mae laughed. "I will not be interrogated without a lawyer present!"

The three women all chuckled as they continued handing out drinks. When the next wave of auction attendees had passed, Lola turned back to her. "I don't want to press you too hard, Mae." She laid her hand on top of Mae's. "But we're here for you if you need us. You know that, of course. But it's just good to remind each other sometimes."

Mae smiled. Lola was right. It was easy to forget every now and then that she had good friends around her. People who loved her and cared about her. Maybe unloading some of these problems was a good idea. She still couldn't figure out why she was so darn reluctant to do so.

Fortunately, she didn't have to puzzle over it for much longer. Because just then, who should walk up and ask for a glass of punch but the one and only Dominic O'Kelley.

"Good evening, ladies," he said in that rolling Irish brogue.

"Well, if it isn't Mr. O'Kelley!" Debra said merrily. "How are you, darling?"

Dominic nodded and smiled. "In good health and good spirits, thank you. And yourself?"

"Well, it's always nice to be in the presence of a famous novelist."

He blushed and bowed slightly. "Not so famous, I promise you. Middling at best, and for that I am thankful."

Mae watched the whole proceeding ruefully. She knew Debra was just trying to get a rise out of him, not actually flirting or anything like that. She was probably trying to get a little bit of a rise out of Mae herself, too, now that she thought about it. Neither Debra nor Lola had come out and said much of anything—as a matter of fact, with the exception of the always-blunt Sara, no one had commented directly on what might or might not be blossoming between Mae and Dominic—but Mae knew that both of her friends suspected that there was something there. The two of them loved poking fun at Dominic, if only to hear him demure in his melodious voice and exotic turns of phrase. Mae was perfectly content to hang back and let them banter with him.

But Dominic wasn't quite so content. He turned to her, and Mae could swear that his smile grew a few degrees warmer. She felt the flush rising in her cheeks. "Good evening, Mae," he said softly.

"Hello, Dominic." She felt like a shy girl at the dance, batting her eyelashes and trying to disappear from the sight of the handsome boy asking her for a turn.

He swept a hand around the room. "Have any of the items on auction caught your eye?" he asked.

"Oh, the flowers from Soiree Floral downtown are magnificent. But I never bid," she added. "I have rotten luck when it comes to things like that."

His eyes flashed behind his glasses. He had dressed up for the occasion, Mae noticed, in a dark green button-down shirt and gray slacks. He looked exactly like what he did—bookish, intelligent, handsome, polite. Like a gentleman. There was also something distinctly Irish about him. Mae could never quite put her finger on it, but his homeland radiated from him like a strong cologne. "Perhaps tonight is your lucky night, then," he said.

"You never know, Mae," prodded Lola. "Maybe your luck is turning!"

Mae doubted that very strongly. She'd never thought of herself as very lucky. At least, not in the little ways, like winning raffles or catching all green lights on her drive somewhere. She was lucky in the ways that mattered—like finding Henry, like being gifted the Sweet Island Inn. The problem was that those things seemed to exist only on borrowed time. Toni's call seemed like just the latest iteration of that pattern. *Giveth and taketh away,* or something like that.

"Anyway," Dominic said, straightening up and fixing his glasses higher on his nose. "I am sure I am disrupting you ladies from your work. I think I'll take a turn around the room and see what might be up for purchase. Have a wonderful evening, Debra, Lola, Mae." He looked at each of them in turn and nodded politely, saving a warm smile and Mae for last. Then he turned and meandered slowly away, hands clasped behind his back.

As soon as Dominic was out of earshot, Debra turned to Mae and seized her by the wrist. "He *loves* you!"

"I couldn't agree more," said Lola, nodding.

"Oh, that's just Dominic," Mae protested. "He's like that with everyone. He's really a very courteous man. They don't teach manners here like they do over in Ireland."

"No way," Lola insisted. She was shaking her head decisively. "That's not manners. That's real."

Debra nodded. "Very real."

The heat in Mae's cheeks intensified. She turned her attention to the table to pour some more cups of punch, though that was hardly necessary, given the rows and rows of already filled cups that were arranged neatly before them.

She could sense Lola and Debra exchanging meaningful glances over her head, but she kept her eyes down. She and Dominic were just good friends. She'd been telling herself that since he first showed up on her doorstep, and she really did believe it. Or at least, she once did.

But maybe that wasn't completely true anymore. Maybe something really had been blossoming between them when Mae wasn't paying attention. Was that such a bad thing?

Perhaps not, thought Mae. Perhaps that wasn't such a bad thing at all.

16

BRENT

Saturday morning.

It had been a whirlwind two weeks. Someone must have alerted the tourists to Nantucket's unseasonal spell of amazing weather, because they had come flocking in record numbers for this early in the spring. Marshall kept joking that they'd just heard that Triple B had started working charter trips and that's why they were arriving in droves.

Brent had worked a trip with Marshall at least every other day. It was exhausting work, but it was as honest as it came. He finished his days sunburnt and tired all the way down to the bone. Most nights, he was asleep by the time his head hit the pillow. He hardly had the energy to keep taking Henrietta for their jogs, though he knew that she'd never forgive him if he didn't, so he made the extra effort for her sake alone.

At least the money was good. Either this wave of tourists was unusually generous or Brent really did have a knack for this job, because the tips that were pressed into his hand at the end of each day still managed to take him by surprise. In just a couple weeks, he'd managed to pay the back rent that was due on his apartment, as well as get a new couch, throwing away an old one that had long outlived its usefulness. It felt good not to be concerned that his debit card would get declined while buying groceries at the Stop 'n Shop.

It felt especially good not to have quasi-panic attacks every time he so much as glanced at the water, too. Honestly, his anxieties had been few and far between. As long as he kept his head down and focused on his work, he didn't pay much mind to the fear that still lurked in the back of his head. He might never again be fully at peace while out on the water, but as long as he could keep his wits about him enough to hook bait and chat idly with customers, he'd managed to find a fragile coexistence between himself and the ocean.

Until today.

When Marshall texted him first thing and told him that they were headed out to the Garden of Eden this morning by special request, Brent felt a geyser of panic in his chest. They'd managed to avoid it thus far, but it was one of the more popular spots within reach, so it had been bound to crop up sooner or later.

Brent knew that Marshall was only texting him this heads-up out of courtesy. Being his lifelong best friend, Marshall was well aware of how Brent felt about the Garden of Eden. As Brent strode up morosely to where Marshall had the boat idling next to the marina dock, he knew that his friend could see the discomfort written all over his face. To his credit, Marshall kept things subdued in place of his normal over-the-top bombast.

"Morning, brother." He handed Brent a cup of coffee. "Sleep all right?"

"Good enough," Brent grumbled. He'd slept like a log, actually. No dreams. That was rare, too.

"Ready for the day?"

Brent rubbed some sleep out of his eyes and looked up at Marshall. It was obvious that Marshall was just concerned about him. Brent sighed. His first reaction was to be defensive, but that wouldn't get either of them anywhere. "Ready as I'll ever get, I suppose. Had to happen sometime, right?"

Marshall nodded. "Yeah, probably. But if you aren't ready, I can do it myself."

Brent shook his head firmly. "No. Can't leave you on your own like that. Wouldn't be right."

"Fair enough," Marshall said, pleased, though he'd never admit that.

"Besides, you'd be lost without me," Brent added with a grin.

His buddy chuckled. "Let's not get ahead of ourselves. I preceded you into this world, my friend, and if you aren't careful, I'm gonna kick you out of it before me."

Brent raised his fists. "You're three days older than me. I'll end you in three minutes. Let's go, amigo. Put 'em up."

Marshall roared and charged at him. The two men mock-wrestled, throwing each other in headlocks and bumping back and forth along the starboard side of the boat, each fighting for the upper hand and laughing all the while.

Only when someone cleared their throat from above did they stop roughhousing and separate.

"Uh, 'scuse me, gentlemen. Sorry to break up the party, but I'm looking for Marshall Cook? Got a charter trip booked with him for the day."

Marshall was still panting as he smoothed back his hair and straightened out his shirt. "At your service, sir. You must be Roy McNeil, then, right? Welcome aboard."

"Yessir, that'd be me." The man squatted and reached out a hand to shake. Marshall and Brent took turns introducing themselves. Then

Roy and Marshall started talking. Brent's attention, though, stayed trained on the girl who was standing a step or two off to the side.

She looked to be around Brent's age, early twenties, with long, dirty-blonde braids and a smattering of freckles across the bridge of her nose. Her eyes were warm hazel, and there was a grin playing at the corners of her lips. She had a mischievous look to her smile that seemed perfectly in keeping with her outfit—well-worn denim overalls, cut off high on her thigh, with a bright red bikini top underneath. Fun, but maybe a little reckless. Dangerous, perhaps. His mother would have called her "full of personality."

"I'm Brent," he called up to her somewhat awkwardly.

"Ally," she replied. She popped her gum, then bent to shake his hand. Brent noticed every minute detail—the rings stacked on her fingers, the tangle of yarn bracelets that looked like they'd been bleached of color by hours in the sun, the constellations of freckles scattered along the underside of her forearms, which were a deep, bronze tan.

Brent cleared his throat and let go of her hand after maybe just a beat too long. Her grin twitched. He wondered if she was laughing at him.

"Come on down, folks!" Marshall called over.

Brent helped Ally into the boat, first taking her backpack from her and then grasping her hand to ease her step down from the dock. Roy, whom Brent assumed was Ally's father, hopped down capably. He and Marshall seemed to be getting along like gangbusters already. Marshall always did have a way of conversing amicably with old guys. Normally, that worked out great for their charter trips. But this time around, it meant Brent was left to entertain Ally. That wouldn't be a problem, except for that he felt strangely mute and bumbling in her presence. She had this way of looking at him, with that flash in her eyes and the grin playing on her lips, that made him feel like he was on display.

"What brings you guys into town?" Brent asked her. Anything to fill the silence. Marshall was clambering behind the controls, firing up the engine, and pulling the boat away from the dock, still chatting with Roy all the while.

"Here until July," Ally said. She smacked her gum again. "Sort of a quasi-vacation thing. Mom and my sister are at the spa today, but that's boring, so me and Dad decided to come have a little fun of our own out here."

"Gotcha," Brent replied lamely. He reached down and fiddled with a few things that didn't really need to be fiddled with. "What do you, uh, do?"

She laughed. Brent's face immediately turned red. He turned and pretended to scan the water. They were picking up speed, and the island was retreating behind them. "I'm in college," she explained. "Well, I was. Just graduated. So I'm here now until I figure out what's next in my life."

"You and me both," Brent said.

Ally laughed again. "You a little lost too, sailor boy?"

He chuckled. "I guess you could say that." *Sailor boy.* She was so personal, so familiar, right off the bat. Brent wasn't like that in the slightest. He took a long time to warm up to people before he let his personality shine through. Ally didn't seem to have any such qualms. They were two minutes into knowing each other and she was already teasing him, laughing at him, poking fun. It was a little unsettling, to be honest. But he didn't *not* like it. There was something really appealing about her energy. Like they could cut the BS and get to know each other right away. No veneer, no façade. Just straight-up truth, uncut honesty.

Again, unsettling. Brent had way too many demons rattling around in his head to just lay his cards face-up on the table like that.

Luckily for him, they had gotten out of the no-wake zone that surrounded the marina and made it to open ocean, so Marshall picked up some speed. Ally said something to Brent as they accelerated, but the wind whipped her words away. She laughed, though—he could tell she was laughing without having to hear what joke she'd made.

The next few hours passed quickly. They hit up a couple spots that sat between the marina and the Garden of Eden, which was their ultimate destination. At each one, Brent dutifully set up Ally's rod and told her about what they might expect to catch. She didn't have much in the way of fishing experience, but she was a quick learner. By the time they got to their third location, she was comfortable casting out the line herself. No bites as of yet, but they would come eventually. They always did.

He alternated back and forth between chatting easily with Ally and getting flushed with embarrassment. It was something about her laughter that did it. There was a mischievous edge to it, yes, but it was more that he just couldn't for the life of him figure out if she was laughing *with* him or *at* him. She kept calling him "sailor boy," too, as in, "So are you from Nantucket, sailor boy?"

"Yeah. Born and raised."

"What's that like?"

He looked at her oddly. He'd never really thought about that question, honestly. What was Nantucket like? It was like—well, he didn't know. "It's home, I guess."

"Yeah, but what does that mean?"

"It means, uh—well. I suppose it means that ... it's just all I've ever known, I guess. What's it supposed to mean?"

"You're the one who said it. Have you ever left?"

Brent nodded. "A couple of times. New York, Boston."

"Do you mean 'a couple' as in literally two?" She looked aghast.

He shrugged nonchalantly. "Yeah. Why do you ask?"

She grabbed his forearm. "Because it's a big freaking world! You gotta get out of here. Nantucket isn't all that, you know."

Brent just laughed and shook his head. "I like Nantucket. It's nice here."

"How do you know you wouldn't like somewhere else better?"

"I just know. This is my home."

She sighed like she was a teacher dealing with a difficult student who just wasn't getting it. "You're crazy, sailor boy. You gotta get out. See some stuff."

But the thought had really never occurred to Brent. Leave Nantucket? Why would he do that? He knew Nantucket. He understood Nantucket. His family was here, his whole life. What would leaving do for him? As far as he could see, not much.

"Where've you been?" he asked, if only to change the subject.

Ally cast a hand around. "Not enough places yet! I will, though. Soon."

One of the rods hit just then, cutting off their conversation before he could ask where she wanted to go and when. She leaped up to grab it from the holster and started reeling in excitedly. Brent stood back and brooded while Ally struggled with the rod, offering advice every now and then. *Give him some slack. Now, yank it in! Get that hook set!* The fish got away before she could reel him in, but Brent was hardly paying attention.

He had a sudden flashback to Eliza calling him a Nantucket hillbilly. That always made him chuckle. If that's what he was, then so be it. He belonged here. That was the beginning and the end of it.

Brent was so caught up in his thoughts that he barely even noticed when they got to the Garden. Marshall pulled in where he wanted to set up camp, right by the underwater drop-off, and killed the engine. Brent looked around. It was just another patch of empty ocean, like any other. Why had he feared this so much? There was a lot of ocean on this planet. A lot of bare, meaningless water. There was no reason to be scared of this, any more than he'd be scared of the patch of water a quarter mile over from here.

His dad wasn't here anymore. No part of him was. All the anxiety that had been racing through him since Marshall's text that morning vanished as suddenly as it had come. What a strange sensation. It was like a little kid who built up this nightmarish fantasy of the boogeyman in the closet, only to be confronted with nothing more than some shirts on hangers when his parents came in to open the door for him. Fear, peaking up to a crescendo that ultimately fell flat and vanished without a trace. He'd been expecting—heck, maybe even *hoping*—for a big, cathartic moment. But as he gazed around the horizon, he felt nothing. Neither fear nor pleasure. It was weirdly disappointing, as if he'd had nausea that passed without the satisfaction of purging it. Life wasn't like a movie, as it turned out. No soundtrack in the background telling some hidden audience that this was a big moment for him. It didn't feel like a big moment at all. It felt like nothing.

Only when he looked at Ally did he feel something. Not much of anything—just a hint. Just a spark. Just kindling, the vague suggestion that a fire could be built here. Maybe. If he played his cards right. Face-up, without fear.

He didn't know whether he could do that. But as he stood at the site of the accident that had taken his father's life and looked at this girl— a girl he'd just met this morning and yet someone he felt like he already knew so well—he felt like maybe, just maybe, he had a chance.

17

MAE

The days after the auction passed slowly and strangely. Mae would never admit this out loud, whether to herself or to anyone, but she had made it somewhat of a point to steer clear of Dominic since the conversation at the punch station with Lola and Debra. She still met him on the porch in the mornings for their sunrise coffee ritual, but she often made her excuses and left early to attend to her innkeeper's tasks.

That was exactly what she did this morning. She hadn't said much as they'd sat there. After she offered one or two words to his first couple questions—*How did you sleep? Do you have big plans for the day?*—he'd seemed to catch the hint and fall silent. She felt guilty. He hadn't done anything wrong by any stretch of the imagination. It was Mae herself who was the problem.

The issue was that Lola and Debra had stirred up a tangled ball of emotion that Mae had spent a year fussing over and was no closer to figuring out than she had been when she started. The heart of the question went something like this: How was she supposed to live her life now?

It was an impossible question; a recipe that needed every ingredient in the house and was never quite finished cooking. *How was she supposed to live her life?*

She supposed it was best to start with what she knew for certain: that she loved Henry, she had loved him since the moment she'd met him, and she would continue loving him for the rest of her life. That had never, ever been in doubt. It was as real and as constant as gravity, as the sun rising, as her love for her children. Here or not, alive or gone, it didn't matter—her love for her husband held true.

She knew also that with that love came sadness. And just like her love, that sadness would also be here forever. She had spent forty-plus years growing old with Henry, and she'd expected that to continue until both of them were confined to their rocking chairs on the front porch. It felt almost as though he'd abandoned her in the middle of a painting they were both working on. They had painted the broad strokes, the outlines of things that were unlikely to change. Four beautiful children, each perfect and yet flawed in their own perfect ways. A home in Nantucket. A daily give-and-take, a set of rituals, a way of moving around and with each other in their kitchen, their bedroom, their little world. He'd built all of that with her, but he'd been taken by fate before they had a chance to finish coloring in the details. There were so many beautiful subtleties to their lives that had not yet had an opportunity to emerge. Now, they never would—at least, not precisely the way they would have were Henry still here. It made her heart ache.

But there was still painting to be done, wasn't there? There remained blank spaces on the canvas of Mae's life that she had not yet gotten to. And if she stayed buried in the past, if she rooted herself next to Henry's grave, enmeshed herself in his memories, they would stay blank forever. Didn't she owe it to herself, to her children, to Henry, to paint those spaces in?

She fervently believed that she did. No matter which way she cut it, she could not bear to put her life on hold and mourn indefinitely. She was a hummingbird, gosh darn it, and hummingbirds did not sit still. They were physically incapable of it. That was how Mae felt. As though she'd spent a year flying in place, and if she did not take off for a new horizon soon, then she would simply fall from the sky and never, ever fly again. Her heart ached at that, too.

So, back to the question that had kept her up late every night for a year: How was she supposed to live her life? She knew her children would be part of it. She knew that Nantucket would be part of it. But what else might fill in the spaces?

Could Dominic be one of those things?

That thought frightened her, because it came so suddenly and unexpectedly and yet so, so forcefully. Perhaps Dominic had filled in a space in her life before she ever realized that that was what he was doing. How could she have been so blind to what he had come to mean to her? It took Lola and Debra pointing it out to make her really look the thing in the eye and make sense of it.

Dominic was a stroke of paint on the canvas that hadn't yet quite taken shape. It was up to Mae now to decide what to do with that stroke. And that was a scary thought. Because taking up her brush again meant, in some way, that she would be leaving Henry behind. Not all of him, of course. But part of him would stay in the past while she walked into her future. She didn't think she was ready for that. She wasn't sure if she would ever be.

So she stayed away from Dominic, and she kept herself occupied, and she decided that she would think about it later, when she wasn't quite so busy.

That Saturday, after replying curtly to Dominic, she bid him a quick goodbye and went into the inn to take care of the few little things this morning that required her attention. Her phone rang almost as soon as she stepped inside. It was Eliza.

"Hi, honey," she said, grateful for the distraction.

"Hey, Mom." She went muffled for a second, then fixed the phone. "Sorry. Anyway, listen: it's been a hectic morning over here. Winter is being a handful. She has a little bug, I think, or maybe she just didn't sleep well, I'm not sure. And packing is taking forever and a half. We had to come over to Howard Street to get a few things. I know we had plans so you could see her before we leave, but do you mind just coming over here instead? It would make my life a lot easier."

"Oh," Mae said. "Oh. Well, okay. Sure, hon. Whatever you need."

"Thanks, Mom. See you in a bit." She hung up before Mae could say anything else.

Mae stood on the threshold for a moment. She heard Dominic sigh behind her on the other side of the porch door.

Oddly enough, her heart was pounding. She knew why.

She'd been very apprehensive about going back to the Benson family home on 114 Howard Street. As a matter of fact, she'd avoided it whenever possible over the last twelve months after moving to the innkeeper's quarters at the Sweet Island Inn. If she needed something or other from the house, she usually sent Brent or Sara over to fetch it for her.

She was reluctant to go back because she knew that returning to the home she'd shared with Henry was always going to be hard for her. That was another reason that her heart had plummeted so dramatically when Toni had told her about her plan to sell the inn. Did that mean Mae would return to Howard Street? Was she mentally, emotionally, or spiritually prepared for that? She honestly wasn't sure.

But she had to see her daughter and granddaughter before they embarked on this wild adventure of theirs, so it didn't seem like she had a choice. Best to just swallow her fear and get things out of the way as quickly as she could manage.

Once she had bagels set out for breakfast and beach towels stacked up by the door for her guests to use for the day, she left a note on the refrigerator that said she'd be back in a little while. She decided to take her bicycle from the inn over to Howard Street. It was a nice morning, warm and sunny. She let her mind wander as she rode slowly down the road.

There was so much happening all of a sudden. It felt like the whole family had been in something of a holding pattern for a year. And now, out of nowhere, it had burst into a million different directions, like a fireworks display. It was getting a little hard to trace all the patterns.

Eliza, Oliver, and Winter were headed off for an eight-month sojourn with a rock band. Mae's heartstrings twinged at the thought of being separated from her granddaughter for so long. She'd come to rely on Eliza's wisdom when it came to various administrative tasks around the inn, too, so she knew she would miss her eldest daughter's intelligence and foresight. But she felt deep in her soul that this was the right thing for Eliza. She'd spent so long coloring in the lines, so to speak—living her life according to rigid expectations, both those others placed on her and the ones she placed on herself—so to see her follow her heart and live spontaneously seemed like just the ticket for unlocking a path to real happiness. Oliver was a kind man, too. He treated her Eliza well. This was the best thing for both of them.

But just as Eliza was leaving, Holly would be returning home, and bringing Mae's other grandchildren with her. That was a welcome surprise. Mae had always loved Pete, ever since he and Holly had first fallen for each other all those years ago. It would be a joy to have them all back home on Nantucket again.

Then there was Sara. Mae hoped desperately that her grand plan for this restaurant was coming from the right place—a place of hope and ambition, rather than a place of desperation. There was no way to know for certain. But no matter what, Mae knew that she would be behind her one hundred percent.

Lastly, as always, was both the simplest and the hardest of her children. She knew that Brent thought of himself as a straightforward man. He was born on Nantucket, he lived on Nantucket, and he would always do so. But she wondered sometimes if there was a side of himself he hadn't yet discovered. *Let him be his own man,* Henry said often when she worried about what route her son would take in life. She tried to do that as much as possible. But it was hard to see him struggle. In those moments, all she had to offer was love. She had to believe that that was enough to see him through to the light at the end of the tunnel.

By the time she arrived at Howard Street, she felt somewhat better, having catalogued everything and given each winding branch of her life a dose of careful consideration. She still had a little undercurrent of anxiety as she walked her bicycle up the lane and propped it against the fence, but she swallowed it back and put a smile on her face. Eliza opened the front door as she approached. She had Winter in her arms. At the sight of her grandmother, Winter cooed and reached out a hand.

"Aww, my love!" Mae exclaimed. "Come to Grandma." She nestled Winter in her arms and poked her nose with a soft fingertip.

"She's been something else this morning," Eliza said, sighing. "Woke up every hour on the hour. I'm dead tired. And this packing is—well, nightmare doesn't even begin to cover it. How is a woman supposed to pack for both herself and a three-month old baby for almost a year on the road? I'm exhausted, and we're not even halfway."

Mae laughed. "Babies are a handful. And babies on the road doubly so. Tell you what—you go finish packing. I'll entertain the little angel for a while."

Eliza scoffed. "Little angel—man, she's got you fooled." But Mae could tell that she didn't really mean it. Try as she might to act the role of a sleep-deprived new mom, Mae knew that her oldest daughter was as competent as they came. She was more prepared than anyone else to handle the fickle moods and needs of a newborn. But that didn't mean she wouldn't appreciate a few minutes of peace and quiet. After all, what else were grandmas for?

"Come, come," Mae murmured to Winter in a sing-song voice. "Let's go see what trouble we can get into." She followed Eliza into the house.

"Hi, Mrs. Benson!" called Oliver from the living room. He was seated in the middle of a monsoon of clothes, bottles, open suitcases, and a million and one other things that were halfway to being packed or unpacked.

"Good morning, Oliver," said Mae. "Looks like you two have quite the project on your hands."

"You can say that again." He laughed. "I wasn't prepared for this."

"I'm sure you will be just fine. Just be nice to each other, all right? I remember one of the only times that Henry and I ever truly fought was over packing for a trip. Lordy, that was a nightmare."

"Oliver's already getting on my nerves this morning," Eliza accused, but she was laughing.

Oliver, for his part, held his hands up. "Who, me? I'm innocent of all charges."

Mae just shook her head. "I'm staying out of this. You kids be adults now. And be nice to each other!" she called over her shoulder as she headed for the stairs with Winter in her arms.

It was quieter upstairs. The wooden floors creaked under her weight, exactly as she remembered them. It was like hearing a familiar song from years and years ago come on the radio—a little sweet and a little sad at the same time. She walked slowly down the hallway. "Look," she said to Winter, raising her granddaughter up so she could see the framed picture Mae was pointing at. It was a family photo of Henry, Mae, and all the kids, taken at Winter Stroll almost two decades ago. Brent was a toddler, all bundled up in enough layers of scarves and beanies and a parka so thick that it swallowed him whole. "That's your mommy," she whispered to Winter. "And that's your uncle, and your aunt Sara, and your aunt Holly. That's Grandma. And that right there—that handsome fella—that's your grandpa. It's a shame you never met him, love."

Winter just looked solemnly at Mae.

"A shame indeed. You would have liked him. And he would have *loved* you, I can promise you that much. He was always a sucker for babies." Mae let loose a long exhale and kept walking down the hall. Her old bedroom was waiting at the end. It hadn't been used in months. She pushed the door open with one toe. It swung inward on silent hinges. She stopped at the threshold.

Everything was more or less how she left it. Bed made, dresser cleared, window shades pulled closed. One beam of light had snuck through the tiny sliver left between the curtains. It lit up a column of dust rising from the floorboards. The scene was oddly beautiful.

Mae felt suddenly uneasy. She didn't want to step in. It felt like disturbing something that ought to just be left alone. But that was silly. This wasn't a mausoleum. It was a bedroom, nothing more and nothing less. She walked in and sat down on the bed.

Winter looked around. She was starting to get better and better at controlling her head. Mae ran a gentle thumb along the soft slice of belly that lay exposed beneath the hem of Winter's shirt. Babies were always so soft and unblemished. And that baby smell ... she bent over and inhaled that unmistakable freshness, like powder and breeze.

"I used to live here with your grandpa," she murmured. Winter was gazing at her, unblinking. "For a long time. Your mother lived here with all her siblings, too. We were a very happy family." She frowned and corrected herself. "We are *still* a very happy family. But I do miss your grandfather. I miss him very much some days."

If she expected something to happen—for Henry's ghost to emerge from the closet or speak to her from the netherworld beyond—she was disappointed, because the only thing to answer her was silence.

She took a slow breath and looked around. She knew every inch of this room. Henry's gilded pocket watch, a gift from his own grandfather, still sat in its velvet box on his bedside table. The ceiling fan would still whine if you put it up to its highest setting. In the far right-hand side of the closet hung her wedding dress and Henry's tuxedo. She closed her eyes and remembered the day they were married. She remembered nestling her head against Henry's chest as the band played "The Way You Look Tonight" for their first dance. She could practically smell his cologne and the faint tang of whiskey aroma.

And then, inexplicably, she thought of Dominic. It was too much to say that she suddenly felt open to the possibility of loving again, but perhaps she just felt a little less uneasy about it than she had once before. Something about remembering Henry gave her this sense of —well, not exactly closure, but something akin to it. Like Henry was finally beginning to settle into a place in her heart where he could stay for the rest of her life. Like maybe there was a path forward. Only time would tell, she knew, and it wasn't as if she had ever gone through this experience before. She had only her own sense of rightness and wrongness to light her way. And right now, in this moment, she felt a powerful aura of rightness. It seemed to emanate from the things in this room, like the comforter and the bathroom mirror and the lamp in the corner were all vibrating at the same frequency as her own memories, and all of them were in harmony.

"I loved your grandfather very much," she said again to Winter. The baby said nothing back, of course, but she didn't need to. This time, when Mae said it, she felt like she could hold onto her past and her future at the same time. They weren't in conflict. There was nothing that needed to be untangled. There was Henry, forever and always, and there was the wide-open possibility of blank canvas, with the bright, alluring brushstroke that was Dominic, yearning to be explored.

A few hours later, after Eliza and Oliver had managed to wrangle their belongings into some kind of packing arrangement, Mae handed Winter back over to her mother and returned to the inn. She noticed a strong smell when she walked in the door. It was a fresh, floral smell, and when she rounded the corner into the living room, she saw why.

At least a dozen massive floral arrangements took up every conceivable flat surface. The room was positively bursting with color and scent, like a jungle had taken up residence in the inn. And standing in the middle of it with his back turned to her, carefully adjusting a bouquet of white roses in a glass vase, was Dominic.

He must have heard her enter, because he turned to her and smiled. His eyes flashed with an inexplicable river of emotion. "I recalled you saying that you quite admired the work of Soiree Floral at the silent auction," he explained gently. "And, I must admit, I tend to be quite lucky when it comes to winning things like that. So I took the liberty of putting my name forward." He smiled again.

Mae's heart swelled. He was a good man. The flowers were beautiful. Her life was knotty and unpredictable, more so than she had ever realized before. But in this moment, everything seemed so simple.

So she smiled, walked forward, and pulled Dominic into an embrace.

18

BRENT

Later on Saturday evening.

Brent was roused from sleep by his phone ringing.

It had been a very, very long day. Roy was a restless kind of guy, the sort of fisherman who's always convinced that "this spot is totally dead" and the next one will be the good-catch jackpot. Grass is greener on the other side, basically. Which was all well and good if that was a client's preference, but it meant that they'd spent the whole morning and the better part of the afternoon going from spot to spot to spot, barely taking any time to actually set up camp for very long at any of them. Despite that, they'd still managed to catch a fair amount of fish, so Roy was pleased enough with the day's haul. Nonetheless, it made for tiring work for the crew of Captain Cook Charter Fishing Co. Even Marshall, who'd barely stopped talking long enough to take in a full breath since the day he was born, was reduced to mumbling tired goodbyes by the time they returned to the marina. Brent had taken care of clean-up post-haste and jetted off home for the comfort of his bed.

"Sailor boy," said the voice on the other end of the line.

Brent sat bolt upright. "Ally?"

He was sure he was dreaming. But if he was, this was a weird dream. Not very imaginative. If he was going to be in charge of scripting his own dream, he sure wouldn't have set it in the same crummy apartment that he had to face during waking hours. But he looked around and confirmed that yes, he was still at his place—on the couch, as a matter of fact; he'd been too tired to drag himself even as far as the bedroom before keeling over and falling asleep. That meant he wasn't dreaming.

He pinched himself as hard as he could, just to be sure. "Ouch!"

"What?"

"Um, nothing," he muttered. He threw the ratty blanket off him. He stubbed his toe on the coffee table in the process and let out a blue streak of curse words.

"Wow, 'sailor boy' was really spot on, nickname-wise, wasn't it?" Ally remarked over the phone. "Do they teach you all those words in pirate school?"

"Who? I mean, how? What is happening?" His voice was still thick with sleep, and though he'd confirmed that he was in fact awake now, he hadn't processed much else. Well, besides the fact that Ally was on the other end of the call. Then again, that still didn't quite make much sense.

"You sound awfully confused. Should I call back?"

"No!" he blurted, way more forcefully than he intended. "No, no, it's fine. I was just—I'm awake."

She laughed, and he had the same annoying, niggling question he'd had all day—was she laughing *with* him or *at* him? He still hadn't landed on an answer. It was driving him nuts. *She* was driving him nuts.

Truth be told, he hadn't thought much about women since Rose. It wasn't a stretch to say she'd broken his heart last year. He was man enough to admit that now. She'd opened the door to a happy little life and then slammed it shut in his face. That wasn't all Rose's fault, he knew. She had baggage. Emotional scars, and the fear to go with it. But still, that didn't stop him from getting hurt by what she had told him. *I can't do this. I'm sorry.* He still shuddered every time he thought about the note she'd written.

He wondered where she was now, what she was doing.

Then, with a massive act of willpower, he wrenched his attention back to the present. Ally was on the phone. He could hear her breathing impatiently.

"What're you doing?" she asked him.

He looked around. Henrietta was curled up on her bed in the corner, but she was awake and eyeing him, as if trying to decide whether or not he ought to be taking this call. "I am—I *was*—sleeping. Your dad worked us hard today."

Ally laughed again. "He does that. He's a softie though."

"For you, maybe."

"Definitely for me," she agreed. "I'm his little angel."

"Why do I get the feeling you aren't all that angelic?"

For the third time in the last minute, she laughed. She laughed an awful lot. Brent was starting to realize that he liked that about her.

"Guilty as charged," she admitted. "As a matter of fact, that's why I was calling. Wanted to see if you could show me how to get into a little trouble around here."

"How'd you even get my number?" he asked, bewildered.

"Your boss gave me your business cards."

"Marshall is *not* my boss," Brent corrected sternly. When he realized how petulant he sounded, he relaxed and chuckled at himself.

"Boss, boyfriend, whatever. We don't have to put a label on it if you don't want to."

He knew she was messing with him, but it prickled him nonetheless. "He's not that either."

She changed the subject. "How's your girlfriend?"

This time, he was ready to banter. "Imaginary," he shot back.

"I hope she's nice."

"She is. Pretty, too."

"She sounds lovely. I hope you two have a wonderful life together."

Brent settled back onto the couch, smiling despite himself. "What kind of trouble are you trying to get into, anyhow?"

He could hear her grin through the phone. "Now you're talking my language," she said. "Depends—what do you have on tap?"

He started to answer, then caught himself. "I shouldn't even be on the phone with you. You're a client. This is a bad idea."

"*Was* a client," she corrected. "Trip's over. I left my client status on the boat. Now, I'm just an innocent citizen looking for something to do on a Saturday night. Where's the harm in that?"

Brent sighed. Something about this screamed trouble—Ally herself screamed trouble—and yet, he found himself getting drawn in. She just seemed like pure, unadulterated fun. Was that such a bad thing? Was that so wrong? He was a twenty-three-year-old man with no plans on a Saturday night. Was it such a bad thing to go see what Nantucket was up to tonight?

"So what's it gonna be, sailor boy?"

An idea popped into his head. He grinned. If he'd had a mirror in front of him, he knew exactly what he would see in his reflection—a grin that looked exactly like Ally's. Henrietta whined in the corner.

"Ever throw an ax?"

Thunk. The ax buried itself in the wooden target just left of center.

"Bull's-eye!" Ally cried, throwing her hands up in victory.

Brent laughed. "That's a little shy of a bull's-eye, cowgirl."

"Yeah, well, I'm shooting from the men's tees, so I get a little bit of a bump to my score."

Brent scratched his head. "I don't remember agreeing to that?"

Ally poked him in the chest. "You didn't have to. I'm the guest. I set the rules around here."

"I don't remember agreeing to that, either."

She sashayed away to the little table they were occupying at the far end of the ax-throwing lane. He watched her walk, trying not to be too obvious about admiring her. She was wearing a long blue sundress, despite a little bit of a chill that had set in once the sun went down. She didn't seem to mind the coolness of the air. Her tanned shoulders were exposed by the thin straps. Brent could swear that the sun on the boat that day had brought out a few more freckles across her collarbone.

She was pretty, there was no denying that. But, in all honesty— Scout's honor and all that—that wasn't her chief appeal to Brent. She just didn't seem to care about anything at all. It was like she was doing cartwheels through life without ever once worrying if she might fall. Brent couldn't exactly relate. But her energy was intoxicating nonetheless.

"Well, we're all out of axes," he said as he joined her at the table. "What's next?" She took a long sip of the beer. He'd stuck to his guns and ordered a seltzer, though he wanted badly to join Ally's party and drink the pitcher of beer she'd ordered. Still, he knew that that way held only trouble. No, best to let Ally do the drinking.

She smacked her lips as she drained her glass. "Thought I'd ask you the same question."

He weighed the options. "There's a billiards hall down the way if you shoot pool or throw darts or whatever. Could go dance at the Chicken Box, or—"

"I've got a better idea," she cut in. She had that fiery gleam in her eyes. Before she even opened her mouth to say what the idea was, Brent knew he was in. All the way in, head-first-into-the-deep-end in, hook-line-and-sinker in. That was a dangerous thing to feel, but he felt it anyway, and on a night like tonight, he wasn't going to second-guess it. Just go with the flow. Do the cartwheel. Take the plunge.

"Oh yeah?"

"Let's go swimming."

He laughed. "Sounds like fun, if you're into hypothermia. It's still only April. Might've been a warm spell, but the water is still—"

"I'll drive!" She snagged his car keys off the table and took off running. Brent stood still for a minute. When he realized she wasn't coming back, he dropped some cash on the table to pay for their ax-throwing and drinks, and took off running after her.

Ally had the car pulled up in front of the bar by the time he got out there. She flashed the brights on and off a half-dozen times, then laid on the horn a half-dozen times more. The music was cranked on high, too, some booming pop song on the radio. Brent was mortified.

People were leaning out from the bars and restaurants up and down the street, trying to see who was causing such a ruckus. He ducked his head as he hustled into the car.

"What on earth are you doing?" he exclaimed. "People are watching!"

Ally laughed. Her eyes were gleaming. "Let 'em watch!"

He knew this was a losing battle, so he changed the subject. "We're not swimming," he argued. "That's crazy talk."

"Maybe you oughta learn to talk crazy sometimes, sailor boy," she shot back with a wild grin.

"This is—you're—jeez, just ... You shouldn't be driving!"

"Why not?"

"You were drinking!"

She ran a hand through her long blonde hair and shrugged him off. "I had like two beers. I'll be fine. Relax; this ain't Catholic school. It's okay to break the rules sometimes."

He didn't have much of a chance to keep arguing, because just then, she floored the accelerator in his truck and they went sailing down the road. Ally seemed to be following the signs for the nearest beach. Brent, for his part, was white-knuckling the door handle. She didn't seem to be too drunk to drive by any means. He was actually fairly impressed by her ability behind the wheel, though she was for sure way more reckless than he ever would've been. They took corners at breakneck speed, but she never once faltered. It wasn't fear of crashing that kept Brent squeezing the daylights out of the handle. It was fear of Ally herself.

She was too open. She didn't seem to have any demons at all, at least not like he did. She wasn't worried about guilt or responsibility or any of the things that weighed so heavily on Brent's soul most hours of the day. As far as he could tell, she was mostly worried about wringing as much fun and emotion out of the world as she could, like squeezing every last drop of water out of a wet towel. She laughed loud and drove fast and drank quickly. And when she decided she wanted to go for a swim, she didn't check the temperature first. She just dove in.

Coincidentally, that seemed to be more or less exactly what she had planned. When they reached the parking lot for the beach, she threw the car in park and leaped out, leaving the keys in the ignition and engine running. Brent cursed again, retrieved the keys, and chased after her.

But the strangest thing happened as he ran down the path to the beach. It felt like he got lighter with every step. Like gravity was loosening its hold on him, or maybe he was just—for the first time in the last twelve months—outrunning his demons. The wooden boardwalk turned into sand, and as he burst out of the dunes, he saw Ally running ahead of him. The moon was bright tonight. It lit up the beach in a smooth white glow. Where it hit Ally's skin, it shone back, almost brighter for having touched her somehow.

She didn't stop. Brent thought she would've at least taken off her dress, maybe, but she didn't seem to even consider the possibility. She just kept running, from the soft sand into the wet sand and to the edge of the water. She didn't stop there, either. He could hear her laugh as the waves tickled her toes, then her ankles, then her knees. The hem of her dress was floating behind her in the water, and still she kept going, until she couldn't touch the bottom anymore. Then she started swimming straight out, like she was headed for the horizon.

He was frozen in place, right where the ocean met the sand. It looked dark and foreboding out there, even with the full moon skimming off the wave caps. He had two choices, as far as he could tell. He could sit and wait for her. Or he could shuck off his shoes and run in after her.

Staying on shore was safe.

Running after Ally was unknown.

But he'd been playing life safe for a long time now. *Maybe you oughta learn to talk crazy sometimes, sailor boy.*

Brent stood on one foot and ripped off his boot, then did the same with the other. He threw them over his shoulder and ran until the water was hugging his torso and he couldn't run anymore. He started swimming then, taking big, slashing strokes with his arms. His shoulders ached and he swallowed a fair amount of saltwater, but he didn't stop. Not until he finally reached Ally, treading water out past where the deep swells turned into whitecaps.

"I wasn't sure if you were gonna come out this far," she said. The moon lit up her face.

Brent smiled back. "To be honest, I wasn't sure, either."

"Well," she said, touching her chin as if she was deep in thought. "To the victor go the spoils, right?"

He wasn't sure what she meant. But when she reached out to grab his soaking wet shirt and pull him towards her to plant a kiss on his lips, he wasn't too worried about it anymore.

19

HOLLY

Sunday afternoon.

Everything was happening so fast! Holly felt like she was in one of those cartoons where something zoomed by her so quickly that it made her head literally spin around on her neck. One second, she was crying on her couch and terrified that her husband, her high school sweetheart, the love of her life and father of her children, was cheating on her. The next second, they were in the car on the way to go house-hunting in Nantucket. It still didn't quite make sense, but Holly was in such a good mood these days that she didn't even want to question it.

"Think the kids will be nice to your parents?" she asked.

"I gave them both a lecture on behavior before we left," Pete said. He was behind the wheel of their minivan as he pulled onto the highway, bound for the ferry to Nantucket. "Two lectures for Grady."

Holly grinned. She always knew when Pete was hiding something. "And ..." she prompted.

He smiled sheepishly. "And I promised him that I'd buy him a new video game if I got a good report from Pop-Pop and Memaw." When Holly started laughing at him, he protested, "Gotta show 'em both the carrot and the stick, you know? C'mon, now, that's just good parenting."

"What did you bribe Alice with?"

"Had to get creative with that one. Five homemade certificates, redeemable anytime for ice-cream night with Daddy. Limited to one use per week, no school nights."

"Very creative indeed," she admitted. She loved when Pete was like this. Ever since he'd told her about his grand plan to move the family to Nantucket and turn their lives around, it was like this massive weight had been lifted off his shoulders. He was her Pete again. He sang in the shower, he rehearsed elaborate high-five routines with Grady, he brushed and braided Alice's hair with Bobby Fischer-like intensity. He was the man she loved, and she *loved* that she loved him. She loved everything these days. The very air itself seemed sweeter, the sun seemed brighter.

She was going *home.*

It took her by surprise how excited she was about that. She knew she loved Nantucket, but she never expected that she'd miss it this much. With all the time and attention it took to raise two kids as a stay-at-home mother, she'd pretty much just buried those feelings in the back of her head. As if she didn't even have the energy to realize that she wanted to be back in the place she grew up. The tap water didn't taste right in Plymouth, she was just now noticing, and the traffic lights were different. People usually didn't wave and smile at you on the sidewalk here, and even when they did, it felt fake and forced and just plain weird. Not like the charm of her hometown.

Going house-shopping was an unexpected treat, too. Holly loved houses, interior decorating, all the things that went into that. She was shy to admit it sometimes—she was enough of a girly girl already, wasn't she?—but sometimes when the kids were asleep and Pete was working, she would stay up all night watching HGTV house remodeling shows and shouting at the TV whenever she disagreed with their design choices. She couldn't wait to see what might be available for them. She knew for sure they'd find something special. But, even more than the new house itself, what she was excited about was possibility. Hope, in other words. It was practically a foreign emotion at this point. But, goodness gracious, it felt *wonderful.*

So wonderful, in fact, that she rolled down the window of the car as they merged onto the highway and let out a whooping cry of joy. The wind blew her hair into a crazy mess as they accelerated up to fifty, sixty, seventy miles per hour, but she couldn't care less. Pete looked at her.

He chuckled. "What's gotten into you?"

"I just love you," she said. She was giddy, silly. Had Pete always been so cute? Had he always looked so good in his glasses? Had he always had such nice, strong forearms? She loved her husband so much in this moment. She leaned over the center console between them and planted a kiss on his cheek.

Pete put one hand on her knee as he drove with the other one. "I love you, too," he said. It felt like they were back in high school, just driving aimlessly around Nantucket with nowhere to be and nothing to do but love each other.

It had been so long since Holly had felt this free.

She never wanted it to end.

~

It was going to be a beautiful day in Nantucket, so Pete and Holly decided to leave the car on the mainland, take the fast ferry in, and just use bikes to get around. Holly was squirming in her seat with excitement the whole way over. Fortunately, the fast ferry from Hyannis took only an hour, so they were there in no time at all.

She took a deep breath as they disembarked. "We're home!" She threw her arms around Pete's neck. "I can't believe we're moving back."

"I can. It's gonna be great."

Brent met them at the ferry terminal with a pair of bicycles from the house on Howard Street stashed in the bed of his truck. He looked like he'd had a late night, but when Holly asked him what he got up to, he just mumbled something nonsensical, gave them a tired smile, and took off home.

"Wonder what kind of mischief he got into last night," Pete remarked. "That was awfully abrupt, even for your brother."

Holly shrugged. "Who knows? He's been all over the place these days. Hopefully, it was good trouble."

"He looked kinda happy though, didn't he?" Pete said. "Like ... more relaxed. More so than he was at Christmas, at least. He looked pretty glum then. Maybe he met someone."

"You never know!"

Equipped with bicycles, they went riding off. Holly had assembled a list of open houses that were available for viewing that day. She figured they'd eventually secure a realtor when they narrowed down what exactly was possible within their price range. But she knew the island like the back of her hand, and she was so excited that she wanted to be very hands-on with the early part of the house-hunting process. So off they went to their first stop.

The first few houses were all not quite right for one reason or another. One needed quite a bit of work to the kids' bathroom, while another had shag carpet and mirrored walls installed everywhere that might have been fashionable fifty years ago, but now felt horribly dated. Still, it was fun to walk through the houses holding Pete's hand and imagining what it would be like to live in this one or that one.

Pete seemed to be having a good time, too, though he didn't quite share Holly's fondness for the intricacies of interior design. She'd wax melodic about crown molding or accent walls, and he would just nod and smile. "I see what you mean, dear," he'd say. Whether he saw or not didn't really matter. She was just glad that he was here with her.

As they went from house to house, they started to see a few of the same faces. That was to be expected. Nantucket was desirable real estate, after all, so Holly had known that there would be other shoppers at these open houses. One woman in particular stuck out to her, though. She was probably around Holly's age, but she had a tight, pinched face, and her lips were pursed tight like she was forever holding back a rude comment. She was dressed in very expensive clothes and carrying a handbag that cost as much as Holly and Pete's car. She seemed perpetually dissatisfied with everything in each house where they crossed paths, too. But she was perhaps most dissatisfied with Holly herself.

On more than one occasion, Holly overheard her whispering evilly to the realtor she was with—an older lady with dyed blonde hair who was similarly decked out in wildly expensive attire and positively dripping with pearls. They seemed to be trading acidic barbs about the people around them.

At the last house before they went to find some lunch, a split-level bungalow done up in classic Nantucket style, Holly was wandering on her own through the sunken den area when she heard the woman mutter to her friend, "They let just about anyone in here these days, don't they? Ought to filter out the riffraff. Serious buyers only."

Holly almost spit out the sip of water she was drinking. She froze in place. But, taking a deep breath, she forced herself to keep walking and pretend to look out the window to the backyard. As she did, she risked a glance back at the two clucking hens.

She could swear that they were talking about *her*.

It was like someone had punctured her good mood with a needle. She hissed through her teeth and told herself to calm down. She mostly just couldn't believe that anyone would say something so unbelievably rude about a complete and utter stranger. Riffraff? You gotta be kidding! Maybe you are just overreacting, she told herself. Or maybe the woman was talking about someone else. But Holly didn't think so. She knew in her gut that the comment had been directed at her. And Holly overhearing it must not have been an accident, either.

Pete came wandering up, hands in his pockets. "Whatcha think about this one?" he asked nonchalantly.

She didn't say anything, just seized him by the elbow and steered him into the foyer. When she repeated what she'd heard the rich woman say, he blinked slowly. "You sure she wasn't just making a joke?"

"A joke?" Holly asked, flabbergasted. "No, hon, I don't think so. She's just a witch."

"Let's not jump to conclusions, babe," he counseled. "I'm sure it was taken out of context. Don't worry about her, though. I'm sure we'll never see her again."

"Maybe ..." Holly said, but she barely heard him. She knew with complete conviction that this woman wanted to hurt her feelings. And she had a sneaking suspicion that this wasn't the last time they'd cross paths.

The realtor who was running the open house called from the living room. "Hi, everybody? Can I get your attention for just a moment? I'd love to give you a quick rundown of the house, if you all don't mind gathering in very briefly. Then I'll let you get back to devouring the snacks I set out." The woman had an easy smile, but Holly was too steaming mad to smile back.

She and Pete crowded into the living room with the dozen or so other people who'd been wandering through the rooms. The realtor started listing off the home's history and some of its features, but Holly's attention was locked on the woman who'd insulted her. She had very few wrinkles on her face. Holly's thoughts jumped immediately to Botox. A woman who dressed like that and carried a purse like the one she had wouldn't think twice about resorting to a little chemical assistance in the fight against wrinkles.

Holly knew that she ought to feel bad about having such petty thoughts towards someone else. Didn't that make her no better than this woman? Perhaps it had just been so long since she'd been so viscerally taken aback that she didn't have a reaction ready. "Just breathe," she whispered to herself. "Let it go."

Just then, the woman raised her hand and interrupted the realtor mid-speech. "Hi," she drawled. "I'm Cecilia Payne. My husband and I are moving to the island. I just wanted to clarify that you couldn't possibly mean the price you just quoted. I must have misheard you."

The realtor looked confused, but to her credit, she quickly got her bearings and her smile brightened again. "Yes, ma'am," she said apologetically, and she repeated the figure.

To Holly's horror, Cecilia laughed out loud. It was a mean-spirited laugh if she'd ever heard one. Holly's heart went out to the realtor. She had such a happy, easygoing smile, but at the sound of this Cecilia woman's laughter, it vanished altogether. She suddenly looked uncomfortable to be up in front of everyone.

"Let's go," Cecilia muttered to the woman she was with. "I wouldn't pay half that amount for this dump." The two of them whisked around the corner and were gone.

Holly gritted her teeth. She had a new enemy, and her name was Cecilia Payne.

20

ELIZA

Morning of the next Friday.

The day had finally come. The bags had been packed, the goodbyes had been said, and now there was only the ride to the airport remaining before they took off on their new adventure. To be honest, Eliza still couldn't believe this was happening. Of all the unexpected twists her life had taken over the last year, this was perhaps the most unexpected of all.

She wondered what her dad would have had to say about the whole thing. He'd probably joke, and say something like, *Trying to be a rock star by proxy, eh?* He'd be supportive, though. She knew that much. He had always wanted her to be happy, first and foremost. And the truth was that she really was happy. It was like she'd finally let go of something that she'd spent her whole life squeezing onto with all her might, and only now were the rest of her muscles finally relaxing.

She had a beautiful daughter. She hadn't heard from her jerk of an ex-fiancé in nearly a year. She was in love with a handsome artist who loved her in return. And they were about to spend eight months chasing Oliver's dream.

This was exciting.

She looked up at Oliver as he hefted their multitude of suitcases into the van service they'd arranged to take them to the airport. He caught her looking and smiled back. "What're ya staring at, Benson?" he asked with a grin.

"Just you," she answered simply.

"Do I have something on my face?"

"Hmm," she said, pretending to think. "Let me see." She reached up, grabbed his chin, and turned his face left and right as if she were studying his skin for smudges. Then, suddenly, she swooped in and planted a kiss on his forehead. She'd just applied some ChapStick, so it left a faint smear where her lips had been. She laughed. "You do now."

Oliver laughed, too. "You got me there." He looked down at Winter, who was contently snuggled in a wrap that secured her to Eliza's torso. "She sleeping?"

"Out like a light," Eliza confirmed. "Let's hope it stays that way for the flight."

"Fingers crossed," Oliver said. "Otherwise, we'll have to jettison her over the Atlantic."

Eliza smacked him on the shoulder.

"Kidding, kidding!" He laughed easily.

"You better be," she fired back at him, brow wrinkled in mock-anger.

"Besides," he continued cautiously, pretending not to look at her. "We both know I'd jettison you first."

She hit him again, harder this time, but both of them were laughing.

~

The flight went quickly. It was just a short jump over to Boston. They'd hardly reached altitude before the pilot was already relighting the "Fasten Seat Belt" sign and prepping them for landing. Winter slept the whole way through, and jettisoning wasn't necessary.

Once they disembarked, they gathered their carry-ons and followed the crowd down the bridge and into the airport. "There he is!" called a short, stocky bald man with a goatee after they'd almost finished winding their way through the security corridors. He was standing on the other side of the glass TSA partition, next to a suited man holding up a sign that bore Oliver's name in big block letters. "Our burgeoning star."

"Hey, Warren," Oliver said coolly. The men met at the end of the partition and clasped hands. "This is my girlfriend, Eliza. Eliza, Warren is the rep from the record company. He'll be stopping in on the tour from time to time to make sure everything is going okay."

"Pleasure to meet you," Eliza said, taking Warren's outstretched hand and shaking. He was extremely personable by aura alone. One of those people who seemed instantly trustworthy, everybody's best friend.

"Likewise," he said, returning her smile. "And who's this little bundle of joy?" He peeked into the wrap that held Eliza's little girl.

"This is Winter," Oliver said.

"I didn't know you had a daughter!" exclaimed Warren.

Oliver just smiled enigmatically and said, "Something like that." Eliza's heart melted, just a little bit. They'd been very wary of this subject over the last year. Winter wasn't Oliver's by blood, of course, but he loved her like she was, and Eliza loved him all the more for it.

"Well, it's great to finally get you all here. I have big hopes for this tour. It's gonna be a lot of fun, and it being a family affair just makes it that much better." He turned and pointed out the man in the suit who was holding the sign. "This is our driver, Avery. He's gonna take us all to the hotel to get settled in and meet the band. Don't worry about your luggage—we have guys for that. Come this way!"

The rest of the evening went by in a flash. Pretty much as soon as they arrived at their hotel room for the evening, it was already time for Oliver to go do soundcheck at the venue for the band's performance that night. So he'd turned right around and left, leaving Eliza with a kiss on the cheek and a nervous fluttering in her stomach.

She knew he was going to do great. After all, how many times over the last year had she stopped by one of the bars or restaurants around Nantucket where Oliver played, just to listen to him at the piano? He was a beautiful player and a beautiful singer. Even when he was just messing around on the electric keyboard at home, he was like an angel. One of Eliza's favorite activities was peeking around a corner and listening to him work on his own material. When he didn't know she was watching him, he'd get this cute intensity to him. Furrowed brow, stopping and starting constantly to scribble notes to himself in the margins of his sheet music, muttering under his breath, "Yes, yes! Wait, no, dang it," and on and on.

He wasn't nervous at all. Eliza didn't think he was really capable of feeling nerves. Still, she felt like someone ought to be nervous on his behalf, so if he wasn't going to do it, then it seemed like the responsibility fell to her.

She had a nice dinner of room service, fed Winter, who was taking all the new scenery in stride, and then got dressed. The show that night would be at a smallish bar-slash-concert venue that often hosted acts like the Fever Dreams—up-and-comers, basically. After getting them settled in, Warren had filled Eliza in on the details. They'd have a car service come scoop her and Winter up when it was time to go to the show. The car was due at 8:15. That was three minutes away. Eliza left

Winter to play with some little toys for a few seconds of tummy time so she could duck into the bathroom and finish doing her makeup.

"Be right back, love," she said to her daughter. Turning into the bathroom, she looked into the mirror. She hardly recognized the woman who was looking back at her. Long, curly, flowing hair, verging on messy but artfully so. She had on ripped black jeans and a high-collared black velvet top. The sleeves were cut off at the shoulder, revealing just enough of a Nantucket tan. She applied a few strokes of eyeliner, mascara, and a dark lip color. When she was mostly satisfied with the job she'd done, she stepped back. She looked like what she was—the girlfriend of a soulful pianist headed out on a national tour—plus some dates in Canada. More to the point, she looked nothing like what she had once been: a work-obsessed Wall Street finance professional who took life way too seriously.

That was a good thing.

Then, it was time to go. She grabbed Winter, who was dressed for the night in a onesie with a printed slogan on the front that read "Mom says 'Please don't buy me a drum set.'" Oliver had thought it was the funniest thing in the world. They made their way out of the hotel room and out to the front of the hotel, where a black car was waiting for them.

Fifteen minutes of traffic later, they were walking through the band entrance and into the backstage area. Oliver was seated at a keyboard with his back to them. He had earphones in, too, so he didn't hear Eliza walk up. Biting back a smile, she kissed his cheek from behind and put Winter on his shoulder in one fell swoop. He jerked up for a second, surprised, but when he realized who it was, his face split into a huge smile.

"Look who decided to show up!" he teased.

Eliza poked him in the chest. "Rock stars are never on time."

He just smiled and pulled her into an embrace, gently sandwiching Winter between them. "Glad you're here, babe. It's gonna be fun."

"You nervous?" she asked, looking up at him. His eyes were so alive and dancing in the overhead fluorescents. His excitement was contagious, too. She felt her heartbeat pick up a little bit. This was such a huge night for him. She was glad to be a part of it.

He chuckled. "Not really. It's just like any other night, you know?"

"You're crazy. I think your brain is broken. I'd be a puddle of nerves."

Oliver tweaked her earlobe. "Nah. You've got the harder job tonight, after all."

"Oh yeah? What's that?"

"Listening to me criticize myself after the show."

"Oh, jeez," she groaned, rolling her eyes. "Can't wait for that part of the evening."

"Only kidding, babe." He laughed, then bent down and kissed her softly once more. "All right, I wanna go through everything one more time. I'm on in fifteen, so I gotta be ready. See you out there?"

She smiled. "We'll be watching. Right, Winter?" She took her baby back from Oliver's arms, but not before he pressed a final kiss to her head. Winter waved a hand erratically.

"I'll take that as a yes," Oliver joked. "Have fun, you two!" He turned back to the piano and wiggled his earbuds back into his ears as Eliza and Winter walked off to the side and found an unoccupied couch. She fished out the pair of baby-sized noise-canceling headphones she'd bought for the tour—didn't want Winter to get spooked by the loud music once the concert began.

It didn't take long before it was showtime. Eliza stayed in her seat out of the way as roadies and musicians buzzed around everywhere carrying instruments, wires, sound equipment, clipboards. There was an exciting thrum of energy in the air, strong enough that she felt like she might get zapped if she stuck out a hand. Her heartbeat picked up a little faster when she saw the show manager come fetch Oliver and take him to the wings of the stage. He flashed her a thumbs-up and mouthed "I love you," which she returned, before following the arrows taped on the ground that led her to the VIP viewing area along the side.

She settled Winter on the rail in front of her, keeping a hand on each of her daughter's chubby little thighs. The stage was dark, as was the crowd, though the latter was swaying and tossing like the Nantucket ocean at night. She couldn't say exactly how she sensed this, but the vibes emanating from the attendees felt so positive, so warm. Buzzy and crackling, like heat lightning on a beautiful summer's evening. She realized suddenly that she was holding her breath in anticipation.

She didn't have to wait long, though, because just then, a spotlight switched to life. The curtains parted, revealing Oliver seated at a massive grand piano. He had a microphone stationed in front of his face.

"I'm Oliver Patterson," he said in a soft, alluring crooner's voice. "Let's have some fun." The crowd roared, and Oliver hit the first few chords. They came crashing through the mountainous loudspeakers stacked up on either side of the cage, striking Eliza in the chest like a tidal wave. Winter cooed delightedly. She couldn't help but grin.

She knew he had won the crowd over as soon as the first note left his lips. It was just obvious—everyone here was on the same team. Her team, Oliver's team, the Fever Dreams' team. They were in it together, making not just music, but rather a moment, a night frozen in time where it was so easy to just let go, wave your hands in the air, sing along even if you didn't quite know the words. It was special, it was beautiful, it was perfect, it was theirs.

The first few songs flowed one into the next. The energy in the room built higher and higher. Eliza found herself shimmying her hips from side to side and bobbing her head. Never in her entire life had she been much of a dancer. But Oliver had danced with her that first night they'd met, hadn't he? It was like he saw the dancer in her and was determined to bring her out. Well, mission accomplished, because he was a dozen yards away from her and yet the tug of his personality was still enough to get her moving and shaking and laughing at everything and nothing at all. It felt more like a dream than real life.

Winter, too, seemed to be loving it. She saw the people in the crowd clapping their hands and started mimicking them, which she'd never done before. Eliza laughed, delighted.

The songs got faster and more energetic. Oliver had intentionally started slow, but the pace picked up and so did the energy. Finally, after one rousing track that had the whole crowd wailing along to the final chorus, he stopped. He'd been singing for almost twenty-five minutes straight without stopping to do much talking or bantering with the people in the venue at all. Now, though, the lights dimmed to a soft blue and narrowed in on his face.

"Before I do this last song," he began, "I want to do something I've never done before."

The crowd hooted and hollered. "Do it!" one man shouted.

"Where are my girls?" Oliver asked with a wicked grin on his face. "Where are Eliza and Winter?"

Everyone in the crowd was looking from side to side, a little confused. The spotlight was sweeping around in search of them. Oliver, too, was scanning his gaze from left to right, trying to figure out where the two of them were standing. His fingers kept stroking soft notes as the hunt went on.

Eliza could've killed him then and there. Her heart had leaped right up into her throat. Winter, of course, had no idea what was happening. But Eliza felt an awful surge of anxiety and panic. She'd spoken in public plenty of times, but this was different. In her previous life, when she was giving a training to Goldman Sachs employees or presenting to an executive board of potential clients, she had a mask on. A confident, assertive mask, but a mask nonetheless. She didn't have a mask ready for this moment, though. The whole night already felt so raw and vulnerable. If she walked out onto that stage, everyone would see her for who she was, not who she wanted to portray herself as. There was no hiding from the spotlight.

But there was also no turning back.

The spotlight operator and Oliver found her at the exact same moment.

"There she is," Oliver murmured into the microphone. The crowd followed his gaze, saw her standing behind the railing off to the side of the stage, and roared in approval. "Think we could encourage her down to the stage with me, ladies and gents?"

Another booming wave of applause and cheering erupted into the rafters.

A roadie came and found her. "This way, miss," he said, urging her down. Eliza thought about just making a break for the exit, but as she dutifully followed the man through the guts of the backstage area, she could still hear the crowd making noise, bantering back and forth with Oliver, who was still playing gentle single notes.

The roadie held open a curtain for her. Beyond that veil was the stage, the spotlight, Oliver. Behind her was the exit. No one was going to stop her if she left. She wasn't a prisoner, after all.

But her future lay forward.

So, taking a deep breath and swallowing back the fear that threatened to take her over, Eliza—with her baby cooing in her arms —strode into the light.

When they saw her, the crowd reached a new level. It was almost deafening, but it wasn't threatening. Like she'd sensed from above, it was a warm, friendly energy that wrapped her up like a blanket.

"Aren't they beautiful?" Oliver asked. Everyone answered thunderously in the affirmative. "Glad you agree," he replied, and they all laughed. "So for my last song, I wanted to do something a little more special, a little more intimate. If you folks could dim the lights for me just a touch more ..." The lights went down per his request. It felt like everyone was huddling inwards together, getting close, more personal.

The single notes Oliver was playing turned into chords, which turned into the opening salvo of a song Eliza had never heard from him before. "I wrote this one just a few nights ago. Haven't shared it with anyone yet. I hope you all like it. Eliza, Winter ... this is for you."

Eliza was frozen in place. The song was hauntingly beautiful. But as it went from introduction to verse to chorus, it warmed up. By the time Oliver launched into the bridge—a high, soaring melody that sent shivers down her spine—she knew that the spell he'd been trying to weave was successful. It was a love song in the truest form, because it was telling her—not just in the lyrics, but in the music itself—that it was written for her and about her.

Eventually, it ended. The last note faded away, there was a beat of silence, and then the crowd exploded. Oliver stood up from the piano, came around to Eliza and Winter, and kissed them both.

Yes, Eliza thought to herself. *This could work.*

21

BRENT

Late afternoon, Monday.

Brent hefted his tool bag in one hand and wiped some sweat off his forehead with the other. He was a sleep-deprived zombie at this point. He thought about turning back and going home to sleep until Friday. But he'd made a promise and shaken hands on it. A Benson man never went back on a promise.

So he raised his fist and rapped his knuckles on the door.

He heard some shuffling and a muffled "Coming!" from within. Then the door of the house swung open. The man on the other side of it, Frank O'Leary, was tall and broad-shouldered, with dark, curly hair and five o'clock shadow. "Brent! Good to see you, brother. Come on in."

Brent nodded hello and followed him in. The house was half completed at best. Patches of drywall were unfinished, half the appliances were still strewn underfoot, and much of the flooring was still yet to be installed.

"It's a mess in here, I know," Frank said apologetically. He was a nice guy. Talkative, for sure, and demonstrative while he spoke, with hands flying everywhere to make his point. He and some old college buddies of his had booked Marshall and Brent for a charter fishing trip the weekend before. While they were out on the water, Frank had mentioned that he was building his own house on some land he'd bought on the island. Apparently, he had run into a snafu that required some delicate handyman's work.

"Boy, have I got the guy for you!" Marshall had crowed triumphantly. "Triple B, come make our guest's acquaintance."

Brent and Frank had got to talking. When he finally got around to the actual details of what needed doing, Brent had known right away that he could help the guy out. And when Marshall mentioned offhand that their charter boat, the *Tripidation II,* needed about a week out of the water for some annual repairs in dry dock, it had seemed like a good opportunity to keep making cash while charter tips were held up.

"Yeah, no problem," he'd told Frank with a shrug. "I can do that for you."

"Well, would you get a load at the confidence on this guy!" Frank had said to his friends, laughing and slapping his knee. "I like it a lot."

That made Brent smile inwardly, out of surprise if nothing else. He hadn't had what one would call "confidence" in a long time now. Not since Dad.

He knew what was causing it, though.

Ally.

They'd spent just about every night together since their first. Sitting on the beach, taking bike rides everywhere and nowhere. She was a wildfire. As it turned out, Brent might have been catching a little bit of her swagger without ever realizing it. Maybe that wasn't such a bad thing.

All of that had brought him here, stepping carefully through the chaos of Frank's half-finished homebuilding project. He was tired from staying up late with Ally the night before. They'd started off shucking oysters down at Brent's favorite raw bar and ended up kissing on the couch at his apartment until sometime around dawn, so he hadn't got much in the way of sleep. But a promise was a promise, so here he was, tools at the ready.

Frank gave him the details of the project—some wiring and plumbing that needed to be routed, and a tricky problem with how a certain load-bearing wall had been blueprinted that turned out to need a little bit more finesse than was originally called for. Brent sized up the situation and saw instantly how he was going to fix it. He smiled. His dad would've loved to see a moment like this.

"Yessir, I've got a plan. Shouldn't take me more than a few hours, I don't think."

"A few hours! Man, I love it. I had a good feeling about you."

He chuckled. "Appreciate that. Feel free to keep doing whatever you gotta be doing. I'll be out of your hair by sundown."

"Will do. Want a beer or anything like that?"

"Just a water would be swell, thanks."

"You got it," Frank said. "Coming right up."

Brent set his bag down on the floor and got to work. He let his mind drift to Ally as his hands stayed busy. She was like a comet that had come streaking out of nowhere and lit up his world. It felt like he was learning so much about life from her, although that was just about the cheesiest thought he'd ever had. He squelched it as soon as it came unannounced into his head.

But it was true either way. She did stuff head-on. No fear, no hesitation. She reminded him of Sara in that regard, although even Sara had more foresight in her little finger than Ally had in her whole body. Again, he wondered, was that such a bad thing? He was tired of being cautious, of being afraid, but he hadn't known quite how to let those things go. Perhaps Ally was just the right person at just the right time for him.

"What's that song?" Frank asked as he strode back into the room with a bottle of water in his outstretched hand.

"Huh?"

"The one you were whistling."

"Oh," Brent said, blushing. "Didn't even realize I was doing that, to be honest. My dad taught me that one. He used to whistle while he worked. I don't think it even has a name. If it does, I sure don't know it."

"Sounds like something my grandpa woulda whistled in his woodshop back in the day."

"Might be one and the same. My dad was an old soul in his own way."

"You've got a little bit of that in you, too. I can tell."

"Is that so?"

"I know 'em when I see 'em, my friend. You've got more years in your head than you do on your body, if that makes sense."

Brent had a vague idea what he was talking about. Once upon a time, he might've agreed. But now, with Ally in his life, he felt the blaze of youth lighting him up. So he just nodded to Frank and got back to work.

The hours wound their way past. Brent was just about finished by the time the last of the sun's rays were disappearing behind the horizon. He stood up, dusted off his hands, and examined his handiwork one last time.

"Done already?" Frank said. He'd been in and out of the room over the last couple hours, taking care of this and that, checking up on Brent all the while.

"Yessir," Brent responded. "That oughta hold you up nicely."

"I'll be darned," Frank laughed, shaking his head back and forth in disbelief. "Mr. Cook really steered me right. You were worth every penny, young fella." He handed a thick stack of twenty-dollar bills over to Brent. "Everything we agreed upon and a little extra, just for being a pleasure to work alongside."

"Thank you very much," replied Brent. He'd gotten a little more comfortable with accepting tips, but it still rankled him somewhat. Still, a job done well deserved recognition. He felt proud of what he'd done here. "If you have any problems—with this or with anything else—you just give me a call and I'll be down here to get it all straightened out for you."

"Believe me, I will," Frank said at once. "And I'll be singing your praises to anyone who'll listen. Thanks again, brother."

The two men shook hands once more. Then Brent grabbed his tool bag. Whistling the same tune his father had taught him a long time ago, he headed out.

His good mood lasted about three steps past the front door.

That was when he looked to his left and saw Rose.

22

HOLLY

This was it. They'd found it. The perfect house.

Holly knew it before they even stepped foot inside. It was like getting zapped by lightning as soon as they crossed the property line. She squeezed Pete's hand a little tighter. It had been a long two days of touring dozens of houses, but the excitement she felt right now was going to make all that worth it.

The home was situated on a vibrant green lawn. Nothing huge, but enough space for Grady to chase a soccer ball back and forth when the weather was nice. There was a young tree that had been planted square in the center of the backyard, too. Holly could already close her eyes and picturing it growing alongside her family.

The house itself was done up in gray shiplap siding, with plenty of windows to let in natural light. As they walked up the driveway into the home, Holly felt herself getting giddier.

The front door swung in and revealed the interior. The crown molding was just a touch fancier than she would've preferred, and she might like to change a few coats of paint here and there. But otherwise, it was pure gorgeous. The floors were the kind of hardwood that got its beauty from years of Nantucket summer and winter. She could already picture what she would do with the space of the living room as they wandered through it. She'd always been fond of classic Nantucket interior style, so she wouldn't stray too far from that. A natural jute rug would add some nice beige elements to the room and look fabulous in the sunlight streaming through the windows above the reading nook. A white linen slipcover couch here, a wicker end table there, and some clean-looking lantern lighting to go overhead. She loved the exposed wooden beams that ran the length of the living room and into the kitchen, as well as the cubbies and bookshelves built into the left-hand wall. Blue and white accents could be strewn about liberally—throw pillows, artwork to hang up, perhaps even an accent wall.

They looped through the kitchen, which was gleaming with white cabinetry, and back to the staircase. They moved to the second floor and stuck their heads in each of the bedrooms. The master was awash in April sunlight, and the two bedrooms for the kids shared a Jack and Jill bathroom setup, which would be perfect.

Best of all, Cecilia Payne was nowhere to be seen.

Holly felt like doing a little two-step, maybe jumping up and clicking her heels together. This was the home for her family. She knew it.

She looked at Pete. "This is it."

He smiled and nodded. "This is it."

As soon as they stepped back outside, Holly picked up her phone and dialed the realtor she'd already exchanged a few preemptive emails with. She filled her in on everything and told her they wanted to put an offer in immediately.

"Fingers crossed!" Judy chirped. "I've got a good feeling about this one for you two."

"So do I," Holly said. "I hope we get it."

"I'm sure you will."

They said their goodbyes and hung up. Holly immediately called her mom and told her all about it. She, too, was excited for them. "Why don't you and Pete come by the inn and have a little treat to celebrate?"

"Wanna go by Mom's?" Holly asked Pete, cupping the speaker of the phone.

"Sure thing," he said. "It's not too far from here." Picking up their bikes, they wheeled over that way. Mom greeted them at the door with a hug, a kiss, and a brownie for each.

"Oh wow, Mrs. Benson. These are better than ever. Did you change something?" Pete gushed.

Holly rolled her eyes. She knew he wasn't actually sucking up; he was just being Pete. Fortunately for him, Mom ate that kind of thing up.

"I'll never tell," Mom joked with a wink and a friendly poke in Pete's side. "Come, come. I got a little something special out for you two." She led them onto the back porch, where a bottle of champagne and three glasses were waiting.

"Mom, you're ridiculous," Holly groaned, laughing. "We haven't even heard back from the sellers yet!"

"I have a mother's intuition about this one," said Mae simply as she handed the bottle to Pete to uncork.

"What's being a mom have to do with real estate?" Holly sassed.

"Sometimes you just know."

Mom was in rare form today. She seemed to be practically glowing, actually. "Did you do something with your hair, Mom?"

"Nope."

"New makeup?"

"Nuh-uh."

"Dress? Glasses? Earrings? Perfume?"

"Nothing is different, dear," Mom insisted.

Holly didn't believe her. "*Something* is different," she said. "I'm gonna figure out what." Before she had the chance to go hunting for the source of her mother's radiance, her phone buzzed. It was the realtor, Judy.

"That's strange," Holly remarked, frowning. "I didn't expect to hear back from Judy for a few days at least."

Pete looked up at her through a mouth full of brownie. "Could be good?"

"Let's not get our hopes up," warned Holly, though her hopes already couldn't be any higher. She held her breath as she picked up the call and said, "Hello?"

"You're not going to believe this!" Judy exclaimed.

"Go on?"

"The sellers accepted your offer!"

Holly squealed. Mom and Pete looked up at her in alarm. "Already? That's insane!"

"You're telling me!" Judy laughed. "In thirty-five years of doing this, I've never had an offer accepted so fast. Good timing, I suppose!"

Holly sure wasn't going to complain. She thanked Judy and said she'd get to the paperwork as soon as they were back home in Plymouth.

This didn't feel real. But if it was a dream, she didn't want to wake up. "Pour me a big glass, babe," she said teasingly to Pete, who had begun distributing the champagne into the three glasses that Mom had brought out. "It's time to celebrate. We're coming home!"

23

BRENT

Rose hadn't seen him yet. She was unloading groceries from the trunk of her car. He recognized that beat-up old VW Beetle, painted the most hideous yellow he'd ever seen in his life. He'd teased her about it on the night of their first date, over eight months ago.

"It's cute," she had said defensively back then. She stuck out her bottom lip like she was offended.

"It looks like it's warning people away from a nuclear disaster," was his response. She had laughed and punched him playfully in the shoulder. Right now, standing transfixed in the doorway of Frank's house, he reached up and rubbed the spot where she'd hit him. He swore he could still feel the faintest ghost of an ache there.

He felt like he was having an out-of-body experience. Just like he had when Ally first called him the night of their fishing trip, he pinched himself hard. It hurt just as bad as it did the first time. He cursed and dropped his tool bag. It landed on his foot, claw end of the hammer first, which hurt, too. He cursed again, louder. When he bent down to grab his throbbing big toe, he rammed the top of his head on the wall of Frank's house. That hurt most of all. He cursed a third time.

Only then did Rose look up and see him.

He felt like the idiot Coyote in those old Roadrunner cartoons. Forever hurting himself, looking like a fool. He certainly looked like a fool now. He could see Rose through his watery eyes. She was narrowing her gaze at him. The last of the sun was hitting her in the face at just the right angle so that she had to hold her hand over her forehead and squint to make out the source of the noise.

When she saw it was Brent, she blanched.

He could actually see the color drain from her face, though she was still two dozen yards or so away from him. "Brent?" she said softly. He knew that she didn't believe what she was seeing, either.

The pain in his head and foot subsided gradually. He straightened up, wincing, and picked up his tool bag again. "Rose," he mumbled by way of greeting. So much for being smooth and confident. He felt exactly the way he did when they first met on the beach all those weeks and months ago: like a bumbling dummy. Thick-lipped and slow-witted.

"Are you all right?" she asked, clearly concerned.

"Yeah. Fine. Dandy. Living the dream."

"Ah." She pursed her lips. Not in a mean way, just in a Rose way. "What are you doing here?" she blurted. "I mean, shoot, that was really rude. I didn't mean it like that. I just meant, uh ..."

"I was doing some work on your neighbor's house," Brent cut in to explain. "Don't worry, I didn't stalk you or anything."

"I didn't think you did," she said, crossing her arms. "I wasn't accusing you of that."

"Felt like you might be."

"Well, I wasn't."

They stood there awkwardly, each staring generally in the other's direction but trying not to make exact eye contact. It was like two middle schoolers at a social function who were doing their darndest to pretend the other didn't exist, though both wanted badly to go up and ask the other one to dance.

Brent was doing a pretty good job of pretending, actually. Mostly because he'd spent the last eight months doing just that: pretending that Rose didn't exist and had never, ever been a part of his life. It was easier that way. Just ignore her, erase the memories, forget her laugh and her smile. It didn't do much good for the ache in his heart, of course, but there were plenty of other things to which he could attribute that daily pain. No sense in adding his longing for Rose to the mix.

Although, to be fair, that didn't stop him from longing for her. She popped up in his dreams every third or fourth night. Not doing anything that made much sense—though Brent's dreams never made much sense. But just popping up, hanging around, sort of haunting the joint. He was fed up with it.

Even more than being fed up, though, he found himself actually getting kind of mad. Of *course* she'd reappear in his life just when he'd met someone else who excited him. Ally shows up and then boom, scarcely two weeks later, here comes Rose. He knew it wasn't her fault. But he blamed her for reappearing anyway.

"How are you?" she asked, shifting her weight to one side and letting her arms fall.

"Fine," was his curt reply. "Just working a lot."

"Working is good." She fell silent again. He noticed that she was gnawing on her bottom lip. That was a cute habit of hers, he remembered.

He thought about saying goodbye and walking away. End this now, before it got out of hand. But then his mother's voice came unbidden into his head, telling him not to be rude. *She's a nice girl, and you ought to treat her as such,* Mae's voice scolded.

He growled under his breath. Fine. He'd be cordial.

"How are you?" he asked.

"I'm fine, but I'd prefer not to shout our pleasantries back and forth over the bushes, if you don't mind. Do you want me to come over there, or should you come here?"

"I'll come there," he grumbled. Hefting his bag in his grip, he jumped over the bushes and walked up to her. Her scent struck him even from a dozen paces away. That perfume, floral and delicate and sweet. It addled his brain immediately. He tried to shake it off. *Just be cordial, say hello, and then leave, before your stupid mouth gets you into trouble,* he thought to himself.

They stood in front of each other. It was as close as they'd been since the night of their first date. When she had told him she was ending things, she had done it with a letter left on the beach for him to find. He hadn't seen hide nor hair of her since then. That in itself was kind of amazing. Nantucket wasn't that big. He figured she'd moved off the island or something. But apparently not. Fate had just kept them separated—until now. What were the odds of them meeting like this? A random encounter after a random handyman job? Had to be one in a million. Brent wasn't a betting man, but even if he was, he wouldn't have ponied up much on them crossing paths again here and now.

"So you're fine," he repeated stupidly.

Rose smiled. "Yeah, I'm fine. Getting ready for the summer. It can't come fast enough."

"Oh. Right. End of the semester and everything." Rose was a kindergarten teacher at the local elementary school.

"Yeah. Those kiddos can really wear you out after a long school year."

"I bet."

"Mhmm."

Silence. A beat.

"How's Susanna?"

"She's good," Rose said, nodding. "Just turned five last month. She's at a friend's house right now. I have to go pick her up in just a minute."

"That's good."

"Yes. I think so too." She looked over Brent's shoulder to the house behind him that he'd just come out of. "Will you be doing a lot of work on Frank's house?"

Brent shook his head. "Just the one project for now. He said he might call me if he needs something else done, though."

She laughed, that soft, tinkling laugh of hers that sounded like a wind chime. "I would bet on you getting a call sooner rather than later. Frank strikes me as a 'shoot first and ask questions later' kind of guy. Not the best trait in a contractor, but it makes me smile."

Brent chuckled. The awkwardness was subsiding a little bit between them, though he still wasn't quite sure what to do with his hands. He kept adjusting them back and forth between his pockets and the grips on his tool bag. "I could see that. My dad was wired the other way. Measure twice, cut once, you know? Frank's a nice fellow, though."

"Very nice."

Another beat of silence.

"I should probably get this stuff inside before the ice cream melts," Rose said, gesturing down to the plastic grocery bags at her feet. "Susanna would pitch a fit. I would too, actually."

"Let me help you," Brent offered, remembering his manners.

"Oh no, really, it's—"

But he was already stooping down and gathering up the rest of the bags.

"All right," she relented. "This way."

He followed her inside. The house smelled like Rose. He saw Susanna's toys scattered over the living room carpet and fresh flowers in the vase by the entryway. He wondered briefly if Rose had bought them for herself or if someone else had bought them for her. The sudden flash of anger he felt at the thought of another man bringing Rose flowers surprised him. He hadn't ever been the jealous type. Besides, it wasn't like Rose and he were dating or anything even close to that. So why get so worked up? He took a breath and let it go.

"You can set those down right here," she said, patting the countertop. Brent did as she said, then stepped back and thrust his hands in his back pockets again.

"I should get going," he said.

She turned back around from putting something in the freezer and looked at him. "Okay," she said finally. It felt like she was sizing him up. He wondered if she found what she was looking for. She opened her mouth like she wanted to say something else, then thought better of it. What was she going to say? *I'm sorry? I miss you?* Yeah, right. Whatever it was, he didn't need to hear it. He was in a fragile place right now. It didn't take a genius or a therapist to surmise that much. The last thing he needed was to expose his heart again to someone who had already wrecked it once. Leaving right now, before she said whatever it was she was on the verge of saying, was the only thing that made sense.

"I'll see you around, Rose."

She nodded slowly, brow furrowed in something like confusion, or maybe sadness—he wasn't sure which. She said, "I'll see you around, Brent."

He nodded back. Then he turned and left, far more confused than he had been when he entered.

Like Rose had predicted, Frank called him the next day, needing Brent's help with something else. So he went back. Rose's car was still gone by the time Brent was finished and leaving for the day. Frank called the day after that, and the day after that, too. Each day, Brent returned.

He didn't see Rose again.

24

ELIZA

Friday night.

Next stop: Baltimore.

This show wasn't shaping up to be as much fun as the first one had been. As soon as they arrived in the city, Winter seemed to come down with a bug, like she was allergic to Maryland. Eliza didn't really blame her. Baltimore wasn't exactly her favorite city in the world. But regardless, her baby was sick, and that meant Eliza was going to have to miss the show for the night.

"Sorry, babe," she said apologetically to Oliver when he was dressed and ready to leave their hotel room to head for the venue.

"It's okay, hon. You gotta do what you gotta do. No worries at all." He kissed her on the top of the head. "Love you both. Be good for your momma, okay, Winny?" he said to the baby. He kissed his fingertips and touched Winter gently on her cheek. She'd finally fallen asleep after being fussy and inconsolable all day long, so he was careful not to wake her.

Then, Oliver was gone. The door clicked shut behind him and silence took over. Winter must have sensed it, because she woke up a minute or two later and started whimpering, then wailing. She must've learned how to cry from someone in the Fever Dreams, because she had never really cried much before this trip. But now, she was finding vocal ranges never before heard by a human ear. Or so Eliza thought, at least. She picked her daughter up and laid her against her chest, then started pacing around the room.

Hours went by like that. It took precisely fourteen steps to go from hotel room door to the sliding glass balcony entrance, then fourteen back, over and over and over again. When Winter was still crying after half an hour, Eliza had started singing a lullaby, one her mother had sung to Brent when he was being fussy way back when. When she forgot a word, she just hummed or made one up to go in its spot, and on and on like that, until finally Winter stopped crying and went back down. Just in time, too, because Eliza's feet had been screaming in protest for over an hour. She held onto the sleeping Winter as she laid down in bed, turned off the lamp light, and fell asleep herself, her sick baby snoozing peacefully on her chest.

Thank the Lord. Motherhood was hard sometimes.

Eliza woke up sometime later. It was dark in the room. The sun had long since gone down. Judging by how well-rested she felt—not very —it was still sometime in the middle of the night. She'd only woken up because she heard a noise. But as she looked around, she couldn't see much of anything, so she wasn't sure what the noise was. Gradually, as her eyes adjusted to the darkness, she made out a shape.

Then, *boom*. The hotel door slammed shut and someone cackled.

"O, is that you? You scared me!" she hissed. "Winter is finally sleeping. Don't wake her up."

"Yeah, yeah, yeah," he said from the entry hallway. He said it in an obnoxiously dismissive voice, as if the hours-long struggle to get her to sleep was no biggie. "She sleeps all the time." His words were a little slurred together, she noticed suddenly.

"This is a little different, I think," Eliza said acidly. She was tired, her head throbbed, her feet hurt, and all she wanted was to go back to sleep. Thankfully, Winter was still slumbering, though Eliza could feel her twitching every few seconds on her chest.

"Mhmm," was Oliver's only response. She heard the twin thunks of his boots coming off and getting thrown carelessly to the ground.

"Do you mind?" Eliza snapped.

"Mind what?"

"Being quiet."

"I am.

"No, you most certainly are not."

"I'm not making a quiet. Sleep much. Loud light."

"You're what? You're not making any sense, Oliver."

All he said again was, "Mhmm."

It took every ounce of willpower Eliza had not to get up and yell at him. He hadn't been here with her when Winter was screaming her head off, had he? No, he was out in front of an adoring crowd, playing music to screaming fans.

"I'm sorry, did you not have a good night?" she drawled sarcastically. She could hear the rustling of fabric and the clanking of his belt as he got undressed for bed. But he was making way too much noise. Being careless about how much noise he was making, actually, which was the part of this whole scene that was really starting to bother her.

"Mhmm."

"I swear to God, if you say 'Mhmm' again, we're going to have a problem."

He didn't say anything to that.

"Are you drunk?" she demanded.

He turned on the light in the bathroom with the door wide open, sending a blinding arc of fluorescent energy directly into Eliza's dark-adjusted eyeballs. Searing pain stabbed into her skull like icepicks. Winter twitched again, harder this time.

"Oliver, I asked you a question." She felt like a nag, and she hated it, but this was ridiculous, wasn't it? No, she wasn't being a nag. It wasn't unreasonable to ask him to be quiet, or not to shine the light in her face. It wasn't unreasonable to request just a few hours of uninterrupted sleep when she could manage to get it. He was in the wrong here. He was. Not her.

"Nah, not drunk, whatever." His words were definitely slurred, worse than she'd noticed the first time around. He dropped his toothbrush on the floor, and when he bent down to get it, kicked over the metal trash can. It clanged deafeningly loudly. Eliza winced.

Winter woke up.

The crying took a few seconds to get going, like the first few chugs of a steam engine. First, her bottom lip stuck out. Her eyes blinked heavily, still sticky with sleep. Her nose wrinkled, then her forehead. Then—three, two, one—waterworks.

Eliza growled in frustration and stood up at once, holding Winter close to her chest. She started singing the lullaby again, but it didn't have any of the magic effect that it'd had the first time around. In fact, it just made Winter cry louder. Eliza's migraine throbbed again.

Oliver stumbled out of the bathroom. His eyes were bloodshot. He was absolutely drunk. Not just a little drunk either, but three sheets to the wind drunk. Busker drunk. Rock star drunk.

That was all well and good. She didn't begrudge him for going out and having a good time without her. She'd told him to, as a matter of fact, and even now, she genuinely meant it.

But that didn't mean he had to come careening in, making a huge ruckus.

"You're wasted," she said.

He shrugged and mumbled something nonsensical.

"Whatever, I don't even care. But you woke her up! It took me forever to get her down, O."

He shrugged again. She took a deep breath and suppressed the desire to sock him in the face.

This wasn't the Oliver she knew. This wasn't King of the Bar, funny, gallant, charming Oliver. This was ... someone else, she guessed. Not the man who cared about her and her baby, the one who always insisted that he get up in the middle of the night when Winter woke up. *Sleep, baby,* he'd tell Eliza. *I'll handle it.* She wasn't even his daughter, but he treated her like she was.

Until now.

She wasn't even sure how to deal with this. It felt so utterly wrong. Maybe she was an idiot for coming on this tour. In fact, the more she thought about it, the more certain she was that it was a terrible decision. A baby? On a rock and roll tour? Who on earth had okayed *that?* What kind of god-awful, irresponsible mother brings her newborn on the road with a man she's only known for a few short months?

"Oliver—" she began. She didn't know where she was going to go with that sentence, but it didn't matter anyway, because he raised a hand to his lips and shushed her.

"Just ... be quiet," he said.

Her jaw fell open, flabbergasted. "What's wrong with you?"

"Mhmm."

That was it. The final straw.

"Get out," she snapped. "Now." She said it in a voice she hadn't used in a long time. More than a year, in fact. It was her Ice Queen Eliza voice. Her Wall Street titan voice. Her Clay voice. It felt rusty and corrosive coming out of her throat. Even as the words left her lips, she felt sick about them. But they also felt strangely good. Like tearing through tissue paper.

Oliver blinked heavily for a few moments. Then his face transformed. His green eyes, still reddened by the booze, narrowed into slits. "Fine," he growled. He whirled back around and shrugged into his jeans, his shirt, his boots.

Then he stormed out of the room without another word. He slammed the door shut behind him, hard.

Winter hadn't stopped wailing. As soon as Oliver was gone, Eliza started crying alongside with her.

Neither of them stopped until dawn.

25

MAE

Saturday morning.

"To where is your attention called this evening, Mae?" Dominic asked quietly.

It took Mae one embarrassingly long, slow sip of coffee to decipher what Dominic meant. "Oh, I don't think I have any plans in particular," she replied thoughtfully. "Perhaps a walk if the weather stays this nice."

"Ah," he said.

Mae eyed him suspiciously over her steaming mug. "Ah?" she echoed. "Just 'ah'?"

Dominic grinned. "I wondered if perhaps you'd like to join me in a small excursion."

"Tempting," Mae teased. "What kind of excursion did you have in mind?"

"I met a fellow in town who has a lovely sailboat. He takes folks for sunset sails about the harbor and such. It sounded quite nice, though terribly lonely if one were to go alone."

"And that's where I come in," she inferred. She was smiling at him. He looked a little nervous, actually. It was cute.

"If you were available, your company would be most welcome. But of course, I can certainly understand if you would prefer not to be trapped on a sailing vessel with only yours truly. That would be a nightmare for some, I imagine."

"Oh stop it, Dominic. You've got such a low opinion of yourself sometimes."

"Rather too high is the problem, I'm afraid."

Mae chuckled. "Nonsense. You're as humble as they come. And besides, you're nice to be around."

He smiled softly and took a sip of his coffee. The steam fogged up his glasses, so he took them off and polished them. Before them, the dawn was unfolding beautifully on the horizon. Soft indigo was giving way to a hazy orange. It seemed that summer had decided to make itself felt sooner rather than later. Mae didn't mind so much. She preferred the heat to the cold, and though it had been a warm spring, she was rather looking forward to a hot May.

"I'll take your word for it," Dominic demurred with a sheepish grin. "But I don't intend to pressure you into anything. It simply sounded like a fine way to pass an evening by."

"It does indeed. Let me just check in with Sara. If I'm out this evening, I'll just want her to keep an eye on things around the inn."

He nodded soberly. "Excellent. In Sara we trust."

"*You* trust, maybe," Mae joked.

Dominic smiled again. His salt-and-pepper beard was looking especially salty today. Perhaps the Nantucket ocean air was starting to make itself felt on him. A year here could do that to a man. It was hardly a bad thing, in Mae's opinion. "Indeed I do," he said. "Therein lies the rub."

~

"He's in love with you."

Sara always had such a way of just *blurting* things that ought not be blurted. Try as she might, Mae hadn't been able to iron out that little wrinkle in her daughter's personality, despite nearly thirty years of effort towards doing so.

Mae sighed and rubbed the bridge of her nose. There was, however, perhaps a glimmer of truth to what her most impetuous daughter was saying. Debra and Lola had echoed nearly the exact same words. If there were signs that Dominic was in fact in love with Mae—or at least heading in that direction—Mae herself had chosen to overlook them. At her age, love was such a fleeting, fragile thing. Romantic love, at least. She loved her children and her friends and the island she called home. But the love of a man? The love of a *new* man? She had left that possibility in the mirror a long time ago. Discarded it like clothes that didn't fit anymore. She hadn't missed it once, nor did she really miss it now. So why did the world seem so insistent on dressing her up in it again?

"I don't think so," she muttered eventually. The two of them were walking down Howard Street. The sun was nearly at its peak overhead. Birds were chirping, the breeze was blowing. It was a fine Nantucket morning in May.

"Wrong," Sara answered at once. "Dead wrong. It's not like anyone is making a big deal out of it though, Mom."

"It feels a bit like you might be, dear."

Sara wrinkled her nose. "I'm just pointing it out. Big difference between pointing something out and making a big deal out of it."

"And yet the line seems so fine, sometimes."

"You're being silly. He's nice! He's handsome! You guys like each other! Just go on a boat, drink some champagne, have a little fun." Sara halted in her tracks and pivoted to face her mom. Placing both hands on Mae's shoulders, she looked at her seriously in the eyes and said, "You deserve happiness, Mom. You of all people deserve happiness."

Mae sighed once more and softened. Maybe Sara was right; maybe she was being silly. Say Dominic did love her, or liked her in a romantic fashion. Who did that hurt? Not a soul, she supposed. She'd made her peace with where Henry sat in her heart. But a woman like Mae had so much heart left to give. She was in the back half of her life, certainly, but that by no means meant that she ought to be put out to pasture. She had energy aplenty, love aplenty, life aplenty. She wanted to share it with everyone she could.

And yet, there was the tingling feeling that remained. It was the fear that Dominic wanted something she wasn't sure she could give. As much heart as she might or might not have left, what if he wanted too much of it? He was a soulful man, the kind of man who would never think to offer her anything less than all of himself. That was what she loved about him, wasn't it? The simple beauty of his words during a quiet morning together. He didn't want much, and yet he wanted everything at the same time. She feared hurting him. Disappointing him. Starting him down a path that she could not follow.

"I don't want to hurt his feelings, love," she murmured finally. The admission took her by surprise, as innocuous as it may have seemed. The fact that she was saying it to Sara was shocking enough. The two of them had never had a mother-daughter relationship quite like that. Sara, as everyone who met her knew, needed to figure things out on her own. She had never come running home to Mommy for help when her heart was broken. That was more Holly's domain.

But perhaps it was just a testament to how fair their relationship had come—albeit in a two steps forward, one step backward fashion—that she could say something as honest as that to her youngest daughter. Surely that was a good thing. Progress, in a way.

"Just go with him," Sara said finally, searching her mother's face. Mae blushed. Sara could have a very piercing gaze at times, like a lighthouse beam sweeping across her and exposing everything. "It's a sunset sail. It'll be fun."

"You're right," Mae admitted. "It will be. Just fun. That's all."

They had circled back around and were standing in front of the house at Howard Street. Mae picked up her bicycle where she had set it, kissed her daughter goodbye on the cheek, and then headed back to the inn.

It had felt like the right thing to do, saying yes to Dominic. But now, standing in the small innkeeper's bedroom at the Sweet Island Inn with just under an hour until they were due to leave for the dock, Mae felt less sure.

Mostly because she had no earthly idea what to wear!

Was this a date? A friendly outing? Something more, something less, something different altogether? Who knew!

When she was younger, back in her college days, she had all sorts of movies and magazines and posters to guide her. Plenty of resources existed to tell her what lipstick to wear, what dress to choose. How to act, what to say.

But no one ever thought to consider that sixty-two-year-old women might want a little guidance, too.

She looked through her closet, unsatisfied with all the options. She rifled through her makeup bag, agonizing back and forth between different possibilities. Too formal, too flirtatious, too young, too old. Nothing felt right. Perhaps it was just a sign of the uncertainty swirling in her own head. She didn't know where to place the upcoming evening in the canvas of her life. Dominic was still that abstract brushstroke. He hadn't yet taken shape. More to the point, she hadn't yet given him a shape to take—mostly on purpose.

It felt like this evening would be the beginning of that process: deciding what Dominic was to her. And that was very, very frightening.

In the end, she settled on a blue cotton dress that swung just above her knees. Tan leather shoes, backless, and a simple gold necklace that went nicely with her hair, which she wore long for the first time in quite a while. She looked in the full-length mirror and stopped to examine herself. She bit her lip as she gazed from head to toe and back up.

What did she want this to say? "Maybe"? That was a horrible answer to the question Dominic seemed to be implying. He was saying, "Can you? Will you?"

And she was saying, "I don't know."

Try as she might, she felt afraid of the gap between them. It felt as though he was standing on the other side of a ledge and saying, "Jump. Have no fear; I will catch you." So much of her wanted badly to jump.

But there was a part of her still that couldn't do it.

He would just have to live with that.

ELIZA

When Eliza woke up again, she saw that Oliver wasn't there. His side of the bed was cold.

So everything that had happened last night was real. It wasn't some grotesque nightmare. Her swollen eyes were in fact from tears she'd shed for hours in the wake of his departure.

She felt crushed. Like Wile E. Coyote getting flattened by a steamroller. Another broken relationship. Her life had taken such a left turn over the last year. From lost to found, and now here she was, lost again. Just when she thought she might be getting back on course —back on a course she never expected to find herself on, as a matter of fact—there it went veering off once more into an ugly gray world of harsh words and lonely tears.

She wanted to cry again. But she'd done enough of that already.

What would her father say? Usually, she knew exactly what he would say. This time, though, when she closed her eyes and tried to drum up some words of advice from the man who raised her, she found nothing.

She felt utterly and completely alone.

Winter was sleeping on her chest. Eliza's skin was drenched in sweat from a long night of cuddling. Her baby's face looked a little less flushed than it had the night before, though. Perhaps the fever was breaking. It might've been an ear infection or just another bug, the kind little girls are prone to.

Something about her little angel turning the corner struck a different note in her heart. When she held her breath for a moment and craned her neck to look into Winter's sleeping face, she felt something different slicing through the haze of depression that threatened to consume her.

She felt hope.

So what if another relationship had failed? The last one had given her this beautiful gift and a new lease on life. This one would have something equally good to offer. She felt that with a resounding certainty.

Not that any of that stopped her from still feeling miserable.

Oliver wasn't here. If he had been here when she woke up, maybe she would feel like they could just work this out. Move past it, together. But something about his absence spoke volumes. If he wanted to be here, he would've been here. He wasn't. He was out pursuing another life. Maybe he regretted bringing her and Winter along. Maybe they were holding him back from the life he'd always wanted for himself.

Maybe, maybe, maybe. So many maybes were spiraling through her head, each uglier than the last.

She needed help.

She reached out and grabbed her phone from the nightstand. She might not be able to call her father for advice, but maybe a breakup —or at least, what felt like a breakup—called for a mother's love anyhow.

She dialed Mom.

Bzz. Bzz. Bzz.

No answer.

Fine. If not Mom, then Holly.

No answer.

Sara.

No answer.

Brent.

Bzz. Bzz. Bzz.

"Hello?" His voice was sleepy. Eliza felt bad immediately.

"I'm sorry, it's early. I shouldn't have called. I didn't mean to wake you up." She started to hang up the phone.

"Eliza?"

"Yeah, it's me. I'm sorry. I'll go now."

"No, no, it's okay," he said. She could hear the sounds of him struggling upright, the rustle of sheets in the background. "What's going on?"

"Nothing," she mumbled.

"You know, I always thought I was better than everyone else at telling when you were lying," he remarked with a low chuckle.

She had to laugh at that too, though bitterly. "Maybe I'm lying a little bit."

"Talk to me then," he said. "I'm here."

Eliza bit her lip. Brent was ... well, he was Brent. He was the same, always, like a Rubik's cube with only four squares per side instead of nine. Simple to solve, you know? Only a few possible combinations.

That wasn't an insult by any means. Eliza loved her brother dearly. But he wasn't exactly her first choice for delving into the intricacies of romantic relationships. Brent's two responses to emotions were usually drink about it or don't think about it. Since he was sober again, the first was no longer an option.

But she needed to say something to someone. Those maybes were still swirling around in her head like a swarm of bats. If she didn't spill her heart out loud to someone who she knew would listen, then they might consume her.

Brent could be that someone.

"Oliver and I had a fight." She quickly explained what happened. When she finished, she waited with bated breath for his response. She wasn't sure why she was so nervous, exactly. All she knew was that what he said next, for one reason or another, mattered a lot.

Silence.

"Brent?"

"Hold on, I'm thinking," he said sternly.

She had to laugh at that. That was a Dad move if ever there was one. A steady, patient thinker. Brent was more like their father than either of them had realized.

"So what do you think?" She couldn't wait anymore. God, since when was she such a fragile, emotional, needy woman? Her time on Nantucket had transformed her, mostly for the better. But there were certainly consequences to learning to relax the kung-fu grip she'd held on her heart.

"He's scared," Brent said finally, with an air of certainty.

"Scared?"

"Scared."

"Scared of what?"

"Scared of you."

Winter rolled back and forth a little bit but stayed asleep.

"That doesn't make any sense."

"It is what it is."

"That's just about the worst expression I've ever heard in my life. 'It is what it is.' I hate that one. It means nothing."

"Yeah, well ..."

"Don't you dare say it again," she laughed, though she was more than half serious.

Brent chuckled along with her. "Look, Liza, I'm telling you: he's scared."

"I'm five-three and my daughter is three months old. We're not exactly a threat." Her tone was dry, sarcastic.

She could practically hear Brent roll his eyes through the phone. "Don't play dumb," he said. "He's scared of what you mean to him. That's a scary thing for a man."

"What do we mean to him?"

"Everything. That's the problem."

Eliza could sense the kernel of truth behind what Brent was saying. "You men are way more complex than women, you know. The whole 'hysterical woman' stereotype is male-sponsored propaganda."

"Don't I know it," he said. "Best smear campaign in history."

They talked for a little while longer. Not about Oliver, specifically, but just about life in general. Brent told her about Ally. She told him about watching Winter sleep.

It felt like they were both giving each other something way more important than the words they were exchanging. Eliza couldn't quite put her finger on it, but there was just something passing back and forth between them that mattered a lot to each of them. She wondered if Brent noticed it, too. What could it be? Love, maybe. Just the simple act of a soul attending to your own. The power of listening. Any of the above, or none. Who could say for sure? It didn't matter in the end, really. What mattered was just that, by the time they said their goodbyes and hung up the phone, Eliza didn't feel quite so alone anymore.

She'd always have her family.

Scarcely fifteen minutes after she'd gotten off the call with Brent, Eliza heard the hotel door open again.

"Sorry, still in here!" she called from bed. "No housekeeping, please!"

Oliver rounded the corner.

He stopped about ten feet away from her—six steps exactly, she remembered from last night's pacing back and forth with a crying Winter. His hands were folded behind his back and he was looking down at his feet sheepishly. "I was going to say, 'Not housekeeping, but I do have a mess to clean up.'" He risked a glance up at her, saw she wasn't laughing at his lame joke, and looked back down. "I brought bagels." He pulled a brown paper bag out from behind his back. "And coffee."

She said nothing. Just looked at him.

She wasn't sure what she was supposed to say, really. Did she need to forgive him? Did it matter?

Was what they had broken? It hadn't been the most dramatic fight in the world, after all. Maybe it just felt so painful because they never, ever fought. But Eliza just couldn't shake the feeling that something irreparable had been shattered between them. She had a vivid flashback to a fight between Sara and Mom, when Sara had purposefully destroyed one of Mom's favorite pieces of china just to lash back out at her. This felt like that, like there was no piecing this back together. Even if they did somehow fix it, the cracks would always be there, barely held together by dollar-store glue. Was that the kind of life she wanted to live? Was that the kind of home in which she wanted to raise her daughter? No. She had run from New York to escape a life built on lies, with the cracks papered over. She had no intention of starting that process anew.

"Are you going to say something?" he asked softly.

"I'm not sure what you would like me to say, Oliver," she replied curtly. She felt that ice queen tide rising in her throat. *Lash out at him. Send him away.* She resisted the temptation—for now. ˙

"You're right. There's no reason for you to make this easy on me." She could see the knot ride down his throat as he swallowed hard. "I guess I should start with an apology." He looked up at her. Those green eyes shimmered. His fingers clasped and unclasped in front of him now, so long and lithe. "I am scared, Eliza."

Her jaw fell open. She'd been so quick to dismiss Brent's assessment of the situation. What did her kid brother know about love?

"What is there to be scared of?" she whispered. "It's just us."

"'Us' is exactly what frightens me. I'm ... I'm living out my dream right now. This—" he swept a hand around the hotel room to mean the tour, the attention, the crowds, the adoration—"this is everything I ever wanted." He paused, looked at her, swallowed again. "But it means nothing without you. And I think I'm realizing that I can't have both. So I want you to know this: I choose you. I choose you ten times out of ten. I'm sorry."

She softened. Melted. He must have seen it, because he came over to her and wrapped her hands in his. Her eyes were tearing up, she noticed, no matter how hard she tried to stop the tears. She knew she ought to press deeper. It was clear that Oliver had things he was struggling with. Even if this was a fragile peace, though, that was what she wanted.

"Do you mean it?" she asked.

He bent down, pressing his forehead against hers. "I mean it," he echoed. "I mean it."

Fragile or not, this was the peace she needed. She closed her eyes and kissed him.

27

MAE

Saturday evening.

It was the loveliest evening that Mae had had in a long time. "You look ravishing," Dominic said when she'd met him downstairs in the foyer to the inn.

"Oh, thank you." To her surprise, she blushed. Lord have mercy— blushing at his first words to her! Was she sixty-two or twenty-six? "You look very nice yourself."

He did a mock bow. "Dressed in my Sunday finest. To be perfectly honest, I haven't the faintest idea how one is meant to dress for a sunset cruise. I thought about wearing my swimming trunks beneath my slacks."

Mae giggled—honest to goodness *giggled.* Then she took his offered elbow and they went on their way.

They made their way to the docks and met the captain, a kindly older gentleman named Harvey who looked every bit the part of a sailor— grizzled gray beard, sun-weathered skin, a strong handshake. He escorted them on board, showed them to the bow, and then made his way back to the wheel.

On the bow was a delightful little spread of cheeses, crackers, fruits, and a bottle of champagne on ice, along with a pair of glasses for the two of them. Dominic popped the bottle expertly as the boat pushed off from its moorings and they made their way out towards the setting sun.

The angle of the rays on the water painted everything the most glorious orange. Mae had seen a thousand Nantucket sunsets in her lifetime, and yet this one was as good as any of them. Clear blue sky behind them, fading ahead into a purple so deep one could dive into it.

"Nature is an artist, isn't she?" Dominic murmured as he poured them each a glass of bubbly.

"She most certainly is."

He added, "And a bit of a showoff, I think." He pointed off to the starboard side of the ship, where a pod of dolphins was frolicking in the warmth of the evening waters.

Mae laughed. "Perhaps a little bit over the top," she said. "But I'm not complaining!"

"Nor am I. A lovely evening with a lovely woman—what is there to complain about?" He raised his champagne to hers. The rims of their glasses kissed with a soft *tink*. "To you, Mae Benson, and your endless patience with my eccentricities."

"You give me too much credit sometimes, Dominic O'Kelley. After all, you *pay* me to put up with you." She smiled mischievously as he looked at her slack-jawed for a second. Then he realized he was teasing him, threw his head back, and laughed. Even his laugh sounded Irish. She loved it.

She took a sip of her champagne. It was cool, crisp, and refreshing. That, plus a bite of a chocolate-covered strawberry, was all she needed to set her mind at ease. Dominic was absolutely right—it was a beautiful evening. She had nothing to worry about.

After all: life was meant to be enjoyed, wasn't it?

An hour passed by at a pace so meandering that neither of them noticed the seconds slipping away like waves on the shore. They talked about everything and nothing, and sometimes they didn't talk at all. The captain, Harvey, stayed behind the wheel at the rear of the ship, piloting them expertly through the gentle waves, so that there was never a bump or a spill of the champagne.

One glass became two glasses became a third. Mae found herself buzzing pleasantly. Dominic's eyes were reflecting the last of the setting sun as he told her about the latest updates in the novel he'd been working on for the better part of a year.

"Sounds like you're almost there," she said.

"So close and yet so far. I do find that the ending almost always writes itself, though."

"Is that so?" She loved hearing about his experience as a writer. It always seemed so foreign to her, that he spent each day of his life imagining people and places that had never existed before. She couldn't imagine what it was like to close one's eyes and be transported to a world of one's own making. She had always been a here-and-now person, a feet-on-the-ground person. Dominic was anything but that. He was a dreamer, and when he spoke of his dreams, he made her feel them along with him. It was a gift unlike any other.

"Yes," he replied. "Sometimes, there is just a certain way that things go. The world falls into place in exactly the right pattern. It is beautiful, in my opinion, when everything is exactly where it is meant to be." He blinked, and when he reopened his eyes, they seemed somehow more serious. Mae felt a shiver run down her spine, like a blast of cool Irish air had come out of nowhere. "Like now, for instance," he finished gently. He paused and then, with deliberate slowness, he reached out to touch her hand where it rested on the ship next to him. "Right now, it feels to me as though everything is exactly where it is meant to be."

This was it. The moment she had longed for and feared all at once. She could almost sense him offering his heart up to her. She knew what he wanted her to say. *Say yes. Say you feel as I do. Say that you care for me the way I care for you.* At their age, those words didn't always need to be said. They hummed in the air, all the more powerful for being unspoken.

Dominic's eyes searched hers. They were not fearful, though it was obvious that he had put himself in a vulnerable position. They were patient, kind, and understanding. All the things she loved in him.

When she didn't answer, he glanced down for a moment, then back up. "I wanted to tell you something, Mae," he said. The waves were slapping gently against the hull of the boat. The sun had almost disappeared, too, and the first starlight was beginning to pierce through the night veil. "I made you a gift of sorts. A bit of a selfish one, but one that I hope you'll understand."

Mae was a little confused at this turn of events. She watched as he reached into the small backpack he'd brought along with him and retrieved something from inside. "Here," he said, offering a rectangular package to her. It was hefty and wrapped in brown paper. "Open it."

She hesitated and looked at him. He smiled and nodded again. "Go on then. It's for you."

"All right," she whispered. She tried to keep her fingers from shaking as she tore off the brown paper.

Inside was a book. A galley copy of a book, actually, according to the stamped inscription on the first page. The cover was blank, but when she turned the pages, she saw on the third one a title inked in the middle. "'A Rose in Nantucket,'" she read out loud. "'A Novel, by Dominic O'Kelley.' Oh, that is a beautiful title!"

Dominic was still smiling gently. "Turn the page."

She frowned and did as he said. When she saw what was written on the next page, she gasped. It was a dedication. To her.

"*For Mae,*" she read. "*Without whom my life would be utterly bereft of beauty.*" She looked up at him. Her eyes were filled with tears. "Oh, Dominic. I'm sorry. I'm so, so sorry."

He understood at once. His face didn't betray it, but she saw the shade of his eyes falter. His gaze fell to his hands, which were clasped in his lap. "It is too much," he said softly, still not looking at her. "I should have known. I am terribly sorry."

Mae didn't know what to say. This horrible, beautiful, heartbreaking, perfect and perfectly wrong moment was everything she had longed for and feared for so many months now. It was love, hers for the taking, if she wanted it.

But it was too real. Too serious. Too much.

As much as she wanted to reach out and take Dominic's hand, she found herself faltering at the critical moment.

She was not yet ready for love.

"Dominic ..." she began, but he shook his head sadly.

"I am terribly sorry," he said again. He was looking at her levelly this time. Not angry or devastated, but merely sad, as one would be to see that a creature had wrecked one's garden in the nighttime. Or that a baby bird you'd been watching grow up through the window had suddenly left the nest without saying goodbye. The sadness of loss that didn't wound as much as it just left part of you missing something you never knew you had come to rely upon.

"Dominic, I—" But he just shook his head again and she fell silent once more.

"I'm going to take a business trip," he said quietly. "I expect to be gone for perhaps six weeks. If I may be so bold, I would like to ask you a favor."

"Anything," she said at once through a throat that felt choked and tight. "Anything at all."

"Will you save my room?"

She nodded. She didn't trust herself to speak anymore. A tear had escaped from her eye and trickled down her cheek.

He smiled at her. His eyes were inscrutable behind his glasses now that the sun had finally set. "Thank you, Mae." That was all he said.

He was gone by the morning.

PART III

SIX WEEKS LATER

28

SARA

Monday night.

After months of boring idleness, there suddenly weren't enough hours in the day. Six weeks had gone by in the blink of an eye. But Sara's task list had grown longer, not shorter.

Who knew that opening a restaurant would require so much work? Well, she had. But still, it was one thing to say she was going to open her own place, and a whole other thing to do it.

She'd picked out a site for it—a former steakhouse and bar with beautiful bones that was badly in need of a facelift. It had come at a good price, which she was able to afford thanks to Mom's generous offer of Dad's life insurance money. While they were signing over the paperwork for the mortgage application, Sara had felt a twinge of guilt. Mom must've sensed this, because she laid her hand on Sara's knee, smiled, and said, "He would've loved to be here with you."

That little sentence had made Sara's heart swell. She felt deep down in her soul that her mom was right. Dad would've loved this, would've supported this, would've been down at the restaurant night and day working to get the place up and running in time for her scheduled opening at the end of June. He might not've been here anymore, but Brent was, and her little brother was doing his darndest to help.

In the process, however, he and Sara were getting pretty close to strangling each other.

"How many times do I have to tell you not to leave the tools out like that?" he said when he arrived. He pointed at the buzz saw, which was lying on its side on a worktable, sharp blade exposed.

"What's the big deal?" Sara said, annoyed. She wiped some sweat off her forehead. The A/C unit wasn't in working order yet, so it was "hotter than hell and half of Georgia," as her dad would've said. Though, now that she thought about it, she was reasonably sure he'd never been to Georgia.

"Someone could get hurt," he pointed out.

"'Someone' oughta watch where they're going, then," she fired back. He rolled his eyes, a habit she despised. "Anyway, nice of you to show up," she continued. "Can you give me a hand moving this thing?" She jabbed the paintbrush she was holding in the direction of the cherrywood bar top, which had been propped against a wall while it awaited installation.

"Apologies for the lateness, boss. Say, did my paycheck get lost in the mail?" he snarled sarcastically. "Oh wait—I'm not getting paid jack for this. I get here when I can, Sara."

"You volunteered, you know."

"I volunteered to help, not to get yelled at every time I set foot in the dang place. It wasn't like I was just dying for an unpaid job."

Sara exhaled angrily through her teeth. "Just shut up and help me move this thing. I have to get a coat on the wall now so it can dry in time for a second coat in the morning."

He folded his arms across his chest. "Maybe I'm not 'volunteering' for that particular task."

She threw her paintbrush in the bucket. "You're acting like a child. Are you serious right now?"

"Are you?" he snapped back immediately. "I don't have a problem helping you, Sara, but the least you can do is treat me with a little respect."

"Who has time for respect? I don't have time for respect! Paint doesn't care about respect!"

"That sounds like a personal problem."

"Well, it's your problem now! Now, for the last time, are you going to help me or not?"

He huffed. "I oughta just leave you to deal with it by yourself."

She resisted the desire to roll her own eyes this time. They were standing in the guts of her empty restaurant, fists clenched like two boxers entering the ring. But bickering like schoolchildren wasn't going to get anything done faster. So Sara sucked up her pride and said, "I'm sorry. I'll put the saw away. Will you please help me?"

Brent slumped over and shook his head tiredly. He looked worn, which made sense, given all the things he was juggling right now. But, much to his credit, he set down his bag and came over to help her wrestle the bar top into a different resting place.

When they were done, they dusted their hands and eyed each other.

"God, I would love a beer," he mumbled. It was his form of brokering peace between them.

"I need something stronger than that."

They both laughed exhaustedly. Brent might have been joking, but Sara sure wasn't. And it wasn't even the work of the restaurant that was driving her to crave a stiff drink. It was the reason she was here in the first place.

To put a word on it: men.

"*Ugh, men*"—a common Sara refrain over the years—didn't even do justice to how she was feeling these days. The problem was that, every time Sara closed her eyes, she pictured Gavin and Russell staring balefully at her. They both had looks on their faces like, *You really gonna do this?*

And, no matter how badly she wanted to deny it, she had to admit— but only to herself, never to anyone else—that she was motivated in large part by spite for the two men who'd put her in this position in the first place.

She knew darn well that that wasn't really a fair assessment. Gavin was a jerk and Russell was—well, Russell hadn't actually done a thing wrong. So why was she so mad at him? He'd moved on, as he'd clearly shown her at the bar two months ago. She should do the same.

But she blamed them both all the same. It was childish to do so, it was stupid, and it was irresponsibly directed towards others when she was the one who'd made the choices she made. And yet, she couldn't stop herself. When she was sweating her butt off while painting or working the buzz saw at high noon in this stuffy shell of a building, she thought about Gavin sticking his nose where it didn't belong, and she got right back to work. Teeth clenched, hair tied back, fire in her heart.

She was doing this for her, yeah. But she was also doing this because screw them, right?

"I'm sorry I yelled at you," she said. "I shouldn't have done that."

Brent looked up at her, surprised. "What day is today?"

"Monday, June—uh, June 14th. Why?"

He whistled. "Because I will forever remember this day as the first and only time I've ever heard you apologize."

She flicked paint at his head in response. He ducked, chortling.

"First and last time. I'm gonna get back to work."

She turned to go back to painting the trim on the lower part of the wall, but Brent grabbed her by the shoulder. "You doing okay?" he asked.

"Yeah," she said, shrugging him off. "Peachy."

He grabbed her again. "Really?"

"Really," she said firmly.

"Because sometimes it's nice to have someone ask you that. Even if you're not gonna tell them the truth."

"Whatever you say, B."

"I know you're anxious about all this. It's a big thing you're doing. But I believe in you. And if it feels like too much sometimes, you know you can talk to me, okay?"

Sara softened. He was just trying to be nice to her. She didn't have many people like that left in her life. She knew she needed to do a better job of hanging onto the ones she still did have. "I know. I'm just —yeah, anxious is a good word. I want this to work."

"It will," he said without hesitation. "I know it will."

It shouldn't have felt that good to hear it. Sara should just believe in herself, right? Wasn't that what everyone always said to do? *Believe in*

yourself! Manifest your own reality! God helps those who help themselves!
True, true, true.

But it didn't hurt to have Brent's faith in her, too.

"Thanks, bro," she said with a smile. "Now, if you'll be so kind, we've got a lot to do."

Brent grinned broadly. "Lead the way, captain."

29

BRENT

Over the last month and a half, Brent had been getting run ragged. He was working charter trips with Marshall by day, building Sara's restaurant with her by night, and trying to find time to hang out with Ally in between.

Being busy was good—he definitely had a little bit of his momma's spirit in him—but he was dead-freaking tired.

What worried him more than any of the things going on in his world was the fear that he was headed for a repeat of last year. Hadn't this all unfolded in exactly the same way before? Hadn't it landed him in a heap of trouble? Sure enough, last summer, he'd been working hard, exploring a fragile new relationship, and seemingly gearing up to turn a big corner in his life.

But that had all come crashing down in brutal, ugly fashion.

Was this destined to do the same thing?

He really, really hoped not. He didn't think he could survive another heartbreak and downward spiral like the one that had crippled him last fall. Between the alcoholism, the depression, and the hunger to get his face kicked in, he'd barely made it through the new year. What was worse was that, at times, he hadn't even wanted to make it.

It had been a while now since he'd felt that way. Those dark nights seemed like little more than a distant memory. He might be exhausted twenty-four-seven, but at least he was getting worn down while doing things he loved.

He loved doing the charter trips. The threat posed by the ocean grew a little less intimidating with each new day on the water. And, as it turned out, he was really good at his job. He knew the Nantucket waters like the back of his hand, and he had a little bit of a natural flair for entertaining guests. Most folks just wanted to be listened to. Brent had a knack for that. He understood where they were coming from.

Plus, he liked to hear their stories. Never before had Nantucket felt so small to him as it did when people came to them from all around the world and told him about their own hometowns. Florida, California, Brazil, South Africa—they'd had clients from every neck of the woods, each one more interesting than the last. When they talked about the food and the landscapes of their homes, Brent could practically close his eyes and taste the seasonings, smell the fresh air, so utterly different than everything he knew. He'd never had what you'd call a travel bug, but out of nowhere he'd found himself daydreaming about getting on a plane and heading for sights unseen with little more than the clothes on his back.

That was where his mind went when he was hammering away in Sara's soon-to-be restaurant. His hands would be busy cutting, measuring, lifting, building, painting, but his mind would be in Thailand, France, Chile.

"Earth to Brent," Sara said, breaking his spell of concentration.

"Huh?"

"I said, can you hand me that wrench?"

"Oh. Yeah, no prob. Here." He handed it over.

"Whatcha thinking about?" she asked a moment later as she tightened a fixture. They were in the kitchen today, installing the industrial equipment she'd ordered from a restaurant supply company with the meager help of a how-to manual and some YouTube videos. Burners, walk-in freezer, sinks, ovens—the works, basically.

"Nothing," he mumbled.

"Liar. You're thinking about your new girly, aren't ya?"

Brent blushed. Thankfully, his newfound tan kept it from showing on his face. Then again, Sara didn't have to see the color in his cheeks to know that she had him squarely pegged. "Nah," he demurred, but she knew he was lying.

The truth was that he was thinking about Ally. Because, every time he thought about some exotic locale, he pictured her there alongside him. It was her fault. She was the other piece of the puzzle that was fueling these daydreams. She'd started talking to him about taking a big trip once her family vacation was over in July. "We could go anywhere!" she'd say.

"We?" was always his reply.

She'd inevitably fix him with that head-tilted-to-the-side glare. "Yes, dummy, *we*. You know that you're allowed to leave this isolated little rock from time to time, right?"

He usually laughed and changed the subject, but the thought stuck with him. It had honestly never really crossed his mind to leave Nantucket, as embarrassing as that might seem. This was home, right? Why leave? It seemed like an obvious conclusion. Now, though, everything was up in the air. He could leave. He could go anywhere.

So why not do it?

That was the thing about Ally—she made everything feel possible. There were no rules around her, or at least none that she really paid any mind to. She was fun, spontaneous, exciting, beautiful. She drew him kicking and screaming into the present moment. He had no choice but to be fully *with* her at any given second. Take your eye off the girl for just a blink and she'd be off to something new. He liked that about her. No thinking. No fear. Just *go*.

All of which begged the question: if he liked Ally so much, why did he keep finding himself thinking about Rose?

He hadn't seen her since their run-in at Frank's house over six weeks ago. Frank had left the island on business of some sort, meaning that Brent's phone had stopped ringing off the hook every day. Without Frank in town, he had no reason to go over to that side of the island, though he was just itching to do so. He couldn't quite put a finger on it.

Maybe it was just how unresolved the whole thing was. Rose had cut things off so suddenly that Brent didn't know if he was ever going to fully recover. Best thing to do was forget about her and move on. That was the only way to heal.

He just didn't really feel like doing that.

"You like her, huh?" Sara prodded.

"She's fun."

"But you *like* her. It's okay to say yes, you know. We aren't in high school anymore. You don't have to keep these things secret."

"I just told you I think she's fun."

"But that's a non-answer," she pointed out. "Do you like her or don't you?"

"Can you just leave me alone?" he snapped.

Sara raised her hands, eyes wide. "Whoa. Sensitive much?"

"I answered your question, you kept pushing, I asked you to stop. How am I in the wrong here?"

"There was nothing wrong with the question. I don't see why you're acting so weird about it."

"I'm not acting weird; you're being annoying. There's a difference."

Sara started to say something, then fell silent.

"Nothing else to say? No? Then let's get back to work. I'm exhausted. It's late. I want to go to sleep."

"We still have to finish getting the freezer hooked up tonight."

"No," he said, shaking his head. "I'm not doing that tonight."

"I want it done tonight," she said firmly.

"And I just told you no. You're really not listening right now, are you?"

"It has to happen tonight."

"You're repeating yourself."

"I'm telling you what's going to happen."

"No, you're telling me what *you* want to happen. Big difference there, too."

"Brent, we're installing the freezer!"

"That's it." He stripped off his work gloves and threw them to the ground in disgust. He ripped off his work belt and tossed that down as well. "I'm leaving. I've got better things to do than sit here and get disrespected like this all the time. When you want to treat me like a human being instead of a slave, give me a ring."

He didn't wait for her to answer, though he knew she was almost certainly cueing up something nasty to say back to him.

He couldn't stand the way she'd been treating him since they started working on the restaurant together. They'd made incredible progress, given the constraints they'd been dealing with. Brent thought she should be grateful for his help and proud of how fast they were moving along.

But it was never good enough for Sara. It always had to be faster, sooner, cheaper, better, *now now now*. He knew she was being driven by dirty fuel—bad emotions, so to speak. She was mad at the men who'd done her wrong and she wanted to do something for herself. Brent was well aware of how his sister operated. Still, that didn't mean he had to put up with the uglier sides of her personality. Family was family. He wanted Sara to succeed.

He simply had no intention of sacrificing his self-respect to make that happen. He'd come way too far to give that up so easily.

Brent marched out of the restaurant and into the night. He didn't have his watch on, but it was maybe eleven or eleven-thirty, judging by the height of the moon overhead. It was a cool, clear night. The moon was bathing everything in milky light. He walked down the road a little ways, still steaming mad. He found a big rock on the side of the road and plopped down.

He thought about Ally. He thought about Nantucket. He thought about Sara. He thought about Rose.

But he didn't get very far on any of those topics before a truck trundled down the street and pulled to a stop in front of him.

"Well, well, well, Triple B! What're you doing out here all by your lonesome?" Marshall seemed to be a little subdued compared to his usual.

"Some folks just don't know when to quit," Brent grumbled.

"Uh oh," Marshall replied. He pulled the truck over to the shoulder, threw it in park, and clambered out. "Come take a seat on Santa's lap and talk to me about it."

Brent chuckled despite himself as Marshall popped down the bed of the truck and hopped up onto it. He patted the spot next to him. "Upsie daisy, here we go." Sighing, Brent got up and sat next to his best friend.

"Visiting your mom?" Brent asked.

"Yeah," Marshall replied. "She was having a bad night." Marshall's mom suffered from Alzheimer's. She had recently moved into an assisted living facility so she could have more regular around-the-clock care, but she was really balking at the change. Brent knew that his mom's unhappiness weighted heavily on his normally happy-go-lucky friend.

"Sorry to hear that, brother," Brent replied.

"I appreciate that, amigo. What's up in your neck of the woods?"

"Sister being a pain, as usual. Power trippin' like a son-of-a-gun."

Marshall laughed a little. "She's just nervous, I'll bet. Ol' Dinosara."

"I know. Still a pain, though."

"You ain't always such a good-times-guy yourself, Triple B. You Bensons get awfully morose when the mood strikes."

Brent punched him in the shoulder half-heartedly. "Yeah, well, runs in the family, I guess." That certainly seemed to be a fair assessment. Mom had seemed downfallen ever since Dominic had left, though she wouldn't really tell any of the kids why. At least Holly was chipper these days. Or at least she was the last time Brent had talked to her.

Marshall asked, "How's your lady friend?"

"Let's not."

"Fair enough. Radio silence, then."

"Much obliged."

"Any time."

"You know, you can let someone else get the last word in every now and then."

Marshall grinned wide. "Where's the fun in that?"

Brent sighed in fake exasperation, shaking his head. It didn't take much to get Marshall perked back up again whenever he was feeling down. He ought to learn from his friend's example. Bad moods always took Brent ages to come up out of. Even now, he was still simmering from his little spat with Sara. He would just have to sleep it off. By morning, he'd be calmed down a little bit, and the two of them would make up and get back to work. For right now, though, he just needed a little time to cool off.

"Mind giving me a ride home?" Brent asked. Sara had picked him up from his apartment, so it was convenient timing for Marshall to show up.

"You got it, partner," his friend replied. "But let's just take a second and look at these stars, first. Nantucket is putting on a show for us tonight."

That seemed reasonable. No sense in shutting himself inside to brood.

Life, after all, was meant to be enjoyed.

30

ELIZA

After their dust-up in Boston, Eliza and Oliver had been good. Great, in fact. They'd followed the tour around and done shows all over the northeast. Boston, Providence, Poughkeepsie—the list went on and on. Three or four shows a week at a minimum meant that Eliza got to listen to her man play his music for adoring crowds night in and night out.

A tiny part of her was jealous of the people who got to hear him for the first time. It was like being sad when you finish an amazing book because you'll never again get to read it with fresh eyes. Every night, she saw new fans fall in love with Oliver. But, to be fair, she fell in love with him all over again every single night, too.

The next stop of the tour was in New York City. They'd be here for a couple of weeks, playing dates at different venues in Manhattan and Brooklyn. Tonight started the way most of their nights did. She, Winter, and Oliver ate dinner together backstage with the band—which, it turned out, was comprised of the funniest collection of goofballs and weirdos that she'd ever encountered in her life. Shane, Nikolai, Greggy the Eggy, and Meatstick—"don't ask," was what she was told, and that seemed like good advice—were hilarious and completely down-to-earth. It seemed that rock-star stereotypes were mostly overblown. The menu for this evening was takeout from a vegan Thai place in Brooklyn. It was actually incredibly delicious. Guay teow, som tam, and a spicy salad with mushrooms in it.

"Sticking to milk—wise move," Shane said, gesturing towards Winter with a head nod and a wicked smile.

"She's smarter than you, that's for sure," Oliver chimed in. "Since when is this a vegan operation?"

"It's good for the soul, my friend," replied Nikolai sagely. "Besides, no one wants to come see a fat rock star."

After the dishes were cleaned, it was time to get ready to go out. As the opener, Oliver was on first, so he took a few minutes to finish getting dressed, practice his vocal scales again, and do one final run-through on the electric keyboard they kept backstage for that purpose.

Then—showtime.

Seconds before he went out on stage, Eliza brought Winter over to Oliver where he was standing behind the curtains. He did the same thing he did every single night—tickled her thighs until she laughed, poked her chubby little belly until she laughed harder, then gave her a kiss on the forehead.

"Good luck, babe," Eliza said, just like she did every night.

And just like he did every night, Oliver gave her a wink and say, "Let's hope I don't need it."

It made her heart sing to see how tender he was with her daughter. She was glad they'd come on this tour. It was a good thing for their— well, maybe she shouldn't quite call it a family just yet. But it felt like they were in the process of becoming one, if that was a thing. Whatever they were, they were glued together by love. That seemed like the most important detail.

As the show manager counted down the seconds until the curtains pulled back, Eliza followed another roadie to tonight's private mezzanine area for friends and family of the performers. She got herself a glass of water from the craft table and settled into a perch on the railing, off to one side, where she had a good view of everything. Winter was being especially well-behaved tonight. In fact, she'd been doing pretty well ever since Oliver and Eliza had their fight. Maybe she'd turned a corner. Or maybe she just reflected the state of her mom's heart. Either way, Eliza certainly wasn't going to complain.

The curtains pulled back, the crowd erupted, and it took no time at all before Oliver had won them over. Eliza sang along, helping Winter to dance, or rather, to wiggle her biscuit-dough-like limbs in the air, which was what passed for dancing for a five-month-old. She saw Oliver searching for them. When he found where they were standing, he smiled. That was enough for Eliza. Just being seen. It felt indescribably good.

But the height of that warm buzz didn't last long.

"Hello, Eliza," said a voice that she had long ago stopped worrying about.

She turned around, heart thudding in her chest.

"What are you doing here, Clay?"

Her ex-fiancé looked exactly as he did a year ago, like he'd been preserved in a cryogenic chamber. Not a hair out of place, perfectly dressed in gray checkered suit slacks and a white button-down shirt, pressed and laundered. His eyes were just the same as she remembered them—flat, emotionless, predatory.

"I came to see the show," he said with a shrug.

"You came to find me."

"This, that, yeah. We're splitting hairs now."

"You stalked me here," she continued.

"You aren't that difficult to find, babe," he replied, like none of this was a big deal and she was the weird one for freaking out. Her heart was so loud right now, it was unbelievable. As if someone was beating a drum inside her skull. Could it have been one of her social media posts? She was usually careful when she posted for this exact reason. Had she made a mistake somewhere along the line...?

She winced when he called her "babe." "Do not call me that."

He ignored her comment. His gaze flicked down to Winter, held close in her mother's arms. "My daughter," was all he said. That was the most frightening thing that had happened yet. Eliza looked around. There were only a handful of other people here. They were all engrossed in the show and not paying a lick of attention to the nightmare unfolding on this dark little mezzanine. She thought about screaming. Calling for help. Surely Clay didn't belong here. He must've bribed his way up here. That would be very much in line with his character. He'd never been afraid of spreading money around to grease his way into wherever he wanted to go.

"She is *not* your daughter," Eliza said unsteadily.

Clay's head tilted to the side. "The law would beg to differ, I think," he said softly. It was like he knew how vicious the things he was saying were, so he said them softly, as if that would take out some of the sting.

"What do you want?" Best to cut to the heart of the issue. With Clay, it was all about equivalent exchange. He was a finance man to the heart, concerned only with give and take. If he'd come here, it meant he wanted something. She should find out what that thing was sooner rather than later.

"I want us again," he answered simply. That was the craziest thing he'd said yet.

"You're delusional."

"I miss you, Eliza."

"No." She shook her head. "You don't."

"I do!" he insisted with a fervent nod. "We were good together. We worked."

She couldn't believe her ears. Shockingly, this was the most romantic thing he'd ever said to her in all the years she'd known him, ever since they'd first met at Goldman Sachs, a lifetime ago. But, given the context, it didn't feel loving or romantic at all. It felt like the boogeyman was trying to get her to move in with him. It felt so utterly, horribly wrong. *Make it stop, make him leave, let me wake up,* she begged to whichever deity was in charge of this nightmare. *Please, God, make him leave.*

But when she opened her eyes again, he was still there.

"We didn't work. You're a drug addict."

"No, no, no," he said, waving a hand as if to say that that was all illusory. "You misunderstood what was happening that day. I am not an addict."

That was a pitiful attempt at an explanation. It didn't matter, though, because she wasn't interested in his explanations anyway. She'd ended things because of the drugs that day she walked in on him snorting a white powder in their home, but the truth was that she should have ended them for other reasons long before then.

"I'm leaving," she said. "Don't follow me." She started to walk around him for the exits. Behind her, Oliver's voice filled the air, amplified a thousand times over. He was nearing the peak of his show. The crowd was loving it. If she closed her eyes, she could just pretend that everything was fine and she was merely watching her love sing for her and her alone. She could hold her baby to her chest and believe, if only for a moment, that Clay had never appeared, that this wasn't happening.

But then Clay seized her forearm in his grasp and jolted her back to the ugliness of the present.

"You're hurting me," she hissed. In her arms, Winter was fussing. She could sense the unease in the air. Eliza heard the first few whimpers that preceded a wail.

"I want my daughter," Clay said. His face was up in hers now. It was all she could see. He didn't look angry, or hateful, or anything at all, really. He just looked like Clay. Like he was stating simple facts.

"Not a chance," Eliza shot back.

He nodded and repeated himself. "I want to see my daughter."

"Let. Go."

He released her. She tucked Winter close and ran.

31

HOLLY

Pete and Holly had been busy as all get out for a month and a half straight. It continued to amaze Holly how much *stuff* one accumulated in a lifetime. Kids' stuff and clothes stuff and junk stuff. Treadmills and old coats and plates they'd been given for their wedding and never, ever used because they were objectively and irredeemably hideous. Boxes mounted up to the ceiling, each labeled neatly and taped closed, and yet it felt like Holly had barely even scratched the surface of all the stuff that needed to be sorted and moved.

It was a daunting task. But Holly didn't care. Because she felt amazing. Ever since Pete had told her the news—well, actually ever since she'd gotten over the shock of all the fear and worrying that had preceded Pete's news—she'd been on cloud nine. Even now, surrounded by the chaos of a half-packed house and two energetic kids who were three days into their summer vacation, she was serene and smiling.

"Grady, don't pull your sister's hair."

"But Mom, she pinched me!"

"Alice, don't pinch your brother."

"Mommy, he said my American Girl doll had an ugly face!"

She turned to them, hands on hips, Stern Mom expression in her eyes. "If I have to say one more thing to either of you, you both lose TV privileges for three nights. Am I clear?"

That snapped them both to attention. They grumbled under their breath in that little kid way, but Holly knew better than to pay any mind. With the living room temporarily at peace, she turned back to the boxes she was loading up and labeling.

The peace lasted about all of five minutes before the front door opened and Pete walked in.

"Daddy!" came the shrieks from the kids, who sprinted towards him. He scooped both of them up—which was fairly impressive, considering Grady's recent growth spurt—and ran full-tilt down the hallway making revving noises like a race car. Holly smiled and shook her head.

It certainly didn't hurt her mood that Pete had been so loving and attentive lately. He had an infectious enthusiasm for everything. Kids' laundry needed doing? Pete was on it, separating colors and darks, running the whites through a bleach cycle. Holly had her hands full and it was getting close to dinnertime? No problem—the Daddy Special was coming up. It was awesome to see him in husband-and-father mode again.

"Whatcha doing, hon?" Pete called from down the hall a few moments later. Alice and Grady had scampered off into the backyard. He walked towards her, loosening his tie, and planted a kiss on her cheek.

"Kitchen supplies," she answered. "Did you know we own three separate blenders?"

"Of course. What serious household doesn't have a backup blender and a backup-for-the-backup blender? Anything less would be irresponsible parenting."

He flopped onto the couch next to her. She looked up at him and frowned. "What's that smile for?"

"What smile?" he said innocently.

"That one," she answered, pointing at his face. "That mischievous, 'I'm up to no good' smile you've got on. I know that one."

He put a hand on his chest like he'd been frightfully offended. "I don't have any idea what you're talking about.:

"Peter Lowell Goodwin ..."

"Uh-oh," he said, looking alarmed. "She busted out the middle name. All right, all right, you got me."

"Well?!" She was biting back a smile but starting to lose the battle.

Pete leaned forward and put his elbows on his knees. He was wringing his hands in front of him, which was what he always did when he was excited about something. He checked his watch, then pointed at the door. Right then, the doorbell rang. He punched a fist in the air. "Ah, flawless timing!"

"Who on earth is that?" Holly asked, bewildered.

"Nancy!" Pete called over his shoulder as he went to answer the door.

"Nancy? The babysitter? Why is Nancy here? It's a Monday night!"

She heard Pete welcoming Nancy inside. Nancy was their go-to babysitter, the daughter of the neighbors a few doors down. CPR certified, a student at the local college, and an all-around nice, trustworthy girl.

"Hi, Nancy," Holly said politely. "Pete, what's happening?"

"Nancy is here to watch the kids. And you and I, my love, are going out on the town."

Holly's jaw fell open. "Are you taking me on a date, Peter Goodwin?"

He grinned. "Play your cards right, and it might even include dessert."

She stood up and wiped a bead of sweat off her forehead. "Am I supposed to go to a nice dinner looking like this?" She gestured towards the old, ratty mom jeans and paint-splattered white T-shirt she was wearing. "I'm a mess!"

Pete laughed. "You've got fifteen minutes. Any longer than that and the lobster is going to get cold."

Holly's eyes sparkled. "Did you say lobster?"

"I did indeed, darling."

Without saying another word, she turned and sprinted down the hallway towards their bedroom.

"To us," Holly said, raising a glass of wine.

"To our family," Pete corrected. They toasted and drank.

Dinner was incredible. Steak and lobster at their favorite restaurant in town, along with a bottle of Holly's favorite cabernet sauvignon. Life didn't get much better than this.

"Think the kids are being good to Nancy?" Holly mused when they'd set their glasses down.

"I think she'll lock them in cages if they're not. She don't mess around."

Holly nearly spit out the bite of food she was taking as she laughed.

They talked about anything and everything while they ate. The upcoming move, Pete's plans for the new law firm, Holly's excitement to get involved in the Nantucket community. It all felt new and fresh and thrilling.

When the check came at the end of their meal, Pete's smile suddenly turned mischievous again. "Guess what I found?" he said.

Her brow furrowed. "What?"

When he pulled out a Batman wallet from his back pocket, she burst out laughing again. "Oh. My. God."

It was the same wallet he'd brought on their first date all those years ago. Stuffed with sweaty fives and tens from his summer job cutting lawns, he'd thrown it proudly on the table to pay for a lobster dinner at a fancy, white tablecloth restaurant back when they were, what— fifteen? Sixteen? She couldn't believe her eyes. Her stomach did a funny little flip. She looked at Pete again with renewed love in her eyes.

"I love you," she murmured.

"I love you too, Hollyday," he said back, smiling as he signed his name to the bill with a flourish. "Let's go home and rescue Nancy from the rug rats."

She took his arm as they exited the restaurant. Pete went up to the valet stand to retrieve their vehicle. Meanwhile, Holly's phone buzzed. It was Judy, the realtor. This must be good news. They were due to finalize closing in three days, so Holly was sure that Judy just needed to confirm some detail or another.

She was very wrong about that.

When Pete came back up, whistling a happy tune, he saw her jaw hanging open and all the blood gone from her face. Holly let her hand fall by her side, still clutching her cell phone tightly.

"Babe?" Pete asked, face wrinkled with concern. "Everything okay?"

She was so hurt and angry that she could barely get the words out. "The seller got a higher offer," she told him. "They reneged. We don't have a house anymore."

32

ELIZA

Eliza wasn't sure how long she sat in the darkness, clutching Winter tightly to her chest and rocking back and forth in the seat. She'd fled from the VIP mezzanine to the little broom-closet-sized room that served as Oliver's private dressing room for the night. The members of the Fever Dreams were each tuning their instruments and gearing up to go onstage once Oliver was finished performing. They'd given her a quizzical glance as she ran in, but she just waved and smiled and acted like everything was fine.

Only when she got into Oliver's room and shut the door did the panic attack truly set in.

It was a flashback to almost exactly a year ago, when this precise thing was happened. Then, she'd been freaking out over the prospect of being pregnant while trapped in a loveless engagement. Clay seemed to have a borderline sinister sense of timing, showing up here, tonight, and sending her spiraling back down into the darkness she'd spent twelve months scratching and clawing her way out of.

"He's not taking my baby. He's not taking my baby." She said that to herself over and over, like a mantra. Saying that made it feel real. It was like swinging a torch at the wolf-like bad thoughts that kept trying to crowd into her brain. Those wolves were all the many ways in which it was, in fact, possible for him to take her baby. He was Winter's father. He was employed. He had rights. Even if family courts would favor a mother, Eliza knew well that Clay would hire the most expensive lawyer he could and wring her dry until he got what he wanted. He was relentless in that way.

And his sights had now landed on her.

Winter, thank the Lord, had fallen asleep after just a few minutes of a minor meltdown. Eliza's frayed nerves couldn't handle dealing with both a crying baby and a vengeful ex. So the only sound in the room was Eliza's panicked breathing, the squeak of the chair as she shifted her weight back and forth, and her repeated words, mumbled at breakneck speed over and over.

"He's not taking my baby. He's not taking my baby."

The door opened a little while later. Oliver stuck his head in. When his eyes adjusted to the darkness, he realized it was Eliza and Winter sitting in there. He breathed out a sigh of relief. "Jesus, babe, I've been looking everywhere for you. No one knew where you went. Are you okay? What's happening?" He flicked a switch and the fluorescent lights overhead shimmied into life.

Eliza squinted her eyes against the sudden intrusion. She looked up at Oliver and said, "He's not taking my baby."

"Liza, what? What's happening?" He came over and knelt next to her, grabbing her hand in his. "Your hands are freezing. Are you okay?"

Only when his skin met hers did she realize how badly she was trembling.

"Clay was here."

Oliver's eyes bulged. "What? Here? How—I mean, why? What?"

"He found me. I don't know how. It doesn't really matter. He said he wants Winter."

He stiffened. She felt the news hit him like a car crash. Or maybe that's just how it felt to her, because his face actually didn't change that much. "You're scared," he said. It was half a guess and half a diagnosis. "You need to breathe, babe."

"He's not taking my baby."

"Babe, babe, shh," Oliver said. He stood and cradled Eliza's head against his torso, smoothing her hair back in a calming repetitive motion. "Take it easy."

It suddenly felt very important for Oliver to agree with her. She wasn't sure why. It didn't really make any sense. But it would mean everything in the world if he could just look at her and say, *No, he's not taking your baby.*

"He's not taking my baby. Right? He's not. Say he's not. Please say he's not."

"Shh, babe," he repeated. He kept smoothing back her hair. "Just breathe for a while."

"Say it, Oliver. I need you to say it."

"Say what?"

"Say that Clay is not taking my baby away from me." She was staring at him with wide Bambi eyes, searching his face. Why was he not answering her? Why did he look so—haunted? Uncomfortable? Frozen? She wasn't sure what the word was, but he didn't look the way she wanted and expected him to look, which was comforting, reassuring, confident.

"I can't."

What? "What?"

"I can't say that."

"Why not?" She wanted to scream, punch him, shake him until he said the words she so desperately needed him to say. If Oliver just said everything was okay, then she would be able to believe him and breathe normally again. Her heart rate would come down. Her skin would stop alternating between hot and cold, hot and cold.

"Because he's her father. He has a right to see her, too."

Her blood was frozen. She could almost swear that there were ice floes in her veins. Had the air in the room gotten colder? Why did she suddenly have goose bumps pricking up along her arms, the backs of her thighs, the nape of her neck? "What are you talking about?" she whispered.

"Every child deserves to have a father, if that's possible."

Oliver had knelt again, so that he was eye level with Eliza in her chair. He'd let go of her hand, too, she realized. "Oliver, please tell me something different. Anything but what you're saying."

"I'm saying what I really believe," he answered firmly. "Every child deserves to have a father. If Clay is her father, then he has a right to her. And you owe it to Winter to give that to her. That chance. That relationship."

"You—You're ..."

"No," he cut her off, shaking his head. "I can't. I'm not."

"Oliver, please ..."

He raised a palm up to her. "I mean what I'm saying. I wish I had that chance."

"What are you ..."

"I've never told you any of this," he said, with the tone of someone staring down the barrel of their past, "but I'm not actually from Connecticut. I grew up there, mostly, but that's not where I'm from."

Eliza held her breath. Her world had narrowed down to this—the warmth of Winter sleeping against her chest contrasted with the frigid air in the room, and Oliver's words, slipping one by one from him like he was fighting a losing war against the story trying to burst from his chest.

"I was abandoned. I had a drug addict mom and dad. They didn't want me. They left me. A dumpster or a fire station, I'm not sure, the story changed every time I heard it. Doesn't really matter though. They gave me up like trash. I went into foster care. It was ... ugly. I was one of the lucky ones, though. I got adopted sooner rather than later. You pass age eight or so and it gets near impossible to get out of there. But I got lucky."

He'd always told her he came from a lower-middle-class family in Connecticut. "Nothing notable" were his exact words whenever she pried into his past. "Not worth talking about." She'd always figured it was just one of those Oliver eccentricities. A forward-looking kind of man. Now, she saw that there was in fact a story in his past. One he was ashamed of.

"They gave me up, Eliza. Do you know how much I'd give to have a relationship with my parents? With my father?"

She didn't know what to say. How could she possibly respond to this? She didn't know anything about broken families or drug addiction or foster care. She'd grown up in a home full of warmth and love and family members who cared for each other.

He pointed at Winter. "If she can have that, she deserves it. No matter how distant or infrequent or whatever. If she has a father, you can't keep them apart. That's wrong. That's not what a good mother should do."

"Are you calling me a bad mother?" she managed to choke out. Now, there was fury swirling in the chaotic mix of her emotions.

"I'm just telling you what's right."

"You're telling me to give up my daughter."

"I'm telling you to give her a father."

"You're supposed to be her father, Oliver."

He shook his head sadly. "I'm not and I never will be. I can't be. That's not how things work."

"It has to," she said. The sadness had won out over the anger, though neither was leaving her anytime soon. "It has to work like that."

He kept shaking his head, again and again, like a metronome. "It doesn't," was all he said. "It doesn't."

Eliza wanted to cry forever. She wanted to sleep forever. She wanted to take her baby and run until she couldn't run anymore, just to get away from all of this.

But she didn't do any of that. She couldn't.

So she did the only thing left to her to do.

She stood up and left.

33

BRENT

Thursday night.

To literally no one's surprise, Frank needed Brent's help again. He'd called at the crack of dawn that morning, chipper as all get-out despite the early hour.

"Mornin', superstar! Figured you'd be up this early. Think I could wrangle you down here this evening? You ain't even gonna believe what's happening in this neck of the woods. I've got problems up to my eyeballs."

Brent let loose a long sigh and a yawn in rapid succession. "Yeah, man, you got it. No worries. I'll be down there this evening, around five or six."

"Swell, buddy, just swell. See you then."

The charter trip was relatively uneventful, but the cumulative fatigue of burning the candle at both ends week in and week out was starting to get to Brent. By the time he pulled up in front of Frank's house and climbed out of his truck, he barely had the energy to pick his feet up off the ground.

Fortunately—or unfortunately, depending on how you looked at it—Frank had energy enough for both of them. He came bounding down the driveway, all smiles, and grabbed Brent by the shoulder. "I'll tell you what, man, you really are a lifesaver. So let me give you the rundown on what we've got going on inside ..."

Brent was only half listening. Partially because he was asleep, and partially because, just before they stepped across the threshold and into the guts of Frank's home-to-be, he looked to his left and saw something he hadn't seen in weeks.

Rose was home.

Brent had never done a faster job in his life. He cut Frank off pretty early in his rambling so that he could focus on diagnosing the problem at hand. It didn't take long to spot the issue. On a normal day, it might take two or three hours to get the work done—another issue with a load-bearing wall; physics really was not Frank's strong suit.

Today, it took forty-nine minutes.

The sun hadn't even finished setting by the time Brent was dusting off his hands and packing up his stuff. "Finished already?" Frank asked, amazed.

"Yessir," was Brent's curt but polite response.

"Well, hold your horses for just one sec. Are you sure you—"

"Yep, got that squared away."

"And what about the—"

"That too."

Frank scratched his head with a tape measure and looked absolutely befuddled. "I gotta ask, son ... how'd you do all that?"

Brent smiled, gently removed the cash from Frank's hand, and gave him a wink. "My father taught me."

Then he was gone, slipping out of the house with a happy whistle on his lips.

He'd had the vague beginnings of a plan in his head as he was working. Something involving knocking on Rose's door and—well, that was actually as far as he'd gotten. The underlying question was ... what did he want?

Actually, to back up a step, the underlying question was, why was he thinking about Rose in the first place? Didn't he have Ally in his life? Didn't he like how fun she was, how spontaneous she was, how much excitement surrounded her at all times? Didn't he like the possibility she represented? He supposed he did. That's what he'd been telling himself and others since they met. It was at least mostly true.

But maybe not one hundred percent. Maybe there was still a little bit left in his heart that was calling out to Rose. He had a long ways to go yet in figuring out just how his emotions worked, but he had come a long way from where he once was. Progress was progress. This was not the time to turn his back on what he felt. More than anything, it was simply time to find out what that feeling meant.

So, he hopped the low bush that separated Frank's yard from Rose's, strode over to her door, raised a fist to knock, and—

The door flew open.

"Rose."

"Brent."

"I was gonna ..."

"Knock? I'd certainly hope so."

Brent tilted his head, confused. "But you were coming out."

She blushed, looked downward like there was suddenly something really interesting happening at her feet. "Yeah."

He followed her gaze. "With two bottles of beer and a plate of cookies."

"Yeah."

He understood immediately. "Who was that for, Rose?"

Her blush deepened, but to her credit, she raised her eyes up and met his. "It's a real hot day. Thought you boys could maybe use something refreshing and a snack."

"So you were coming over to Frank's."

"Yeah, I was."

"We're all done for the day."

"That's a shame."

"I'm not complaining."

"No, I suppose not. Frank does seem a little needy sometimes."

"Sometimes, yes."

The fast-paced rat-a-tat of their back-and-forth died down. They were both left just looking at each other, wanting to say something but not having much of anything to say. It was obvious that there were two conversations happening. One was about cookies and beer and needy neighbors. The other was about things much harder to verbalize than that. Affection. Longing. Loss. Regret.

"Mooommyyy!" came a voice from the back. It was followed by a blonde whirling dervish that attached itself to Rose's leg with a *whoompf* on impact. Rose, for her part, looked grateful for the distraction.

"Yes, honey?"

"I'm hungry. When's dinner?"

"Five minutes, baby," Rose said absentmindedly. "Spaghetti."

Susanna, Rose's daughter, made a scrunched-up face, as if she couldn't remember whether or not she liked spaghetti. Undecided, she shrugged and skipped away without once looking at Brent. When she was gone, Rose smiled.

"Spaghetti, huh?" Brent commented. He was beginning to regret coming over here. This had been a bad idea. What was he hoping would happen? Dramatic music and roses falling from the sky? Slow-motion reunion and he and Rose ran towards each other in a grassy meadow? That wasn't real life. That wasn't how things worked. Real life was messy and uncertain and vague around the edges. It was hard enough to figure out what you wanted in life. It was darn near impossible to communicate that to another person. Especially one who might not want the same things.

He turned to leave before he had any other stupid ideas.

"Wait!" Rose said. She grabbed his bicep. Both of them looked down at her hand on him. There was a sudden pang of tension, like someone had yanked on the invisible wires that held the world together and sent a humming vibration along them. Rose blushed again, the reddest yet, and let her hand fall away.

"Yeah?"

She bit her lip, then blurted, "Yes, it's spaghetti."

Brent raised an eyebrow.

"Do you—would you—do you want to have some?" she asked awkwardly.

Oh, how the tables had turned. A year ago, he was the one tripping over his words. Now, it was Rose's turn to get red in the face.

"I'm not sure if that's a good idea," Brent replied carefully. "I'm not sure if any of this was, actually."

She nodded slowly, like part of her actually agreed with him. Then, just as slowly, just as carefully, with a tiny smile blossoming in one corner of her lips, she said, "My mom taught me how to make it. Family recipe. I'd tell it to you, but I'd have to kill you right after."

He smiled a little too. "I'm quaking in my boots, Rose."

"So I can't tell you. But you can come try it. If you want to. Stay for dinner, you know?"

Brent took in a deep breath and weighed his options. He could turn and go home and forget all of this ever happened. Call Ally and see what trouble they could get into tonight.

Or he could say yes, go inside, and eat spaghetti with Rose and her daughter.

"All right," he said, nodding. She smiled, turned, and gestured for him to come inside. He checked his phone as he crossed the threshold. There was a text from Ally waiting for him.

Whatcha doin, sailor boy? it read.

He put it back in his pocket without replying.

34

HOLLY

Moving day.

Just a week ago, Holly would've said that this day couldn't come fast enough. It had been circled on the calendar in bright red marker for months. But one phone call had poisoned everything.

"They stole it from us," she'd said to Pete again and again. "They stole our home."

He tried to console her as best he could. But the truth was that she was more or less inconsolable. It felt like she'd had this vision of happiness for her life unfolding in that home, and now that the home was no longer theirs, that vision might never come to pass.

"It isn't like we're gonna be living on the streets in a refrigerator box," Pete had replied with a smile one of the first times she said they'd stolen her home. "Although the mortgage would be a lot better ..." She'd fixed him with a cold glare in return. He hadn't made the joke again.

She knew the wise thing to do would be to let it go. But how could she? Someone should pay.

"Not gonna happen, darling," was Pete's reply to that proposal. "We just have to accept it and move along."

That was a horrible answer.

They did still have a home to move to, after all. In the wake of that terrible call from Judy breaking the news of the house thievery, Pete had made quick work of presenting Holly with three of their backup options. She'd chosen one, reluctantly. She was standing in the driveway right now, looking at it.

But there was no magic in this home. Try as she might to picture that blissful domestic happily-ever-after, she got nothing but staticky blackness instead when she closed her eyes. It didn't feel right, mostly because it wasn't.

And yet, there wasn't a thing she could do about it.

"Need a hand with that, babe?" Pete asked, jerking his head towards the box in her hands.

"No, I'm fine," she mumbled. She followed him down the drive and into their home. Inside, she set the box down on the growing pile they'd already transported from the moving truck and stopped to look around.

The ceilings in here were low, and the floors were done in an ugly faux-hardwood linoleum that had last been fashionable before Holly was born. It wasn't a bad place, by any means. It had four walls and a roof and it was still in Nantucket, after all. The seller had been courteous and helpful in expediting closing so the Goodwins could still stick to the schedule they'd had planned. She ought to be grateful for all that.

It just felt really hard to summon any gratitude at the moment.

The afternoon trickled by in a daze. The kids were helpful in five-minute bursts every two to three hours at best, so it fell to Pete and Holly to do almost all the unloading. They'd rented a truck to bring all their boxes and clothes and such. The movers they hired would be here tomorrow with the bulk of the furniture. That meant they were spending the night in sleeping bags. Could be better, could be worse. Just like everything else about this house.

Mom came over in the early evening to check the place out and help Holly with some unpacking. Holly was careful not to be too obvious with her discontent. Mom seemed awfully frazzled anyway, though she wouldn't admit to there being anything wrong with her.

"Oh, nothing, dear. Just been a bit of a long week, that's all."

"You sure, Mom?"

"Yes, yes, nothing to fret about."

Soon after, she'd gotten a call and returned to the inn in a hurry. She wouldn't say what it was about. "She was acting a little weird," Holly remarked as she watched her mother scurry down the driveway.

"You think?" Pete said. His stomach rumbled loudly. "Say, I'm ravenous. What do you think—pizza night?"

"Sure, honey," Holly said distractedly. "Whatever you want."

That's how they ended up on the floor, pizza in hand, playing an ancient game of Monopoly that Holly had unearthed from a junk closet during the packing up of the house in Plymouth. As they argued and rolled dice and tried fruitlessly to explain to Alice and Grady that it wasn't wise to spend all their money in the first ten minutes of the game, Holly took a minute to sit back and force a smile on her face.

She might never get over the house theft. That would be a sore spot for a long, long time, she figured. But in this moment, she realized, she had a lot going for her. They had a home. They *were* home.

Maybe gratitude wasn't so hard to scrounge up after all.

35

MAE

Saturday afternoon.

What an awful week it had been.

It had all started with the arrival last Sunday of Dr. Frederick Patrick Hoffman, Sr. That was how he'd written his name on the website's reservation form, all spelled out like that. Mae had raised an eyebrow at first, but figured it was merely a funny little quirk. Some people were quite proud of their names, after all. Not a thing in the world wrong with that.

Oh, if only she had known what she was in for.

As it turned out, Dr. Frederick Patrick Hoffman, Sr., was every bit as stiff and difficult as his proper name implied. And he was not shy about letting Mae know that his expectations were quite high.

"Mrs. Benson!" came the voice she'd quickly learned to loathe. "The towels you provided this morning were rather unsatisfactory." The man who owned that voice walked around the corner into the kitchen moments later, holding the towel in one outstretched hand, pinched between two fingers like it was absolutely soiled. Though, to

Mae's eye, it was spotless. She'd seen dirtier towels in hospital surgical theaters. It wasn't as though she was slob or a slouch. On the contrary, Mae knew exactly how hard she worked to provide an outstanding hospitality experience for each and every one of her guests.

But nothing was ever good enough for Dr. Hoffman.

"I'm terribly sorry!" Mae exclaimed apologetically. She scurried over and took the towel from his hand.

"I would prefer if you did not snatch things from my grasp," he grumbled underneath his walrus-like mustache, which had gone white with age.

"Oh, please forgive me," Mae said. She was blushing red as a beet now. "I didn't mean any offense." What was it with this guy? He held the towel out for her to grab, then got mad when she grabbed it? She took a sneaky glance down at the towel in her hand. It was soft, pristine, smelled fresh. Merely the latest in a long string of insatiable complaints from the rigid, bone-thin man standing in front of her at military attention.

He harrumphed in response.

Mae was a forgiving spirit by nature, and she'd done her level best to give Dr. Hoffman a proper Nantucket welcome. But she was no pushover, either. And the fact of the matter was that this gentleman was getting awfully close to pushing her over the edge. He'd hardly taken two steps into the inn on the first day before he was commenting on the "dirty crown molding" and the "aroma of dank humidity." His tone matched his manners which matched his name, and she was sick to death of hearing him pick and poke at every tiny aspect of the inn.

So that was one thing weighing on her. But it was hardly the only thing.

There was the ever-present specter of Toni's phone call. She hadn't heard another peep from Toni since they'd last spoken over two months ago, when she first mentioned the likelihood of the inn being sold. That was worrying. Could her home and livelihood be snatched away from her at any moment? The questions kept her up at night. She found it best to think about it as little as possible. But when she was trying to fall asleep at the end of each long day of apologizing profusely to Dr. Hoffman, she couldn't stop her thoughts from wandering in that direction like unruly sheep.

What else was there? Oh yes, of course—the Debra crisis. Mae, Lola, and Debra had a long-running joke that Debra's ex-husband was like Punxsutawney Phil, the infamous groundhog. If he didn't call Debra on the anniversary of their decades-old divorce, it was going to be a good year. But if he called, everyone on Nantucket was in for a very bad time indeed.

Four years ago, he'd called, and they'd had one of the worst winters on record. When their "divorce-aversary"—June 12th—came and went this year without a peep, the ladies had all let out a sigh of relief.

But that turned out to be premature.

Because this year, Ruben just happened to be a week late. And when he called, he called with a vengeance.

Mae had gone over to Debra's for their regular Sunday afternoon stroll along the beach and found her seated in her living room, utterly distraught. Bawling, actually, the kind of boo-hoo crying that almost never came from a strong woman like Debra.

"Oh, honey!" Mae had said at once, rushing to her side. It didn't take long before Debra revealed that Ruben had called and berated her worse than ever. No matter how many times Lola and Mae told Debra to stop taking his calls, they both knew that she never would. Even if it left her absolutely devastated at the end of it.

Ruben was a lowlife nobody. Emotionally and verbally cruel, he had leached off Debra's warmth and vivaciousness for years before she finally mustered up the courage to ask him for a divorce. But apparently, married or not, he had no intention of letting her live her life peacefully. Whenever he called, he told her how worthless he thought she was, how much better he was doing without her, and on and on like that, until the poor woman nearly started to believe the things he was saying to her.

Lola had quickly come to the rescue as well. The women had done as much as they could to get Debra's spirits back up after the horrible phone call. Nothing seemed to be working, though. Not wine or food or an afternoon at the spa. Ruben had done a thorough number on his ex-wife. Even her best friends didn't know what else they could do to dispel the funk into which she'd plunged.

So that was a headache and heartache all on its own. On top of that, it had been raining for days straight. Just an endless torrent of gushing, fat raindrops, the kind that almost hurt when they hit you on top of the head if you happened to be caught out in a storm.

The other thought that Mae kept coming back to over and over was: *I miss Dominic.* That, too, she tried to run away from, but it kept sneaking up on her in idle moments. She wondered where he was, what he was doing. He'd been quite short on details when he left. "Six weeks" was the only bit of information he'd provided. That seemed not so bad when he'd mentioned it—especially considering the challenging circumstances under which he'd left—but now that six weeks had passed and he still had not returned, Mae was starting to feel nervous. It was like being trapped in the desert without supplies. A rain shower would come eventually—but when?

When she'd finally scrounged up a clean towel that passed Dr. Hoffman's inspection, she left before he could find something else to complain about. She took off her apron, hung it on the hook in the kitchen, and drove over to Pete and Holly's new house.

"Hi, Mrs. B!" Pete greeted her as she came in and set her umbrella by the door. "Still raining?"

"It certainly is! With little sign of stopping, I'm afraid."

"You're starting to talk like Dominic," Holly remarked wryly from her perch at the kitchen counter.

Mae blushed. "Nonsense."

"Mhmm," Holly murmured knowingly.

Mae decided to change the subject. "How is the move going, Pete?"

He swung his arm around the living room. "Feast your eyes on our cardboard kingdom."

There were still many boxes piled high in two of the corners, though "cardboard kingdom" might've been a little bit of an exaggeration.

"This house is just all wrong." Holly sighed. "I don't know where to put half that stuff."

"Hollz ..." Pete interrupted warningly.

Mae thought it best to keep her mouth shut here. There was obviously some unhappiness surrounding the move, though she hadn't had enough free time to check in with her middle daughter to find out why that might be. All she could see was that Holly seemed downright miserable. Actually, a little angry, too. She made a mental note to follow up when she could find a moment.

"Well, I'm here, so put me to work!"

"I'm actually gonna take the kids to a movie," Pete said apologetically. "Not trying to duck out on the work or anything."

"Not to worry," Mae said with a reassuring smile. "We'll be just fine."

"Besides," Holly added, "you've got the worst job anyhow. They've been cooped up because of the rain all day. And I just caught Alice sneaking candy from the snack drawer. Have fun, love you, bye!"

They all chuckled as Pete groaned.

Once he and the kids were en route to the movie theater, Mae and Holly got to work. They started by tackling more of the kitchenware that remained packed up in the boxes. They chatted as they worked. Mae told Holly about Dr. Hoffman, the guest from her nightmares.

"... And then, when one of my other guests called him 'Mr.'—well, you should've just seen his face! That mustache bristled and he launched into a fifteen-minute lecture on how to properly address him. I mean, my goodness! I try not to say a bad word about my fellow humans, but that man is something else entirely. Bless his heart."

Holly shuddered. "Sounds awful. I—"

"Oh, I'm so sorry, one second, dear. My phone is ringing. If it's *Mister* Hoffman ..." Mae frowned when she saw the caller ID.

"Hello?"

The voice on the other end of the line told her the news in a rushed, urgent voice. Mae's face fell at once. "A fire? At the inn?! Oh goodness gracious! I'll be right there!"

36

SARA

Sara's head had been in the clouds for weeks now. Starting a restaurant from scratch did that to a person, apparently. There were just so many things she had to keep track of. Shipments arriving and recipes to test and permits to get, all of which were constantly being rearranged and pushed back or moved forward. It was enough to drive a girl crazy.

But no one had ever called Sara lazy. She was determined to make sure that remained the case. She had organized binders bursting with photocopied invoices, contracts signed in triplicate, permits and certificates of inspection galore. She had filled composition notebook after composition notebook with different recipe concoctions and drafts of the restaurant's future menu.

And, across the top of everything, she printed in careful block letters the same thing each time: *Little Bull.*

That was the name she'd picked. It had taken a couple hours of sitting in a corner and scribbling all over a yellow legal pad before it occurred to her. She'd rejected a million and one names in a row, until suddenly, *boom,* it popped into her head. *Little Bull.* It felt so right that she literally shivered, though the air outside was warm and damp lately with all the rain. She'd immediately sketched out a rough logo, too, of an angry bull with steam rising out of his ears.

Honestly, the whole thing spooked her as much as it thrilled her. It felt like someone else had taken control of the pen in her hand and dragged it across the page on her behalf. She'd looked over her shoulders, but the room was empty.

"Little bull" had been her and her father's joke, their thing. Naming her restaurant after it was both a tribute and an act of gratitude. After all, a sizable chunk of the money she'd needed had come from Dad's life insurance payout. She owed it to him to immortalize his memory in the heart of her new undertaking.

So, *Little Bull.* Giving the restaurant a name like that brought it to life. It made everything feel so freakishly real. This was happening.

But she had other people to thank, too. Eliza and Holly had both contributed what they could, which was both generous and unexpected. Even Brent, who hardly had two pennies to rub together, had sheepishly handed her a check one day for five hundred dollars. "It's the best I can do," he'd mumbled. She tried over and over to reject it—he was pouring hundreds of hours into building out the restaurant with her, after all; he certainly didn't owe her a dime—but he just looked her dead in the eye and said, "If you don't cash it, I'm just gonna go down to the bank and wire the money right into your account myself. Take the money, Sara." So she'd finally relented.

That was how it became *Little Bull—A Family Business.*

That felt right.

They were getting closer and closer now—only a week until opening night!—and Sara was a bundle of nerves. Actually, that wasn't quite correct. She was way too busy to be nervous. But if she stopped for even the slightest of moments to try to take a breath, the nerves came to life within her, sizzling like hot oil in the pan. *What if it fails? What if you embarrass yourself? What if people hate it?*

She had months of successful Friday Night Feasts in her memory to bolster her confidence. But there was a big difference between feeding a dozen people one night a week, and feeding several hundred. Could she pull this off? *Would* she pull this off?

Only time would tell.

With her head so full of thoughts, Sara had to do a double take when she rounded the street corner and saw a crowd of people outside of the Sweet Island Inn, along with a fire truck flashing its lights. She'd been on her way to the inn to see if her mother needed help with anything. With Dominic gone, Mom seemed awfully lonely, so Sara had made it a point over the last month or two to swing around the inn whenever she could and check in.

Apparently, this wouldn't just be a social visit.

As Sara rushed closer, she noticed the acrid smell of something burning. She saw a pillar of smoke rising into the sky, too. She'd been so preoccupied with restaurant thoughts that she hadn't even noticed it until now.

The crowd—maybe two or three dozen people, some of whom she recognized as neighbors and friends of the inn—watched as two firefighters strode into the building in full gear.

Sara's heart leaped into her chest. This inn was *everything* to her mother. If it went up in flames, Mom's heart would burn along with it. She had to help. That thought blared across her mind like someone laying on a car horn.

GO! HELP!

Without thinking any further, she took off running towards the front door.

She was maybe fifteen yards away when she felt an arm snake around her waist and yank her out of mid-stride.

"Whoa!" came a deep, rasping voice in her ear. "Easy there. You can't go in yet, ma'am."

"That's my mom's inn!" Sara yelped. "I have to help."

The arm set her down, but maintained a point of contact on her shoulder. Sara looked up to see the face of a young firefighter, partially obscured by the helmet he was wearing. He had dark, curly hair, sapphire-blue eyes, and five o'clock shadow straight out of a GQ article. When he spoke, she saw the flash of blindingly white teeth. And dimples. He was right on the line between movie-star good-looking and just normal-person handsome. Sara couldn't quite decide which side of that line he fell on.

All those thoughts flashed by in an instant before Sara returned to the matter at hand. "Let me go!" she snapped, pushing away his hand. She started to walk back around the man, who'd placed himself between Sara and the inn, but he stepped back in front of her and shook his head.

"No, ma'am," he said again. "We need to clear the building first. There could be structural damage. It's not safe."

Sara looked desperately over his shoulder. This couldn't be happening.

A new thought began to repeat in her head. If the inn went up in smoke, Mom wouldn't have enough money to repair it, because she'd already given most of Dad's money to Sara.

She felt a wave of guilt crash over her. In a bizarre way, she felt like this was her fault. She shouldn't have been selfish. She should've just let her siblings have their own special moments instead of demanding her share of the spotlight.

Stupid, childish, immature.

She felt faint. The world was fading away. Was there an earthquake all of a sudden? The ground was shaking ...

Sara came back to consciousness sometime later. She looked around, dazed, and realized she was seated in the back of a fire truck. The man who'd stopped her from entering the house was holding an oxygen mask over her face. He saw she was awake and frowned.

"How are you feeling?" he asked, concerned.

"Dizzy," she admitted.

"You fell," he explained. "Fainted, actually. You almost hit your head, too. Good thing I caught you."

"You caught me?" she repeated dumbly. *What kind of terrible rom-com is this?* She laughed inwardly. Her life was getting more and more ridiculous by the day. Fainting into the arms of a handsome firefighter? *Give me a freaking break.*

Suddenly, her memories came flooding back in. The inn—the fire— Mom. She sat bolt upright and tried to rip the oxygen mask off her face. "My mom—I have to ..."

"You have to *sit*," the man said, pressing her back into the seat. "Breathe."

She tasted the copper tang of blood in her mouth. Her head throbbed. She tried to look outside the window, but with the way the truck was parked, she couldn't see much of the inn building. It seemed like much of the crowd had dispersed, though. Maybe that was a good sign?

"What happened?" she asked. "Is everything okay? Where's my mom? Who are you?"

The man chuckled and settled back in the seat across from her, though he kept glancing over every now and then to check the numbers flashing on the screen Sara was hooked up to that displayed her pulse and oxygen saturation. "That's a lot of questions at once," he said. "Which one would you like me to answer first?"

Sara still felt weak. Too weak to retort back to this guy. "Is everything okay?"

"Fine," he answered at once with a reassuring nod. "Oven malfunctioned and made a whole lot of smoke, but nothing too damaging. It'll just smell a little crispy in there for a few weeks until everything airs out, that's all."

She let out a sigh of relief. Malfunctioning oven didn't sound so bad. And this man seemed very calm about the whole thing. She wasn't quite sure yet whether that was just his professional demeanor—*don't upset the fainting chick!*—or if things really were no big deal. "Okay, next. Who are you?"

"Joey Burton." He tapped on the little name tag affixed to his suspenders.

"Why aren't you inside fighting the fire, Joey Burton?" Sara had been half kidding, but the words still came out a little more harshly than she'd intended. She felt bad when Joey winced.

"Still a rookie," he said. "Vets go in. Rookies man the perimeter."

"Ah. A rookie."

The oxygen flowing into her lungs from the mask was going a long way towards making her feel better. It was hard to say whether the fluttering she felt in her stomach now was caused by the smoke inhalation or by the man sitting across from her. Was he wearing cologne? It was faint, but Sara could swear she smelled it coming off him.

"I'd like to go see if I can find my mom, please," she said.

Joey started to say something, then hesitated. He glanced once more at the screen displaying Sara's vitals. "All right," he relented. "You look all right. But don't go far. You gotta sign paperwork before I cut you loose."

She waved in response and walked off the fire truck. Outside, she saw her mother talking with the two firefighters who'd gone inside. The smoke seemed to have stopped pouring out of the inn's open windows, so Sara figured that the situation was under control. But Mom looked so tired. Depleted, really. Sara remembered her saying something earlier this week about a terrible guest, but she'd been too busy to be much help with the whole thing.

"Mom!" she called over as she walked up to the trio.

"Oh thank goodness," Mae said, grabbing Sara's hand. "Are you all right? The nice men here told me that you fainted!"

"Yeah," Sara said, feeling foolish. "Just smoke or stress or something, I don't know. I'm fine now, so no need to worry about me. Are you okay? Is the inn okay?"

"Everything is fine, ma'am," one of the firefighters replied. "The situation has been handled."

"Thank you gentlemen so much for your quick response," Mom was gushing. "I'm so glad this island has heroes like you on hand!"

"You're quite welcome, ma'am," replied the second one. He had a C on his helmet, probably for "captain," if Sara had to guess. "We'll just need you to come this way, Mrs. Benson," he added. "We've got some paperwork for you to fill out."

The captain and Mom walked off, leaving Sara to stand awkwardly alone with the second firefighter. His face was smudged with smoke. Fortunately, Joey came up at that moment. Sara almost laughed. He looked a little silly, waddling around in those huge pants.

"Lieutenant, one of the neighbors asked us to move the truck so they could get their vehicle out of their driveway. Permission to move it?"

"You ain't drivin', Rook." The man laughed. He plucked the keys out of Joey's hand and walked off, whistling.

"That seemed a little harsh," Sara commented.

Joey took off his helmet and ran a hand through his curls. "Yeah, well, it's the chain of command. Gotta put in the time."

"How old are you?" she asked.

"Twenty-six."

She blanched. "You're a baby."

His brow furrowed. "Don't you start on me, too."

She had to laugh at that, but she couldn't deny that she felt weird thinking about how cute he was. He was still a little whippersnapper compared to her thirty years old, wet behind the ears and all that. Or that's how it felt, at least. Either way, she ought to focus on her business. The last thing she needed was yet another male distraction.

She opened her mouth to say something else. Before she could get the words out, though, Joey's stomach rumbled louder than Sara had ever heard someone's stomach rumble before. Instead of speaking, she burst out laughing.

Joey, for his part, looked absolutely mortified. "I ... uh ..." Between the hazing from his lieutenant and the stomach noise, his "cool guy firefighter" bubble was more or less completely burst in Sara's eyes.

"Hungry?" she asked with a mischievous twinkle in her eye.

"I'm always hungry," he admitted.

"I'm a chef," she blurted suddenly. She felt a little dumb for saying it in that way, like she was bragging.

Joey didn't seem to notice, though. His eyes just lit up. "Oh yeah? At a restaurant? Which one?"

"Opening my own soon," she said proudly. "In a week, actually."

He whistled low. "Well, how 'bout that? I'll have to come check it out."

"You should do that."

"Rook!" came a holler from a few dozen yards away. "Get over here!"

Joey looked down at Sara and smiled shyly. "Duty calls," he said. "It was nice meeting you, Chef Sara."

"Nice meeting you too, Hungry Joe."

He grinned and ran off, leaving Sara looking after him with a weird, unsettled feeling flowing through her.

37

ELIZA

Late at night on Saturday.

Six sleepless nights. Six stress-filled days.

Every time she closed her eyes, she saw Clay. She saw his flat, emotionless gaze. She felt like a helpless little fish in the water. He was the shark, circling her, toying with her, waiting only for the right moment to strike.

That was stupid, of course. He was just a man—an egomaniacal jerk and drug addict, to be more precise—not a shark. Not a predator. Not anything she had to fear.

But she wasn't scared for herself. She was scared for her daughter. Winter, who had been so angelic in the days and weeks after she and Oliver had their fight in Boston, had taken ten steps backwards. She was now a screaming whirlwind most hours of the day. It wasn't helping Eliza's state of mind any to see her daughter's face screwed up in unhappiness. Nothing seemed to help; neither food nor change of scenery nor Eliza's comfort.

"Change of scenery" was a little bit of a misnomer, though, because Eliza had become terrified to go outdoors. She'd come home after the show where Clay showed his face, packed up her bags, and gone to a different hotel. That was all she could think of to do. She needed space—safe, clean, isolated space—away from Clay, away from Oliver, away from everything that seemed to be clawing away at her blissful happily-ever-after.

She didn't know what to make of the things Oliver had said to her after his show. How could he take Clay's side, of all things? How could he say that she should give up her baby—whether for a minute or a day, it didn't matter in the slightest—to that *monster*? She'd told him everything there was to know about Clay. Oliver knew what kind of man Clay was. And yet, he had still looked her in the eye and said that Winter needed her father.

No. No, no, no. Screw that. Eliza was not about to let Clay so much as look at Winter ever again. She'd hire a lawyer, she'd flee the country, she'd book a rocket ship to the freaking moon before that happened.

Oliver and the Fever Dreams had continued to play their shows around the city as the days ticked by. But Eliza and Winter went to none of them. They stayed hunkered down in their hotel room, taking turns crying with the blinds drawn low.

It took Eliza a few days before she thought about calling someone and asking for help. It just wasn't in her nature to reach out like that. She was her father's golden child, wasn't she? She knew how to handle anything life threw at her. She'd figure her way out of this, too, of course. But maybe it wasn't advice that she was in search of. Maybe she just needed to hear someone say that everything was going to be okay. If someone else said those words out loud, perhaps she could believe them. Because saying them to herself in the mirror over and over every night wasn't doing the slightest bit of good.

Eliza's thumb hovered over her mother's cell-phone number in her phone. She had only to tap the screen to call. She was lying in the dry bathtub with Winter asleep on her chest.

It was late, near midnight. Eliza felt guilty for considering calling at all. This was stupid. Her mother was in her sixties. The last thing she needed was her oldest daughter calling her because she had a fight with her boyfriend.

But when she tried to let go of the phone, she just couldn't do it. This time around, Eliza needed help. If she dropped this cell phone, she was just going to keep crying and panicking and having half-remembered nightmares about Clay coming to snatch Winter away. Days had passed already and her anxieties had not lessened one notch.

For perhaps the first time in her life, Eliza Benson needed help.

So she pressed call.

"Mom?" she whispered.

"Eliza, honey? Is everything okay?"

She knew she'd woken her mother, and the guilt struck her as expected. But the fear and the sadness outweighed it.

"Mom, I'm scared."

She started telling the story. Once she started, she didn't know how to stop. It was like all those months ago when Oliver had first asked her what her story was at that bar in Nantucket. She'd started, and she kept going, unloading everything like her heart had been overflowing with words that needed to be spoken or else she might die.

And her mother did what her mother had always done: she listened.

When Eliza was done and the tears were dried up, they came up with a plan together. "You're going to get your things," Mom said. "You're going to call a taxi to take you to the airport. And you're going to take the first flight back here. You come home, okay, Eliza dear? You can always come home."

The next morning.

Eliza did exactly as her mother had said. She gathered everything up and repacked her suitcase. She fed Winter. Then the two of them met their taxi downstairs and were ferried away to the airport.

Outside, it rained, as it had done for the past week straight. Every day, the rain had come harder than the day before. Now, it was like a solid object. The sound was near deafening. The puddles had become rivers had become oceans. It was raining like the world was ending.

Eliza didn't feel sad anymore. She felt hollowed out. She didn't have any more tears to shed, for a little while at least. It felt good to be doing something—anything—to get away from this nightmare. Running home had worked the last time she needed an escape. She prayed that it would work this time, too.

But it didn't happen that cleanly. The airport was a madhouse when they arrived. People were everywhere, lines stretched and wound around like mazes, airline employees with little patience and poor manners looking frazzled and hassled. Winter took one look at the scene and promptly started bawling.

Eliza felt like bawling, too. This was not how she'd pictured motherhood when she was a young woman. And it certainly wasn't how she'd pictured this tour with Oliver going. She knew back then, when she'd first told Oliver yes, that she'd been taking a risk. She just never imagined that it would all implode so spectacularly.

After Eliza had stepped into a corner and coaxed Winter into calming down, the two of them returned to the line for the ticket desk. An hour of stop-and-start queuing traffic later, she found herself at the front. "I need a ticket to Nantucket, please," she said. "Plus a baby."

"You're in luck. Only a few seats left."

Finally, a break. It was about time something worked out in her favor. She thanked the clerk profusely, checked in her bags, and took Winter through security to their gate.

Here, too, was absolute mayhem. The storm was throwing everything out of whack. Runways were closed then opened then closed again. Bags were soaked or misplaced. People alternated back and forth between despondent and furious.

Her flight wasn't for a couple of hours, so she hunkered down in a quiet-ish corner and played with Winter. She was desperate to keep her daughter occupied and happy for as long as possible. The last thing she wanted was to be that new mom at the airport who couldn't calm her baby down.

She kept one eye on the monitor as the flights left out of her gate. She kept her other eye on the windows to the outdoors. Somehow, it seemed like the storm was getting even worse. This was a storm of biblical proportions, or at least that's how it felt. Just relentless, pounding, driving rain. It looked like a gusty wind had picked up, too, judging by how the rain lashed against the windowpanes at irregular intervals. Eliza felt nervous. *Please, just let me leave this godforsaken city,* she begged silently.

Fifteen minutes later, the information for the flight to Nantucket popped up at her gate. They were next. There was a plane taxied into the gate, which was fabulous news. Now, if they could just get this thing boarded and take off before the storm got even worse ...

Then came the public address announcement.

"Due to the worsening weather, we have made the decision to temporarily ground all flights originating from this airport. We thank you for your cooperation and understanding. We are sorry for any inconvenience."

No. No no no! She wanted to scream. She wanted to tear her hair out. She wanted to stamp and throw herself on the ground like a little girl. Thank the lucky stars that Winter happened to be asleep, because Eliza had no doubt that she'd start wailing like a siren if she sensed the anger and desperation radiating from her mother.

A crowd was descending on the check-in desk at the gate, but Eliza beat them all to the front. "You've gotta be kidding me," she blurted to the airline employee working. "Everything's grounded? How am I supposed to get home?"

"I'm sorry, ma'am," the woman said with an apologetic smile. "I know this is terrible, but the weather forced us into this position."

Eliza took a deep breath and counted to five before replying. "When is it supposed to clear up?"

"Later this evening, perhaps. We can't be sure."

She looked at her watch. It was eight in the morning.

There was no denying that she was distraught. But her choices were limited. There was no going back into the city. If she had her way, she'd never go back to New York ever again.

She wanted to go home. That meant, for now, that she had to wait.

38

SARA

Brent and Sara had been on good terms since their last squabble, but there was a feeling of tension in the air again. Sara had a nasty feeling that they were headed for another knock 'em down, drag-'em-out screaming match.

The rain wasn't helping matters. It made everything ten times more difficult construction-wise. And it made their moods ten times worse as well.

Sara pounded the flat of her hand on the door. She was drenched already from head to toe, and she'd only been locked outside for maybe twenty seconds. It was raining that heavily. She kept knocking as loud as she could.

Finally, an eternity later, Brent came to the door from inside and pushed it open.

"Gee, thanks," she said sarcastically as she wrestled in a pair of paint buckets that had been left outside last week. "Nice of you to show up."

"In case you haven't heard," Brent replied, pointing up at the ceiling, "it's a little loud, what with the rain and all."

"Did you think I was just taking a little stroll outside or something?"

"I didn't know what you were doing," he snarled.

"Well, I suppose I'll just get a hall pass next time then," Sara snapped. "Or should I have a tracking chip installed like I'm some house cat?"

"You need to chill," he said warningly. "I'm so not in the mood for this today. It's not my fault that you picked a door that locks you out automatically."

"I expected my loving brother to open it if that happened!"

"And I opened it, didn't I?"

"Yeah, but you sure took your sweet time doing it."

He rolled his eyes and turned away. "I'm not fighting with you anymore," he said flatly. "This is stupid."

"No, what's *stupid* is the fact that this rain will not go away. It's been raining for like seven days straight. I'm over it. I cannot even begin to express just how over it I am."

"That, at least, we can agree on."

He turned back to what he was doing. Sara set the paint cans down with a thud and a sigh and looked around. Little Bull was coming to life before her eyes. They'd installed the bar top earlier that week with some help from a few friends. It was the centerpiece of the restaurant, a massive, lacquered wooden surface that looked into the open kitchen. Guests would be able to see the chefs at work. Those who wanted more privacy could choose instead to sit at any of the tables nestled into candlelit alcoves around the outer rim of the room. The recessed lighting overhead looked fabulous, casting warm shadows like abstract art across the floors. Just looking around got Sara excited.

But the punch list was far from complete. It grew by the day, as a matter of fact. She was starting to worry that there wasn't enough time. After a few false starts, they'd barely managed to get the deep freezer operational in time for the first shipment of goods to come in. That was one close call of many. Everything was being done just-in-time, actually. It wasn't how Sara liked to live her life. Eliza had always been the planner, not Sara. But when it came to her restaurant, she wanted everything to be perfect. The stress was eating her alive.

Today's task was painting. They needed to get two more coats of paint on the interior walls between today and opening night next Saturday. Brent was about halfway done with one side. Sara was responsible for the other.

She wrung out her shirt as best she could in the kitchen where the water could sluice away down the drains embedded in the floor. Then she returned to the main dining area, picked up the paint cans she'd rescued from outside, and went over to resume her work.

They painted in silence for a while. Then, Brent started whistling. It occurred to Sara suddenly that she'd never heard a more annoying sound in her life. What was that song? Whatever it was, it was driving her nuts.

She tried to just ignore it for a while. Things were already edgy between them. She felt bad about it sometimes—he was her brother, she loved him, and he was giving up so much of his time to help her, after all. She ought to be grateful. She *was* grateful.

But she was also so sick of fighting with him. She had a vision for how things needed to be done, and Brent just seemed determined to butt heads with her over every little detail. Why couldn't he see the dream in her head? She tried to explain it to him, to show him what she saw when she closed her eyes—the smells, the lights, the colors, the happy guests. He flatly refused to listen to that, though. Or so it felt to Sara.

She dropped her paintbrush in the rinse bucket and walked over to see how he was doing on his half. "How goes it?" she asked, putting on her friendliest voice.

"It goes."

She noticed something and frowned. "What paint are you using?"

He answered without looking down at the can, "Cadet Blue. Just like you ordered."

Her frown deepened. "No, you're not."

Brent looked at her, his face tight with barely suppressed irritation. "Yes, I am."

"No, you're not." Sara snatched up the bucket at his feet and saw in horror that it said "Cornflower Blue," not "Cadet Blue." She shoved it in front of his face. "Look! What does that say?"

Brent threw his paintbrush down onto the floor, flecks of paint flying everywhere, and jumped down off his step stool. "First of all, don't talk to me like I'm a misbehaving kindergartner. Second of all, I picked up this can from the spot where we were storing the interior paints. If it's the wrong color, it's because you put something where it doesn't belong. That's on you, not on me."

"You're joking. Tell me you're joking right now."

"Which part of that sounded like a joke, Sara?"

"There's no way you're blaming me for this. *You* used the wrong color!"

"Because *you* put it in the wrong place! How many times do I have to tell you—"

"How many times do *I* have to tell *you*—"

They were both hollering nonsense at this point. Hands jabbing into the air, faces going red with anger. Until Brent stopped and held up his hands, looking utterly disgusted. "Forget it," he said. "Forget it. I'm leaving. I'm not putting up with this tonight."

"Don't you—"

But he was already marching towards the back door. He grabbed his keys and backpack on the way out, slinging it over his shoulder. Sara hesitated for only a split second before she stormed after him.

The rain outside was relentless. She could barely hear herself as she yelled after him, "This is not my fault!"

He yelled something back, but she couldn't hear. She just stood in the driving rain and watched as he climbed into his truck, pulled out, and drove off, leaving her alone. Her anger grew and grew and grew until, suddenly, it just disappeared all at once, leaving no trace behind.

She couldn't be angry at him. She was just sad. This was going to fail. Her restaurant, her bold play, her impulsive attempt to plant her own flag in the ground and build something she was proud of, was going to fail before it ever got going.

People would laugh at her. Gavin, Russell, everyone. *We knew you couldn't do it,* they'd say. *What ever made you think you were capable of something like this?* She pictured Russell again with that girl at the bar. Her heart throbbed painfully. Then she thought of Gavin, and her fists curled.

Her past was littered with mistakes and missed opportunities. And she was in the midst of creating another one.

All she wanted to do was go sit in the half-completed heart of her restaurant and cry. After that, she'd figure out a game plan. She turned to go back inside.

But when she grabbed the door handle and pulled, she realized with horror that it was locked.

A few long seconds passed with her hand on the handle. The door wasn't budging, she knew that. She and Brent had installed it a few weeks ago. Brent had tested it by throwing himself at it like a linebacker making a tackle. They'd both laughed when he bounced right off. The front door was locked, too, and the metal grate was pulled down over it. So that was a no-go as well. Her cell phone was inside with the rest of her things, meaning she couldn't call anyone for a ride, either.

With no other choices, she went to collect her bicycle. What a stupid decision that had turned out to be, too. That morning, in the only fifteen-minute window of the day where the rain had ceased, she'd decided to bike to the restaurant. *The rain must be done!* she had thought. Like an idiot.

Now, she was stranded a couple miles from her home on Howard Street, in the unyielding downpour. And, as she pulled the bike out from the little overhang where she'd hidden it, she realized that her tire was flat.

She laughed at that. At this point, what else was there to do besides laugh?

She kept chuckling in intermittent bursts as she turned and started pushing her bike on the long walk home. The rain, if anything, fell harder.

As she walked, she wondered. She wondered what Russell was doing right now. Was he curled up on the couch with that little blonde woman? They were probably watching a movie and cuddling. Sara wondered if the woman let Russell pick the movie. If he had, it was probably a cheesy horror film from the nineties. Russell loved those. She started to wonder what Gavin was doing, too, and then she stopped that real quick. He could do whatever he wanted. She didn't care at all anymore. It was funny to her how much she had once cared about every single Gavin thing, and now she didn't care even one iota. If she never saw him again, it would still be too soon.

Her mind was far from Nantucket as she pushed her bike down the street. When she rounded the corner by the fire station, she heard a voice call from just inside the open garage door.

"Oy!"

She figured that everybody was indoors with a loved one, dry and safe from the rain. The voice felt disconnected from reality. Only when the person hollered again did she realize that, whoever it was, they were talking to her.

"Oy! Chef Sara!"

She looked up in surprise. Standing framed in the opening of the fire station garage was the young guy from the fire at the inn. Joey was his name, she remembered. The rookie.

"What're you doing out in the rain, crazy?" he called again, bewildered.

She blinked. "Walking?" she answered dumbly.

He waved her in. Shrugging, she turned and pushed her bicycle up the driveway. After so many long minutes in the rain, it honestly felt weird to be out of it again as she stepped inside.

"You are, uh, a little wet," Joey commented wryly. He had a mirthful twinkle in his eye.

"They didn't skimp on you when they were handing out brains, did they?" she fired back. She wondered if she sounded too bitter, but Joey just laughed.

"My parents might argue otherwise, but I'll just pretend you were being serious. Do you want a towel?"

"Uh, yeah. A towel would be nice. Thanks."

He handed her a thick, dry towel. Sara sponged off her hair and mopped up what she could from her arms, face, and legs. She glanced at the towel when she finished and saw that her makeup was smudged all over it.

"I must look fantastic," she muttered to herself.

"I've seen worse," Joey said.

"You weren't supposed to hear that," she said at once, mortified. She knew darn well that she looked like something the cat dragged in. Makeup running, hair soaked, clothes drenched. She had a weird, twisting feeling in her gut. It took her a moment to recognize it as the kind of embarrassment a person felt when they looked silly in front of their crush.

Did she have a crush on this handsome firefighter? That would be news to her. But as she looked at him and took in his features again—those dimples, my goodness—she realized that it didn't seem as crazy as it might be.

What was wrong with a crush? He was nice, he was cute, he was friendly.

She could have a crush.

As long as she didn't screw this one up, too.

39

BRENT

Brent and Ally were in his apartment, lounging on the couch while a goofy Hallmark movie played on the television. Ally's choice, not his.

He had a lot on his mind. For starters, he was still mad after his fight with Sara in the restaurant, despite several hours having passed.

But more importantly, he couldn't stop thinking about dinner with Rose. Again and again he'd thought about it in the days since. Every idle moment—boom, there was Rose in his mind's eye, shyly slurping a spaghetti noodle or dabbing delicately at her lips with a napkin. It shouldn't have been notable at all. They ate a nice, normal dinner, during which they had a nice, normal conversation, and then they'd said a nice, normal goodbye.

Underneath the surface of all that, though, was an unbearable tension. He tried not to think about it. He honestly tried very, very hard. But that was proving to be impossible.

It was fully dark outside now. The rain had not yet quit. Maybe it would never quit again. Maybe this was just Nantucket today, tomorrow, and for the rest of time—torrential rain around the clock.

"Sailor boy," Ally said, poking him with her foot. "Ahoy, sailor boy."

"Mm?" Brent grunted.

"What're you thinking about?"

"Nothing."

She sat up and grabbed his wrist. "Tell me."

"Nothing. Just, uh... just a stupid fight with Sara. I'd rather forget about it."

"Restaurant stuff?"

"Restaurant stuff," he confirmed.

"You're right. That is stupid."

He laughed and pushed her off him. "Pick on someone your own size, McNeil."

"What's the fun in that?" she said from the other end of the couch. Then she pounced on him again.

Unfortunately for Ally, Brent had done a brief spell on the wrestling team in high school. He'd retained enough of what he learned to capably handle a one-hundred-and-twenty-pound college girl with an attitude. He made short work of her attack, flipping her over and pinning her beneath him.

"Bad move."

"Only if you consider this losing." She winked and bit her lip. That was awfully hard to resist. He leaned down and kissed her. She kissed him back for a moment before putting a pair of gentle hands on his chest and pushing him away, just far enough that his forehead was resting lightly on hers.

"Come with me," she said.

"Huh?"

She rolled her eyes. "Jeez, you're dense sometimes, Benson."

"Come with you where?"

"Away."

He sat back on his heels. "You mean like on your trip. At the end of the summer."

"Well, I leave in a week, so if you consider that the end of the summer, then yeah."

"To Asia."

She sat up with him and took hold of his hands in hers. Her eyes were flaming bright as she looked at him excitedly. "That's just a starting point. We can go anywhere. Throw a dart at a map and we'll go there, I don't care. But come with me."

Brent wriggled one of his hands out of her grasp and pushed back the hair from his forehead. He'd let it grow long this summer, and it had become bleached blond from all the hours in the sun while out on the boat with Marshall.

"You want me to leave my family and my home behind and just go ... anywhere?"

Ally's nose wrinkled. It always did that when she was confused. "It's not like they're leaving, too. You can always come back. That's the whole point of travel."

"Yeah, but it's not just that simple. You want me to just run off for no reason."

"Who needs a reason?" she yelped. "It's a huge world! You've never seen any of it!"

"I've been around," Brent corrected sternly.

"You've been to New York. Once. That hardly counts."

"It counts."

"Whatever, count it, don't count it, I don't care. But come with me." She touched his face. "I want you to come on an adventure with me."

"An adventure."

"Yeah, an adventure! We could be—shoot, I dunno—eating coconuts on the beach in Bali! We could go do backflips off the Great Wall of China! Doesn't that sound incredible? It beats the heck out of this boring old town."

Brent's frown deepened more with every word. Every time Ally had touched on the subject this summer, he'd more or less brushed it off. It sounded great in theory, yeah. Take off for a while. No plan, no agenda, no destination. Nowhere to be and nothing to do.

Why not do it?

He couldn't put a finger on why not. But there was a burning *No* that rose inside him whenever he considered it. Like a physical chain tethering him to the island. The thought of leaving Nantucket made him actually, literally nauseous.

That was stupid. He was being dumb. Ally was right—the world was huge and beautiful and filled with things he'd never heard of before. More to the point, it was filled with things he'd never hear of if he stayed here for the rest of his life.

So just go then. That was the answer, right? Take her hand, buy the ticket, board the flight. See what happened next. Nantucket wasn't going anywhere. He could always come home.

Go or stay, go or stay. He flip-flopped back and forth on it every day, every hour.

It felt like this was the decision point, though. Something about the way Ally was holding his hands and looking at him made him feel like this was it. Time to choose.

What if he couldn't? Half of him wanted to go. Half of him wanted to stay. Which half was right? How could he pick between them?

He knew what this was really about, even if he hadn't ever admitted it out loud. Not even to himself in the dead of night.

It was about Ally versus Rose. Adventure versus home. Himself versus himself. Which Brent would he be?

He didn't know. He couldn't know.

He couldn't sit here forever, either. Ally was staring into his eyes, into his soul, it felt like. She needed an answer.

"I don't know," he said eventually with a heavy sigh. "Maybe."

"Maybe," she repeated. "That's it? Maybe?"

"I can't give you anything better than that." He sounded defeated. He felt defeated. "I'm sorry."

She stood up and grabbed her purse from the table.

"Where are you going?" he asked her without looking up.

"I leave in a week," she said. "If your maybe changes to a yes before then, give me a call." Before she left, she leaned down and took his chin gently between two fingers, tilting it up towards her. "It's a big world, Brent Benson," she whispered. "Come explore it with me." She kissed him softly.

Then she left, leaving him to sit in the darkness and watch a stupid Hallmark movie as his thoughts raced around and around in endless, confusing circles.

40

ELIZA

The rain, the rain, the rain. It wouldn't stop. It wouldn't ever stop. She was going to be stuck in this godforsaken airport forever. Lord, how she hated LaGuardia. It was the devil's airport, no question. Only the worst being ever created could dream up some place this vile in every way. The ground was gross, the ceiling was missing tiles, everyone who worked here for long enough ended up with a stink-faced expression.

Winter was crying again. This time, Eliza could neither blame nor comfort her. She wanted to cry, too. If they weren't in full view of the public, she might've given into the urge. Crying wouldn't do anything, of course. But it might make her feel at least a little bit better.

There were so many things to cry about. She could cry about what Clay had done, what he had threatened. She could cry about how cold and distant Oliver had been when he told her she was wrong for trying to keep Winter away from that megalomaniacal, drug-addicted control freak. She could cry about how she'd never share another moment with Oliver like they'd shared on stage at that first concert, when it seemed like music itself had been created just to bring the two of them closer to each other.

And she could cry about the rain.

But she didn't do any of that. She just sat in the corner with her baby in her arms, alternating between shushing her softly and singing lullabies in a low voice, barely audible to anyone but her and her daughter. The hours ticked past. No planes came or left. People moved around anxiously, though they didn't really come or go either, just swirled back and forth like eddies trapped up on the beach after high tide. It was like the airport was frozen in time. Quarantined from the rest of the world. No entry. No exit. No solution. No hope.

Until, finally, nearly twelve hours after she'd arrived, something hit her in the face. It was a beam of light. She looked to her left and blinked once, twice, as her eyes struggled to make sense of the scene outside. After so much rain, it was like she'd forgotten what the sun looked like. But there it was, reminding her. One lone beam of light coming out of the dark clouds like a hot knife through butter.

As she watched, the rain slowed, then stopped, as if someone had hit a switch to cut off the sky's faucet. It felt like a weight was being lifted off her. She looked over to the check-in desk. There was a swirl of commotion amongst the employees. Renewed energy, fresh purpose.

Eliza had a feeling: it was almost time to go.

She stood up suddenly. Winter stopped crying. "Look, honey!" Eliza murmured to her baby, pointing towards the sky. "Look. It's the sun." She kissed Winter on the forehead and swayed back and forth, dancing to music that only they could hear. "We're going to go home, baby. Finally."

Sure enough, it was just a few more minutes before a cheerful voice came crackling over the intercom. "Ladies and gentlemen, we are happy to announce that the grounding order for all flights out of LaGuardia Airport has been lifted. We will now resume the boarding process. Please pay attention to all overhead monitors ..."

Eliza ignored the rest of the announcement as she gathered her belongings and strode with Winter towards their gate. She was maybe the tenth person in the newly formed line. The employees wasted no time in opening up the gate door and starting to scan everybody's tickets. They would be on the plane, bound for Nantucket any minute now. Seven people left in front of her. Four. One.

"Eliza!"

She must be hallucinating. Fumes in the air, asbestos in the ceiling conspiring to make her hear things. Because she could've sworn that she'd just heard Oliver's voice.

It wasn't until he was standing right in front of her that she finally believed that it was him.

He was panting, hands on knees, and sweating profusely. It looked like he'd run a marathon through the rain. His shoes squelched. He honestly looked borderline ridiculous. Other people were staring.

"Ma'am?" asked the airline employee. She held her hand out for Eliza's tickets.

"No, wait," Oliver said. "Eliza, wait."

Eliza wanted to scream in frustration. If he was going to make a scene, why couldn't he have done it earlier in the day, when she was sitting around with nothing to do? Why wait until now, when she was literally seconds away from boarding the airplane back to Nantucket?

"I'm sorry," she said to the employee. "I'll get back in line in just a second."

She stepped out, still holding Winter, and glared at Oliver. "I'm getting on this plane, Oliver," she warned.

"Just hear me out," he said. He was still inhaling in ragged gasps.

Eliza frowned. "Why are you breathing so hard?"

"Ran."

"Why?"

"Had to talk to you." He took another deep inhale and seemed to calm down a bit. He stood up straight. He looked like trash, but his eyes were as green and vivid as they had been on the night they met. It looked like there was emerald fire behind the irises. So much life there. So much of everything. Fear, doubt, hope, pride, humility. He was a complex man. She once thought she'd have a lifetime to explore those complexities. It turned out she was off by a wide margin.

"What do you want to say, Oliver?" she asked curtly. He'd already said his piece. Everything he needed to say had been said that night a week ago, after Clay had come and threatened her daughter. She knew where Oliver stood, and it wasn't with her. As far as she was concerned, there was nothing left to say.

"I lied."

That, of all things, took her by surprise. "What?"

"I lied. I said I couldn't be Winter's father. That's a lie."

Eliza held her breath. She didn't know what to say to that. Oliver swallowed and continued. "I'm not her biological father, that's true. But I'm a dad to that little girl. I love her. I love her mother, too. That's you, Eliza. I'm head over heels, stupid in love with you. I always knew that, from the second I spilled a beer on you in that bar all those months ago. Which, just to reiterate, was partially on purpose. But I was scared of what it would mean to be in love with you the way I know I am now. I thought I still loved shows and performing and trying to be a rock star. And maybe I'm an idiot for taking so many days to realize the truth, but I finally came around to it, so better late than never, I guess. The truth is that I was scared of committing to a life with you, because it felt like closing the door on other things I've dreamed of for a long time. I guess what I'm trying to say is that you can shut those doors. Lock 'em and throw away the key, I don't care. I want to be your man. I want to be Winter's father. I'll leave everything else in the world behind and never, ever look back if I can be those things to you."

He dropped to one knee.

This couldn't be real. This was the absolute cheesiest thing she'd ever encountered in her life. No one did this in the real world.

But it *was* real. She was standing in LaGuardia Airport with tears still in her eyes from one of the worst days she had ever had. And the man she loved was kneeling on the ground in front of her, holding open a box, in which sat a diamond ring.

"I quit the tour," he said. "Because I wanted to come with you. Wherever you're going, I want to come. I love you. Will you marry me, Eliza?"

She opened her mouth to speak, then fell silent. Tried a second time, but that didn't work, either.

Only when Winter made a noise did the spell holding Eliza captive shatter. She'd spent so many months running away from choices she didn't want to make. Now, she had the chance to make a choice of her own. There was a man who loved her holding open the door to a future together.

"Yes," she whispered. She cleared her throat and said it again. "Yes. Yes, I'll marry you."

Oliver smiled broadly. His green eyes flashed in the evening light now streaming in through the windows. He slipped the ring onto her finger, stood up, and kissed her.

A question suddenly occurred to her. This wasn't 1998 anymore. You couldn't just waltz up to an airport gate because a woman you loved was about to board a plane. "How did you get in here?" she asked.

Oliver's face reddened. "Bought the first ticket I saw," he mumbled. He showed it to her. It was a one-way ticket to Bermuda.

"Stay there," she ordered. "And hold Winter." She transferred the baby to him, then ran over to the check-in desk. She had a quick, hurried conversation with the person working, then traded a few pieces of paper with him.

When she came back over, she grabbed her things in one hand and Oliver's hand in the other. "C'mon," she said to him with a wry smile. "Our flight to Bermuda leaves in fifteen minutes."

Oliver grinned wide. "You're incredible," he said with such wide-open authenticity that her heart practically melted on the spot.

"Don't I know it," teased Eliza. "You better spoil me rotten, rock star."

PART IV

OPENING NIGHT

41

SARA

A Friday in late June.

Sara was looking at herself in the mirror of the Little Bull employee bathroom.

Tonight was the night. If this was going to be a disaster, then at the very least, it would be a beautiful disaster. And a tasty one.

"You can do this," she said to herself in the mirror. She'd been practicing this self-pep talk all week long as she scrambled to put the finishing touches on the restaurant in advance of opening night. "You studied for this. You trained for this. You dreamed of this. You're capable."

The words sounded thin and disappointing out loud as they echoed against the tiled bathroom walls. Her eyes looking back at her from the mirror seemed uncertain. Like, yeah, maybe part of her believed them. But not all of her.

She just hoped it was enough.

She threw one more splash of water on her face, dried it off with a paper towel, and left. The staff in the kitchen was waiting for her. They all sprang to attention when she walked into the room. Six waiters, three bartenders, four line chefs, a sous chef, two dishwashers, two hosts, two expos. A whole army, looking up to their general for their marching orders.

"Opening night." Sara flashed a smile, then quickly killed it. She opened her mouth to speak, but as she did, her brain went suddenly blank. Like the whole concept of language had just up and vanished. *What are words? What am I supposed to say or do now? Should I just mime out my instructions? Do an interpretive dance before we start letting guests in? Jeez, c'mon, Sara, they're staring at you. They're confused. You're supposed to talk now. Say something. Say anything! Sara!*

SARA! A second voice spoke up in her head. Well, not quite in her head. To be honest, it felt like someone was whispering in her ear from right behind her. She thought she felt a pair of reassuring hands press down on her shoulders, too. *Let 'em know what to do, little bull,* said a voice she hadn't heard in over fourteen months except for in her dreams. *You're the boss. So be the boss. I love you.* And then, just as suddenly as the voice had come, it was gone. She squeezed her eyes shut for a second.

Thanks, Dad.

Brimming with renewed confidence, she opened her eyes again. "Opening night," she repeated. "Big night. You all know your roles. We've practiced this. It's going to be good. Are you ready?"

"Yes, chef!" came the booming reply. It almost made her cry. She thought of Lola, teasing her before that Friday Night Feast just a few short months ago. She thought of Russell, snapping to attention in the midst of a flour snowstorm on their date at his house. She thought of her time in all those Michelin-starred kitchens in New York City, and at the Culinary Institute of America. She thought of the blood, sweat, and tears she'd poured into this career.

Whether or not this made it, she was proud of how far she'd come.

"Then let's get to it," she said.

Everyone scattered at once. It was time to work.

Sara wouldn't be spending too much time in the kitchen tonight. She'd spent the better part of the week training all the kitchen crew on her recipes, and she was confident in their execution without her needing to hover too much over their shoulders. Her job tonight would be to dance in the spotlight. As guests came in, she would greet them, move them to their tables, give them the lay of the land and her pick of the menu. It was mostly friends and family who'd be coming, so there wasn't too much reason to be nervous. And yet, she felt that river of anxiety surging within her. She had to stay on top of it. Surf those waves, so to speak, and let them motivate her rather than consume her.

She spent the next twenty minutes overseeing the final stages of prep. Then it was showtime. She washed her hands, dried them, and emerged into the main dining area just as her mother showed up with Brent.

"Oh, darling!" Mom exclaimed as she drank in the décor. "This is absolutely wonderful!" She'd insisted on waiting until everything was completely finalized before seeing it. *I want to be blown away,* were her exact words. Judging by her dropped jaw and wide eyes, it seemed like that mission had been accomplished.

"Thank Brent." Sara grinned. "He did all the dirty work. I just made his life harder." She shot her brother a wink. He smiled back and pulled her into a hug.

"It warms my heart to see you two so close again," Mom said.

Both Sara and Brent rolled their eyes at that, but they just pulled Mom into their hug and stood there for a second, enjoying a greedily snatched moment of calm in the eye of the storm. Reluctantly, Sara let go. "Lots to do," she said.

Mom kissed her on the cheek and held her at arm's length for one more beat. "I'm so proud of you, my love," she said. "Your father is, too."

"That's good. Because it's a family business, you know," Sara replied with tears in her eyes. "Says so on the sign." She hugged her mom tightly one more time. "Now get out of here, before you make me smudge my makeup." Laughing, she guided the two of them to the VIP table in the corner and sent one of the servers over to take their drinks order.

There was a deluge of well-wishers after that. Lola and Debra, along with pretty much every neighbor and family friend that Sara had ever known. She gave out kisses on the cheeks, hugs, shook hands, laughed and smiled and did everything she had spent a decade training to do. It wasn't long before the restaurant was humming with clinking glasses and the hubbub of fifty conversations at once. Sara loved it. It felt like she'd put this Frankenstein body together, and now, with the arrival of her first guests, it was all coming to life.

Little Bull was steaming.

She burst back into the kitchen as the first appetizers were plated and set out for delivery to the tables. Everything in here was flowing smoothly, with crisp efficiency and dedication to the task at hand. She'd picked her staff carefully. It made her proud to see good people doing good work.

Satisfied with what she saw, she scooped up two armfuls of plates from the ready area and took them out into the dining room. She delivered them to their destinations with a smile and a thorough, detailed explanation of how the recipe had been born, what it meant to her. Everything had Nantucket origins with big-city flair. The seafood was as fresh as possible. "It was breathing this morning," Sara whispered to Brent's old baseball coach. "You can still taste the saltwater if you get a good bite." He laughed as she turned to go back to the kitchen.

When she saw who was standing at the hostess stand, though, she froze.

It was Russell. To his left was the blonde girl she'd seen him with at the bar back in April.

She swallowed hard. *Breathe, Sara,* she counseled herself. This was okay. Totally not a big deal whatsoever. She would just go to the back and compose herself, so long as she could just disappear before he saw her ...

Nope. His eyes swung up and locked on hers. He smiled. It was sort of a sad smile, sort of a communicative smile, sort of a hello smile, all at once. Now, she had no choice but to go over to him. She took another deep breath, wiped her hands on her apron, then walked up.

"Hi," she said as brightly as she could muster.

"Hey, Sara." Russell still had that smile on, like he was trying to say as much as he could without saying it out loud. "I don't think you've met my girlfriend, but this is Clarissa."

Girlfriend. Ouch. "Clarissa," Sara gritted out. "It's a pleasure to meet you. Welcome to Little Bull! Can I get you guys situated?"

"It's a pleasure to meet you too," Clarissa said back. She was really quite pretty up close, and her voice was kind and authentic. "I'm actually going to run to the bathroom real quick, babe," she said, squeezing Russell's arm. "I'll meet you at the table." She turned back to Sara. "I'm so excited to try everything. Russell has told me all about you. He said you're a gifted artist. The place looks amazing, too."

"Thanks so much." Sara was softening like butter in the pan. It was impossible to hate this woman. She just oozed kindness.

"All right, be right back!" Clarissa headed off towards the restrooms.

That left Sara standing alone with Russell.

"So ... We haven't talked in a while," he said.

"I know."

"We didn't leave things off in the best of places."

"I know that, too."

"But maybe it was for the best."

"Maybe." Sara looked off in the direction that Clarissa had gone. "She seems lovely."

"She is," Russell nodded. "I'm crazy about her."

Sara winced. That felt like a bit of a slap in the face. But, the more she thought about it, the more she realized it wasn't meant like that, nor should she take it that way. That's just how Russell was. He had to be crazy about the woman in his life. And he needed someone who was crazy about him, too. Maybe Sara could have been that for him eventually. But she hadn't offered enough of herself quickly enough when she had the chance. And when the time had come to either dive into the deep end or pull out altogether, she'd instead broken his heart.

What happened between them was her fault. She knew that, he knew that, everybody knew that. But it had taken her a long time to get over it because—well, she just still had some growing up to do. Maybe tonight, she was taking that next step in her life.

"I'm sorry, you know," Sara said. "For everything."

Russell smiled that sad, knowing smile one more time. "You don't have to be sorry, Sara. Things are going to work out for everybody. I'll always treasure our friendship."

"You make it very difficult to be mad at you, you know," she teased.

Russell pretended to flick his hair back. "Ah well, I am just extremely likable. Or so I'm told."

She pushed him in the chest, then hugged him quickly.

"So we're friends?" he asked her after their quick hug ended.

"Friends," she confirmed. "You're a good guy, Russ. I hope you're happy."

He grinned. "Thanks, Sara. I hope you are, too. And," he added, "I hope your food is good, or I will not hesitate to one-star review this place on Yelp."

"Do it and I'll hunt you down," she snarled playfully, pointing a warning finger at his face. Clarissa reappeared just then, all smiles. Laughing, Sara led them to their table.

When she retreated back to the kitchen, she felt lighter. A weight had been lifted off her shoulders. A chapter had closed for good, yes.

But tonight was the beginning of something new.

42

HOLLY

Date night! Their first date night in Nantucket. Holly was excited. They were going to go pick up Billy, Pete's new business partner, whom she hadn't yet met, and Billy's wife, then all ride together to the opening of Sara's new restaurant.

It had been a rocky start to life back on Nantucket, but Holly was finally settling in. She'd done as well as she could at suppressing her disappointment over the home-buying debacle. At the end of the day, it just wasn't worth holding onto the anger. They still had a home, on Nantucket, with a beautiful future ahead of them.

That's what she told herself at least. Deep down, she knew that she'd been hurt and outraged. She was going to hold onto some of those feelings for a long time yet.

But not tonight. Tonight was going to be a celebratory night. She was also going to get to meet Pete's new business partner for the first time.

"So tell me about this guy," she said to Pete as they climbed into the car for the drive over to the man's house.

"Who, Billy? He's a good guy."

"A little more detail than that, darling."

Pete chuckled and drummed his fingers on the steering wheel. "Uhh, let's see. Billy and I go way back. Freshman year of college. We took an econ class together. Pretty sure we both failed it, but we had a good time trying. He's a smart dude."

"You guys kept in touch after that?"

"No, actually that's a funny story. Remember that trip I took down to Philadelphia? For that conference?"

"Mhmm, yeah."

"Billy was there, too. We ended up reconnecting. It'd been like, seven or eight years since we last spoke, but we picked up right where we left off. One thing led to another, and now, boom, here we are."

"Here we are indeed," Holly said with a smile. She was staring absentmindedly out the window, bobbing her head to the music and rubbing the back of Pete's free hand with hers. Something about the drive felt weirdly familiar, but she couldn't put her finger on it.

"Are you excited?" Pete asked suddenly.

"For what?"

He turned and glanced at her with a wicked smile. "For life here. I'm excited. I want you to be excited too."

"I am," she reassured him. She meant it. His excitement was so infectious, how could she not be excited along with him? This was a fresh start, a new chapter on the beaches of Nantucket. There was nowhere else like here. She was glad to be home, to have Pete by her side and the future at her fingertips.

If only this darn rain would stop, then life would be pretty close to perfect.

"Where'd you say this house was?" she asked, eyebrows furrowed. Again, she couldn't shake the feeling that she had been down exactly this particular route before. She'd grown up on the island, so that in itself wasn't that weird. Yet the sense of déjà vu lingered heavily.

Pete checked the navigation app he was following on his phone. "As a matter of fact, it is riiiight ..."

His words died on his lips. They pulled to a stop in the driveway in mutual stunned silence.

Because the house they were at was their stolen dream house.

"This can't be happening," Holly said numbly. She was so shocked that she couldn't even begin to put words to it. "This cannot possibly be happening."

"Hollz ..."

She whipped her head around to look at Pete. "Are you sure this is the right place?"

Pete just nodded.

This was the place that she'd dreamed of. The place they'd been contracted to buy, until some snake stole in under the cover of night and convinced the seller to renege. It felt like fate was dangling it in front of her. Was this a cruel joke? It had to be, right? This couldn't be real.

But she couldn't sit and brood in disbelief, because just then, the front door opened. A tall, portly man stood under the awning and beckoned them in with a friendly wave. He had thinning reddish-blond hair and was wearing a Nantucket red quarter-zip sweater over a pair of tailored slacks.

"That must be Billy," Holly whispered.

"Yep," Pete whispered back. "We better go. Are you ..." He looked to his wife. "Are you going to be okay, babe?"

"I don't really have a choice, do I?" she asked him.

He shook his head. "Not really. I'm sorry."

It wasn't his fault, of course. But that was a Pete Thing, too—saying what she needed to hear even if he didn't have anything to do with it. She squeezed his hand hard. Then they got out of the car and ran in out of the rain.

"The infamous Holly Goodwin!" Billy boomed once they'd ducked safely into the foyer. He pulled her into a hug, though she was soaked to the skin from their mad dash from car to front door. As they hugged, she looked over his shoulder at the home that should've been hers.

It was, if anything, even better than she remembered it. It was gorgeous, it was perfect, it was *hers*. It was stolen property.

She forced herself to take a deep breath. She could cry furious tears when she got home. For now, she had to be composed. For Pete's sake.

"Hi, Billy," she said. "It's so nice to finally meet you! I've heard so much."

"None of it's true, I swear!" he chortled. He was a laugh-at-his-own-jokes kind of guy, but not in a buffoonish or malicious way. He seemed like a laugh-at-everything kind of guy. He exuded warmth, like Santa Claus in boat shoes. Holly felt herself starting to relax as he took their raincoats and led the way into the dining room.

But that warmth vanished in one split second as soon as they rounded the corner and Holly saw what awaited them in there. Or rather, *who* awaited them.

Billy said, "Holly, Pete, I'd like you to meet my wife."

That was when Cecilia Payne stepped forward to shake Holly's hand.

43

SARA

The evening was going well, all things considered. All but one table had shown up for their reservations, so she was pleased with that. Sara was scribbling down lists of things to improve on some sticky notes at the host's stand—how different dishes were presented, some general tweaks to the flow and movement of her employees and guests throughout the restaurant's space. But the essentials were in place. The food was good, the atmosphere was pleasant, the staff was diligent.

Sara had even stood up and given a short little speech, thanking everyone for coming to opening night. As she stepped down, she was buzzing with energy and good vibes.

All of which came to a screeching halt when the front doors swung open ...

And Gavin Crawford walked in.

Sara's heart jumped into her throat. First Russell, then Gavin. Were all the men she'd ever dated lining up outside and coming in one by one just to try and ruin her evening?

She went right up to him and met him at the front. "Gavin. What are you doing here?"

He smiled like it was the most natural thing in the world for him to show up—here of all places, tonight of all nights. He was wearing his Gavin Outfit, she noticed. Leather desert boots, dark, slim-fitting jeans, a crisp white button-down shirt.

"I had to come support you on your big night, didn't I?" He looked around, marveling at the place. "Look at what you did! My little protégé."

"You shouldn't be here," Sara snapped.

He ignored her as he turned and introduced the man he'd come in with. Sara hadn't even noticed a second person enter at Gavin's side, but as she looked over to him, she saw that he had an air of self-importance about him. He was a short, older man, chubby bordering on fat, wearing a suit vest and round glasses perched on his nose. "Martin Hogan," he said in a voice that was almost like a cat's purr.

Sara gasped. Everyone in fine dining knew who Martin Hogan was. He'd won every food critic award there was to win. He had a weekly column in the *New York Times*, was a contributing editor to half a dozen national food magazines, and regularly flew around the country dining at the best restaurants America had to offer.

He could make or break Little Bull with a single stroke of his pen, if he so chose.

"Mr. H-Hogan," Sara stammered. "It is an honor to have you here with us this evening. I ... I didn't know you were in town."

"He's my guest," Gavin explained with a wink.

Sara was still flummoxed. This was like having the president walk into your Model UN club meeting. It made the stakes feel so much more real. Before he'd entered, she was just feeding some friends and family in a new location. It was basically Friday Night Feasts with a little extra pizzazz. Now, this could be anything. This could be the beginning of something truly special.

Or terrible.

"Cassandra!" Sara called over her shoulder. The head hostess, Cassandra, came bustling over with a welcoming smile. "Would you please show Mr. Crawford and Mr. Hogan to their table?"

"Of course. This way, if you please, gentlemen," Cassandra said, gesturing towards the final two seats at the bar top.

"I'll catch up with you in one sec, Marty," Gavin said. "Gonna chat with our chef here for a moment."

Martin shrugged and waddled after Cassandra. Sara watched him go, silently pleading for him—or anyone, really—to come back so she didn't have to face Gavin alone.

But when he was gone, it was just the two of them, alone at the front of the restaurant.

"What are you doing here, Gavin?" she asked for the second time.

"You were playing awful hard to get," he said with a shrug. "I figured I'd swing by your neck of the woods."

"With the most famous restaurant critic in the world in tow."

"I thought you'd appreciate the gesture." He frowned. "Maybe I was wrong."

"The gesture?!" Sara wanted to scream. "Why are you *here*, Gavin? What do you want from me?"

He put a hand on her shoulder. She wanted to pull away in utter revulsion, but she took a deep breath and steadied her nerves.

How had she ever found this man attractive? He seemed so wildly repulsive to her now. His cologne was overwhelming; he needed to shave that ragged beard; he sounded so slimy when he talked, like a used car salesman trying to coax her into buying a jalopy off the lot. She didn't want him even to look at her, much less touch her.

"You should go," she said. "You should never have come at all."

Gavin sighed and ran a hand through his hair. "This could be good for you, you know."

Her blood ran cold. "What is that supposed to mean?"

"I mean, if everything goes well, I'll put in a good word for you with Marty. Maybe he gives you a little mention in his column ..." He shrugged again. "Could be good for you."

"That's it. I serve good food and you tell him to write me up. No quid pro quo."

He spread his hands wide. "What's the harm in that?"

"There's no way you flew all the way to Nantucket just to do me a favor like that, Gavin. I'm not stupid."

"I'm not asking for much, you know ..."

She held her breath and said nothing. The other shoe was going to drop any second now. She could have set a timer to it. God, he was so predictable. So transparently selfish. Why did he even want her anymore? Just because she was "the one that got away"? Not in anything even close to a romantic way, though. She was just a little pet that had escaped his collection before he was done playing with her. How many other women like her were floating around in Gavin's orbit? He was a manipulator, a con man, a sleazeball extraordinaire ... She was done with his games.

But he wasn't done with her.

"... All I want is a chance to talk," he finished.

"So talk." Her voice was icy. She felt like she had aged years, decades even, since he first walked into her restaurant. She checked her watch. It had been four minutes.

"Well, maybe not here." He rubbed his chin between thumb and forefinger. Another Gavin habit—once attractive, now anything but that.

"Where, then?" She noticed his other hand was playing with something in his pocket. When she asked where he wanted to talk, he withdrew it and she saw what it was: A hotel room key.

So that was it. He was dangling Martin Hogan in front of her—whether as an incentive or a threat, she still wasn't sure—in exchange for quite literally the most demeaning thing anyone had ever tried to coax out of her.

Gavin offered the room key to her. "Let's talk tonight after you're all done here," he said. "Once Marty and I get a chance to taste what you've whipped up." He winked. Again, Sara was amazed at how calm and natural he acted like all this was. As if he wasn't trying to twist her into the shape he liked her best in—subservient and loyal.

But the truth of the matter was that he had her over a barrel. She could refuse, and he would bring down the hammer that was Martin Hogan on her head like an executioner. Little Bull would be done for almost immediately. It wasn't a threat, even—it was a cold-blooded fact. She'd come so far, worked so hard, built so much. And it could all disappear virtually overnight.

Or she could say yes. She could go to his hotel room after closing. She could give in to his coercion. Then Gavin would tip Hogan's hand, and Little Bull could very well explode into something spectacular. That was within his power, too.

It seemed like an easy decision. Say no, spit in his face, kick him out of the restaurant. She was about to do just that, when something caught her eye.

It was the sign over the door. The one that said *Little Bull – A Family Business*. When she saw that, she thought of her family, and her heart stopped in place. She wasn't the only one with something to lose her.

If it was up to her, she'd burn it all down just to spite Gavin's offer. But Mom's money—Dad's money, really—had built this place. Brent's hands had built it. Eliza and Holly's encouragement had spurred her along on dark nights when she needed it most. The Bensons were tied up in the very walls here, like this restaurant was part and parcel of their family.

Say no to Gavin, and all that would be lost, too.

It was lose-lose. There was no way out.

Gavin saw her hesitation and his grin fell. "Decide by the end of the night," he said. "Let me know."

Then he pressed the room key into her hand and walked away, leaving Sara alone at the front of her restaurant with no idea what she was going to do.

44

BRENT

Brent was having an awfully hard time keeping up his end of the conversation. He and Mom had been the first ones to arrive at Little Bull. The place looked great, as he knew it would. Lord knew he'd put enough sweat and labor into making this place fabulous. But he had to admit, Sara's vision brought to life was really something else. She had a talent for this thing. Who woulda known? "Good for her," he kept saying every time Mom pointed out some new marvel she noticed in the details and the satisfied expressions of the diners around her. Not in a sarcastic way or anything—he genuinely meant it. He was proud of Sara. She had done something special.

But he didn't have much else to say because his mind wasn't at Little Bull. It was in the trunk of his car.

Right next to the duffel bag he'd packed this morning.

It was almost everything he owned—clothes, toiletries, shoes—along with enough cash saved up to travel for a few months at the very least.

He checked the time on his cell phone. It was 8:43 p.m. Ally's flight left in three hours. There were still empty seats on the plane; he'd checked obsessively over and over all day long. If he wanted to, he could get up from here, drive to the airport, and take off on an adventure.

He'd already squared everything away—if he left, Marshall would take care of Henrietta and his apartment. He'd paid three months' rent up front and cleaned out the perishables from the refrigerator.

It was possible. If he chose, he could leave Nantucket with Ally. Go explore. See the world he'd never seen.

But he just didn't know.

Because leaving Nantucket meant leaving Rose.

Why was that proving to be so hard? They weren't together. He hadn't so much as seen or spoken a word to her in over a week, not since their unexpected dinner at her house. Nothing had happened at dinner that would make him think they had a future together.

But he had that thought anyway. There was just something there. Something that tied them together. It was powerful and inexplicable and honestly sounded a little stupid every time he said it out loud. He'd never really believed in fate. If fate was real, then why did a good man like his father die? No, forget fate. He didn't need it.

And yet, he couldn't ignore the urge to run out of this restaurant and find her. He wanted to find Rose, hold her, kiss her. It was a stupid, illogical urge. An urge he could not ignore.

Dinner wore on and his brain ran in the same ceaseless circuit: Ally, adventure. Rose, home. Ally, adventure. Rose, home. He wanted to take a fork and jab himself in the thigh just to bring his thoughts back to the present. But he was swept up in a riptide too powerful to resist.

He had to make a decision.

The rain outside was still pouring down on the roof of the restaurant. It was kind of nice, in a strange way. It filled the gaps between conversations, made everything feel closer and cozier and more intimate. Under other circumstances, he might have relaxed and enjoyed his mother's company and the food that Sara had spent so many weeks and months carefully concocting. Under these circumstances, though, he was seconds away from standing on the table and screaming like a Viking.

He had to decide. He had to choose. He had to do it now, now, now.

"I'm sorry, Mom," he said, standing up. His chair scraped back across the floor. He hardly noticed, though. "I've gotta go take care of something. Will you be all right here?"

"Well, okay, yes, darling," his mom said, completely confused. "I'll be fine. Is everything okay? What's going on?"

"I just gotta go take care of something," he repeated. "I'll make sure Holly can give you a ride home, okay?"

"Are you going somewhere?" Mom asked.

Brent thought about it. "Maybe." He left before she could ask any more questions.

He got faster with every step. Dodging around waiters laden with trays of food, he pushed towards the front, through the doors, out into the raining night. The sound was just as thunderous out here, but all Brent could hear was the pounding of his heartbeat in his ears, and the same circular pattern again and again.

Ally, adventure.

Rose, home.

He jumped into his car and fired up the engine. Tires squealed in the wet gravel as he peeled out of the parking lot. The speedometer crept up. Thirty, forty, fifty. He was going far too fast for Nantucket, far too fast for any car in the rain. But he had to go *NOW*. He was held captive by the most powerful urge he'd ever felt in his life.

Ally, adventure.

Rose, home.

He knew that he was going to come up to an intersection soon, and he was going to have to make his choice. One road led to the airport. Ally would be at the gate, he knew. Despite all her spontaneity, she had a horrific fear of missing flights, so she would be there well in advance of her departure time.

The other road went left, to Rose's house. He didn't even know if she was home or not. It didn't matter. The choice wasn't about right this second. It was about—well, it was about forever, in a way. Brent felt like he was in some respects making a choice about the kind of person he wanted to be. The kind of man he wanted to be.

He could run.

Or he could stay.

Ally, adventure.

Rose, home.

Brent was approaching the intersection fast, faster, faster. The tires were barely hanging onto the road now. It was slick with rainwater. He had to decide. Right was Ally. Left was Rose. Any second longer and he'd crash straight into the embankment directly ahead of him.

Life is meant to be enjoyed, isn't it? That was his dad's voice, whispering to him out of the ether like a ghost.

Brent wrenched the wheel to the left.

Time slowed for a moment. The nose of the truck went towards the left, but the wheels on the right lost their traction and separated from the road for a moment. He'd been going too fast and the conditions were too poor. The truck, old as it was, couldn't handle the strain. It tipped, tipped, tipped ...

And as it hung in the air, Brent had just enough time to wonder if he'd made a terrible mistake.

45

HOLLY

Dinner was worse than she expected.

Frigid, awkward, full of sharp edges and sudden dead ends in the conversation. But even the uncomfortable silence was better than hearing Cecilia talk. She didn't say much. Whether she sensed the awkwardness that Holly was feeling or she just thought she didn't need to make much—if any—of a conversational effort, Holly wasn't sure. When Cecilia did speak, though, it was invariably rude. The food was cold or the wine was warm or the server gave her a funny look. Holly held Pete's hand under the table and every time this witch complained or criticized something new, she squeezed his fingers hard, bit her lip, and resolved not to say anything.

Billy was completely oblivious. That laugh of his was like sweet jelly on top of burnt toast, covering up all the charred bits underneath. He told stories, he drank whiskey. That was perfectly fine in Holly's eyes. As long as he was talking, she didn't have to listen to Cecilia, and she didn't have to force herself to say anything, either. Whenever the conversation did come to her, she tossed it off to Pete like a hot potato. She'd apologize to him later. Right now, all she could think about was getting out of here.

The shock of the dual discovery was like a pair of stab wounds in the lungs. She was finding it hard to draw a breath. As beautiful as this evening should have been—her little sister had opened a fabulous new restaurant, after all!—Holly couldn't focus on any of it. Not the food. Not the décor. Not the buzz of happy diners. The simple act of breathing in and out was demanding all of her attention.

Just get through this, woman, she gritted internally. *Not much longer.*

Until the absolute worst-case scenario unfolded. Pete squeezed Holly's hand. "I gotta run to the restroom real quick, if you'll excuse me."

She tried to keep him pinned to the chair. But she knew she had to let him go. She forced a smile to her face and offered up a not-actually-kidding, "Hurry back, we'll miss you!"

Holly watched him go. When he was gone, she turned back to Billy and Cecilia. She was poking at the food on her plate with distaste, the same face she'd use when plunging a toilet or investigating if an animal on the side of the road was dead or not yet. Fortunately, Billy set his whiskey tumbler down with emphasis and beamed out her.

"Got you all to ourselves now, Holly! So, tell me about life with Peter Piper! Dad of the year I bet, right?"

Holly smiled. This was an easy enough topic. She could talk about Pete all day. But just when she opened her mouth to answer, Billy frowned.

He patted his pocket and pulled out his cell phone, which was buzzing in his hand. "So sorry," he told her, waggling it by way of explanation. "I'm gonna step out and take this one real quick. Work never stops when you run your own business, right?" He laughed, stood, and swept out of the restaurant. Holly heard a faint "Talk to me!" as he left.

Then it was just her and Cecilia.

Oh, no.

She looked down at her lap. What happened next surprised her.

She got *mad.*

Holly could count on two hands the number of times she'd really blown her top in the last few years. She was a calm person by nature, and when she did get upset, she was more prone to tears than anger.

This was an exception to the rule. She was seated here, under her sister's roof, with a woman who had stolen from her. A rude, nasty woman. Maybe she shouldn't say quite *everything* that was on her mind with regard to Cecilia, seeing as how that included a few choice words about the kind of person who steals a home under contract or insults a realtor to their face. The two of them had husbands who worked together, after all. This certainly wouldn't be the last time they interacted.

But Holly couldn't let sleeping dogs lie.

"I like your home very much," she began in a low voice.

Cecilia looked over to her. "Oh?"

"Yes, quite a lot. In fact, Pete and I were going to purchase the very same one."

"Is that a fact?" Up until this moment, Holly hadn't ever fully understood the phrase "talking down one's nose." Now, though, she saw exactly what it meant. Cecilia had her chin tilted high and was gazing at Holly with equal parts curiosity and disdain. Almost like a "Why is this person talking to me?" kind of look.

"Yes, it is a fact. We were going to purchase it, until someone else came in and convinced our seller to pull out of an agreed-upon deal."

Cecilia folded her hands on the white tablecloth and leaned forward. "Do you expect me to apologize, Mrs. Goodwin?"

Holly gritted her teeth. Her spine was an iron-rod, her hands were clamps, squeezing the daylights out of the arms on her chair. She'd never hated someone as much as she hated this woman right now. "That'd be a start," she snapped.

To her shock, Cecilia just laughed. It was an ugly, grating sound, like throwing silverware down the garbage disposal. "I will not apologize for getting what I wanted."

"You stole something that wasn't yours."

"I paid a fair price for a home I desired. I see nothing wrong with my actions. If you wanted it so badly, you should've tried harder."

"We had a deal. You swept in like the Wicked Witch of the West and snatched it away."

"You'll have to try harder if you want to rattle me, love. That is hardly the nastiest name I've ever been called," she remarked. "If you are going to be such a petty child, I don't think you and I will get along very well."

Breathe. Breathe. Okay, forget that. "If you are going to be such a heartless wench, I don't think we will, either." The words felt *so. freaking. good.* coming out of Holly's mouth. Like a bullwhip, lashing through the air with vicious intent.

But Cecilia merely laughed again. It was just as jarring the second time around. Holly winced. She leaned forward and fixed Holly with the coldest glare she'd ever seen. "If you are this upset about me getting that house, then I suggest you watch what you say to me. I am capable of doing much more to get the things I want." She straightened back up and sniffed. "Heaven forbid that our paths should cross again. I don't think you'd be very happy with the result."

Billy came back before Holly could figure out what to say to that. He sat down in his chair with the groaning *oomph* that every big man Holly had ever met seemed to do. Then he grinned at the two ladies who sat staring daggers at each other across the table. "You ladies getting along already, I'm sure? Beautiful! Best friends forever. Here's to Nantucket!"

He raised his glass to the center of the table. Pete strolled up just then and sat down with a weak smile. He must've seen the fury on Holly's face instantly, because the smile disappeared as fast it had come. Like it or not, though, Billy's glass was hanging in the air, waiting for them. So Holly and Pete clinked their glasses together and echoed, "To Nantucket."

Holly drained her wine and immediately flagged down the waiter for another.

It was going to take a long time to calm down from this night.

46

SARA

The frenzied dance of a restaurant in the middle of a dinner service reached its crescendo and then began the slow unwinding towards close. Sara let the work consume her thoughts. Just cook, coordinate, take dishes out, greet guests. There was plenty to do. She didn't have to think about Gavin's disgusting offer if she didn't want to.

But how could she ignore it? He was there at the end of the bar every time she looked over. He looked so utterly wrong sitting in her restaurant. He didn't belong here; he'd forced himself in.

Everything she'd ever loved hung in the balance of this one stupid decision. Say yes or say no? Keep the key or throw it back in his face?

How could she choose?

As she thought, her anger bubbled up. She sliced a little harder during the periods where she was helping out on the prep line. She scrubbed harder when she was lending the dishwasher her aid. When she shook the hands of her guests, she squeezed a little tighter and spoke a little firmer. She could feel the steam building in her chest.

The little bull was raging.

Guests began to leave, one by one, thanking her profusely and lavishing her with compliments. This was supposed to be a night of celebration and triumph. Of pride. Of family.

But Gavin had stolen that moment away from her.

Suddenly, the decision crystallized in her head. She couldn't ignore the guilt over what would happen if the restaurant failed and wasted away Mom's money with it. That was a problem for tomorrow. If she failed, she failed, and she would do that on her own terms. She didn't need Gavin's help and she didn't fear his threats. Not anymore.

He no longer held any power over her.

The trickle of departing guests continued until there were just a few scattered tables left. She saw the dining room staff clear away the plates in front of Martin Hogan and Gavin. Whether they looked satisfied or displeased, she didn't care. Let them think what they wanted. She knew her worth.

Now was as good a time as any for doing what she wanted to do. She marched up to Gavin and said his name. He looked at her and grinned broadly. Oh, how she had once swooned over that grin! It used to mean the world and more to her.

Now—nothing.

Sara grabbed Gavin's hand, turned it palm up, and slapped the room key down in his grasp. She kept a tight hold on his wrist as she looked him in the eye and hissed, with as much icy ferocity as she could muster, "Never come to my island again."

When all the guests were gone, the staff was dismissed, and the lights were turned off, Sara stood in the silence and darkness of her restaurant, closed her eyes, and breathed.

She could still smell the food. The brine of the lobster, the tomato tang of pasta sauce. That sticky malaise of beer, cut through by the tannin acidity of a beautiful cabernet wine blend. It was intoxicating. She'd built this, brought it to life, and now she had earned the right to stand in the midst of it all and just breathe.

So what if it all ended tomorrow? She'd made her choice and she knew deep in her soul that it was one she could live with. She would not fail; she felt that so powerfully and confidently. But even if she did—even if Gavin and the rest of the world teamed up to drag her down—she would be okay. She would hold her head high.

No matter what happened next, Sara Benson had already won.

But there was something else she wanted to do tonight. Stepping back into the kitchen, she hurriedly put a pile of leftovers into a Styrofoam box and wrapped it in plastic wrap. Then she scurried back outside, pulling the back door closed behind her. It locked into place with a *clink,* and she smiled at the memory of a week ago. She dashed through the rain to her car and got in, shivering from the damp.

The engine coughed to life. Sara pulled out, headlights slashing through the precipitation, as she drove down the road.

When she pulled up in front of the fire station, she hesitated for just a moment. There was just a tiny droplet of doubt mixed amongst the ocean of emotions roiling in her stomach right now. What if this turned out badly, too? She'd made so many mistakes over the last year. Could she survive another one?

The answer came from deep within her. *Yes.* She could handle anything. Gavin. Russell. Heartbreak. Shame. Building something from scratch and throwing it out into the world like a kite into heavy wind. If it flew, it flew. If it crashed, it crashed.

But she couldn't spend the rest of her life afraid of flying it to begin with.

So she grabbed the Styrofoam takeout box and went up to the front door of the fire station. She rang the doorbell and waited with bated breath. Footsteps approached from the other side. The door swung inward to reveal Joey Burton, the rook, standing there with a surprised look on his face.

"Chef Sara!" he exclaimed, taken aback. He checked his watch. "It's awfully late. What're you doing here?"

She stuck out the box of food towards him. "Since you're always hungry, I thought I'd bring you some food."

He looked down at the box, then back up at her. His grin was broad and infectious. Sara felt something she hadn't felt in some time— butterflies in her stomach. Not fear, not anxiety. Just the butterflies of *maybe, maybe, maybe.* That was a good thing.

"Do you want to come in?" he said.

"Yeah," Sara told him, returning his smile. "I'd like that."

47

BRENT

The truck hung in the air for what seemed like forever.

And then all four wheels slammed back into the ground, the engine roared, and the vehicle straightened out.

It gripped the road again and bore him away towards Rose's house.

He didn't die. He didn't flip the car.

He just kept driving towards the place he'd always been meant to go.

A few quick turns later, he pulled up in front of Rose's house. He was out of the vehicle before it had even come to a stop. He left the keys in the ignition, engine running. He'd get it later. It didn't matter right now.

He ran up to the door in five quick bounds. He pounded on it, closed fist, as loud as he could. "Rose!" he bellowed. "Rose!" He could barely hear himself amidst the rain on the eaves overhead. Maybe she wasn't home. Maybe she couldn't hear him. Maybe she was out on a date with another man, embarking on her own happily ever after that didn't involve him, or maybe she just didn't want to answer the door at all.

Those questions and a million more ran through Brent's head in seconds flat.

Then the door opened.

"Brent?" gasped Rose. "What on earth are you doing here?"

"You made a mistake," he said. The words fell out of his mouth like he'd been meant to say them for his whole life. Like they were prewritten and he was just reading the lines he'd been given. "We both did. Because I'm vulnerable too, you know. Just like you. My heart's been broken, just like yours. But I can't let this go, Rose. I just can't. I know I'm stubborn as a mule sometimes, and you've got every right to kick me off your front step. That's just fine if you do; I understand. But there's something between us that's worth risking everything. I can't ignore it. I can't let it go."

She said nothing, just stared at him with her mouth hanging open.

"You don't have to say a word," he continued. "Just shake your head yes or no. You say no and I'll be gone. You won't ever hear from me again. But you gotta give me something. I need more than a letter. I need an answer. A real one. Right here and right now."

It felt like the world hung in the balance as he waited. Rose looked frozen in place.

"Brent ..."

That was all the answer he needed. He stepped forward, soaked to the bone from the endless Nantucket summer rain, pulled Rose into his arms, and kissed her.

Her kiss tasted like coming home.

48

MAE

Brent's sudden departure had left Mae sitting at the table alone. Truth be told, she didn't mind having a second to sit and think, though she was of course worried about where her son had jetted off to.

Her mind was full as it was. Dr. Hoffman had left two days prior, thank heavens, but the stress of his week-plus stay at the Sweet Island Inn—and all the other horrors that had accompanied him—were still wreaking havoc on her sanity. She felt frazzled in a soul-deep kind of way. Little things made her jump—plates clicking too hard, an unexpected laugh from the table behind her. She tried to smile her way through it. She'd spent her whole life doing just that, after all. But sometimes smiling through it wasn't enough. She needed something else to calm her down. Something more.

She needed Dominic.

She had neither seen nor heard from him since he left. That in itself was hard on her heart. She thought perhaps he'd call. He wasn't a texter—"the written word deserves better," was his concise summary judgment of the whole concept of text messaging. But a phone call or a postcard would have put such a smile on her face. If only. That would've been nice.

Of more concern was the fact that he had said he would be gone for six weeks, but they were nearing eight weeks since his departure and he still had not reappeared. Was something wrong? A car accident, a heart attack, one more cruel twist of fate thrown in Mae's face? If something had happened, would she ever even find out about it? Who would think to call her—his innkeeper? What even *was* she to him? "A treasured friend." They'd said that to each other before. Maybe the news of some unspeakable tragedy would eventually wind its way to her. But she had no choice but to sit and wait.

Sitting and waiting was the worst.

Mae had enjoyed the last of her dinner alone. She had checked in on Holly's table a few minutes before Brent had left. Her middle daughter seemed awfully flustered. Mae suspected it had something to do with the couple she and Pete were dining with. The man appeared friendly enough—he certainly laughed loudly, though— but the woman he was with had a tight, puckered face like she had just tasted something quite sour. Mae was never one to judge a book by its cover, but something about that woman unsettled her.

Sara, too, seemed to have problems swirling beneath the surface, though it could have easily just been the stress of opening night. Mae didn't know much about restaurants, but to her eyes, this had been a resounding success. The room was filled with the "mm" and "ahh" of satisfied diners. The food looked gorgeous; the décor was fabulous. She was so proud of her daughter. Sara, though, did not seem quite as pleased. Mae would have to find out later what was troubling her girls.

All of her children, actually. Brent, Holly, and Sara all looked to be so disturbed this evening. It was as though the storm had brought bad vibes washing over this little island. Her mind went out to Eliza. She hoped her eldest was happy. *That* had been quite the doozy of a phone call to receive. She and Oliver had made up, apparently, and gone flying off to Bermuda, of all places. And something about a proposal ... It all sounded very exciting, but they hadn't had much time for conversation.

The world was just moving so fast these days. Mae wanted to close her eyes and pause everything for a moment. She missed the slow pace of her life from years ago. She had always known that her children would grow up and live rich lives of their own, full of drama, triumph, tragedy. But it was one thing to know that and quite another thing entirely to see it firsthand. There was also the fact that her steadying rock was no longer with her. She was alone, or so it felt.

And she just felt so tired.

When Sara came back around again, Mae beckoned her over for just a moment. "I think I'll go home now," she said. "I'm feeling so tired all the sudden. Do you mind having one of your staff call a taxi for me?"

"Of course, Mom," Sara said.

She looked concerned, but Mae waved her off. "I'm fine, dear. Just sleepy, that's all." Fortunately, there were no guests booked at the inn tonight. Mae would be able to rest easily. She might even sleep in! Oh, who was she kidding—that was never going to happen. But the thought was reassuring in its own strange way.

A few minutes later, Cassandra, the hostess, came over and guided Mae to the taxi. Mae thanked her profusely. She was such a nice girl. Mae was really very fond of all the staff Sara had chosen.

The taxi brought her home to the Sweet Island Inn. She paid the driver and thanked him. But when she went inside and hit the light switch, nothing happened. Mae frowned. She went and checked the circuit breaker in the basement and found to her surprise that the power was out. "Oh, goodness me," she mumbled under her breath. The storm must have knocked a tree into a power line or something like that. What fortuitous timing that Dr. Hoffman was gone. He would've had a field day with this latest complication.

Mae lit a candle and carried it up to her bedroom. She brushed her teeth and washed her face by the light of the quiet, flickering flame. Outside, she heard the rain slow down. By the time she was ready for bed, it had stopped altogether. What a miraculous sound that was! All week long, the rain had devastated the island. She had come to accept the sound of raindrops crashing into the roof as a permanent fixture in her life.

Now, it was gone. The clouds broke apart faster than expected, leaving slats of moonlight shining down. One came in through the space between her curtains, casting a soft white light throughout the room.

Mae blew out the candle and laid down to go to sleep.

But sleep would not come.

She tossed and turned for some time. She'd been so bone-deep exhausted at the restaurant. Now, when she could slip away into a happy slumber, it evaded her. She kept at it for at least an hour before she sat upright.

Perhaps she should go for a walk to calm her mind. The beach would be lovely now that the rain had stopped on her end of the island, and it was just a couple of blocks away. She always loved the sight of the moon over the midnight ocean. She pulled on a sweater and sweatpants, slipped her feet into her sneakers, and went quietly out of the house with a flashlight in hand.

Making her way through the dunes, she stepped out onto the wide expanse of the Nantucket beach. It was every bit as quiet as she expected, like the world hadn't yet realized that the rain was gone.

The moon was bright and clear, as were the stars. The only noise was the shush-shush-shush of the waves on the sand, and her own footsteps and breathing.

She settled down cross-legged. The sand was a bit wet, but she didn't mind. Its coolness felt good. She let the gentle breeze pass by as she exhaled.

She wanted so badly to stay here forever. But that choice might soon be taken from her. Any day now, Toni would call again with the news that the inn had been sold and it was time for Mae to begin again somewhere new. Mae was surprised that it hadn't happened already. She wondered what could be stalling that. Toni had sounded like she was on the verge of selling during that first call. Had she changed her mind? Well, best not to think like that. It wouldn't do Mae any good to get her hopes up, only to see them crushed again when the inevitable happened.

In a way, Mae understood Toni's desire. This place held only hurt for her after Henry's passing. Mae could never blame her sister-in-law for wanting to leave it in her past.

But for Mae, this beach, this island, this place ... this was home. It had embraced her, given her life and happiness and children and the gorgeous moon rising huge and luminescent over these beautiful waters. No matter what happened, she would find a way to stay here as long as she possibly could.

She belonged to Nantucket, and Nantucket belonged to her.

"I thought I might find you here," said a man's voice from behind her.

Mae nearly jumped out of her skin. She'd been so absorbed in her own thoughts that she hadn't heard him come up. As she turned and saw Dominic standing a few steps behind her, hands in his pockets and smiling, she had to blink a few times before she believed what she was seeing.

"Are you a ghost?" she asked.

Dominic laughed. "No, that fate has yet to befall me, though there is no telling what the future holds."

"I suppose that's a good thing," she said, with remarkable poise given how badly he'd scared her. "But you shouldn't go sneaking up on old ladies like that. You're liable to give someone a heart attack!"

"My apologies," he murmured, chastened.

"You're liable to give me a crick in my neck, too. Won't you come sit down instead of standing behind me like that?"

"As you wish." He came over and settled into a seat next to her. "What a gift has been given to you here."

She looked at him quizzically. "What do you mean?" Mae asked.

He swept a hand around to include everything that lay before them. "This is magnificent. Nature's finest work. She outdid herself when she shaped Nantucket."

It was Mae's turn to laugh. He was always waxing quixotic about the beauty of the island. Like on the sailboat before his sudden departure. He'd said something remarkably similar, actually. It made her smile. For such an introspective, even melancholy man, he had a cute trait of seeing the world through the fresh eyes of a child sometimes. "That's quite poetic, even for you, Dominic."

"I'm in a poetic frame of mind these days. I've been thinking quite a lot about the world and the things that make it up," he said.

"Now you've really lost me." She chuckled. "I'm just an old lady and an innkeeper."

He turned to look at her. His eyes were bright and inquisitive. "I didn't tell you why I left, did I?" he asked.

"No, I don't believe you did," she replied carefully.

He rubbed at his jaw uncomfortably. "I apologize for that. I was uncertain about the outcome of my trip, so I didn't want to sow false hope."

"Hope for what?"

"I overheard you," he mumbled like he was embarrassed. "I am quite sorry for that. It was never my intention to eavesdrop on you or anything of the sort."

Mae shivered despite the warmth of the night air. "Overheard what?"

"About the sale of the inn. Your sister-in-law."

She gasped, then stifled it. "Oh," was all she could say. Why did it feel like Dominic was keeping secrets? He'd been so open with her from the start. What had changed?

"And—I do hope you'll forgive me for this one day—I took it upon myself to see if there was something I could do about it."

Mae had no idea what he was talking about. "I'm sorry, I don't understand."

"I left to attend some meetings with my agent and sell the rights to my book," he explained. "That was the purpose of my excursion. It took quite some time—Hollywood types are as fickle as they come, I'm afraid. But ultimately, we were successful."

What this had to do with the inn and with Toni, Mae didn't know. But she stayed quiet and let him talk. It seemed like he had such a burden to get off his chest.

"I was fortunate to receive a generous offer. And I was likewise fortunate that I did overhear you that day, despite my guilt in doing so. Because, if you'll let me, Mae ... I'd like to buy the inn from your sister-in-law and gift it to you."

Mae's jaw fell open.

Dominic's eyes searched her face, looking for an answer. She knew what he was asking her. It wasn't just about the inn, or about Toni, or about Nantucket, even. It was about the two of them. He was saying, *Here I am. Will you accept me?*

The stars and the moon and the ocean and the night and the island all held their breath while Mae weighed the question in her heart. Somewhere out there, she thought she could sense Henry's smile, too. Urging her to live her life. To look forward. To move into the future, not stay mired in the past.

So, seated next to this foreigner on the beaches of Nantucket, Mae did just that.

She leaned forward and kissed Dominic.

And it felt right.

~

Get Book 3 in the Sweet Island Inn series, NO WEDDING LIKE NANTUCKET.
Click here to start reading!
(Or keep reading below to get a sneak preview.)

The wedding of the year versus the storm of the century. Who will win?

Things are finally looking up for the Benson family.

After a year of tough choices and big leaps of faith, it seems like love, success, and happiness are right in their grasp.

But with a wedding on the horizon and a successful new restaurant growing faster than anyone ever expected, everyone certainly has their hands full.

In fact, it's starting to cause problems.

Little cracks are appearing in the surface.

And the historic storm brewing offshore might turn those cracks into craters.

Can the Bensons and their loved ones band together in time to make this summer their best yet?

Or will jealousy and uncertainty spoil the big day?

Find out in NO WEDDING LIKE NANTUCKET.

Welcome back to another summer at Nantucket's Sweet Island Inn! It's the happiest time of the year, so sit down, stay awhile, and fall in love in the third volume of the heartwarming Sweet Island Inn series from author Grace Palmer.

Check it out now!

A beautiful Sunday morning in June. Seven days until Eliza's wedding.

MAE

These days, Mae Benson sometimes—not very often, but sometimes—slept in.

It was only on days when there were no guests at the Sweet Island Inn and no pressing chores to do. Only on days when she didn't have plans to meet a friend for brunch or volunteer at the pet shelter or the soup kitchen. Or if she'd stayed up late drinking a glass or two of wine on the front porch the night before.

So, not very often. But sometimes. And that alone was a world of difference from what she'd done for the first sixty-two years of her life.

As she entered year number sixty-three, a lot of things were different, actually. Mae was now the permanent co-owner and co-operator of the Sweet Island Inn, a beloved bed and breakfast on the beautiful island of Nantucket just off the coast of Cape Cod. She was a grandmother three times over. And she was beginning a new relationship.

"Beginning" was a heck of a word, though. As was "relationship." And "boyfriend," and "date," and "love," and all the myriad things that went along with falling for someone new at such an unexpected stage in her life. Just a few years ago, Mae would have thought that all those things had long since disappeared in the rear-view mirror. Oh, how wrong she had been!

Life came in circles, as it turned out. Seasons. And this was a beautiful springtime in her world, the kind where all the flower buds were just pushing their way up out of the topsoil. Things in Mae's universe were tender, blooming, and determined to reach the sunlight.

Speaking of sunlight, the rays coming through the blinds in the inn's master bedroom were letting her know that she had slept in plenty long enough. She rubbed the sleep from her eyes as she sat up and looked to her left. Her boyfriend, partner in crime, and fellow co-owner of the Sweet Island Inn, famed Irish novelist Dominic O'Kelley, was fast asleep next to her. Even unconscious, he looked the same as he always did—dapper, intelligent, reserved, with a soft smile playing across his lips.

She decided to be kind and let him sleep in for a little while longer. He'd been up late last night writing the first pages of his new novel. Staying as quiet as she could, Mae slipped out of the bedroom.

There were no guests at the inn today, nor would there be any for the rest of the week. It was closed for a special occasion: the wedding of Mae's oldest daughter, Eliza. Seven days from now, her firstborn would be standing on the altar, across from a man who had stolen her heart when she'd thought it was irretrievably broken. Just the thought of that moment made Mae smile.

With no guests requiring her attention, there was only herself and Dominic to take care of. Downstairs in the kitchen, she put on a kettle to heat water for the French press and found a yogurt in the fridge to quell the hunger in her belly. No guests—that was all well and good, but Mae did miss having them. She loved how far people traveled to stay under her roof and explore the island she called home. She considered it a privilege to be able to host them. It was a responsibility she took quite seriously—"her life's calling," she said whenever anyone asked. After all, Nantucket was beautiful. Paradise on earth. In her humble opinion, everyone ought to see it at some point in their lifetime.

When the kettle began to squeal, Mae poured it over the coffee grounds and set a timer to let the coffee steep. She looked around, twiddling her thumbs. It was so oddly silent with no one here. No squeaks from the floorboards upstairs, no children running underfoot. The only thing that moved were the leaves of a rosebush outside the kitchen window, stirred by the early June breeze.

It still made her head spin to think about how fast this inn had become home. Two years ago, she had been living a different life. Then she'd lost her husband, Henry, to a tragic boating accident. In the wake of his death, Mae had taken up her sister-in-law's offer to manage the Sweet Island Inn in her absence. She had made the transition here from the house on Howard Street, the one she'd raised her family in, the one that Henry had built with his bare hands. That was an abrupt change. But it felt like the inn was her home from the second her bags first hit the ground. Funny how that worked—how home could travel with a person, change shape and size and smell, but still feel much the same every time you walked in the door.

Dominic joked sometimes that she was like a hermit crab. She'd shed one home—albeit not quite by choice—and picked up another. The old home felt somehow foreign to her now, despite how many of her memories and how much of her DNA was bound up in its walls. So foreign, in fact, that she'd recently begun the process of selling it. That thought—getting rid of the house on Howard Street—would once have seemed laughable.

But it wasn't. Not anymore. The Sweet Island Inn was home now. The house on Howard Street was merely a building she once had loved.

Everything she loved now was here with her. This inn, its spirit, its guests, her boyfriend, the island of Nantucket as a whole.

"Good morning, Sleeping Beauty!" she chirped brightly as the boyfriend in question made his way sleepily downstairs. Dominic was wearing a muted gray cardigan and olive green slacks with house slippers on his feet. Mae loved teasing him about the slippers. "Such an old man affectation," she'd say. "As befits an old man," was his inevitable grinning reply.

He crossed from the bottom of the stairs to the kitchen, then let his fingers tap dance gently across the back of Mae's hand where it rested on the kitchen countertop. "What mischief are we getting into today?" he asked playfully.

"Mischief? You've got the wrong girl for that," Mae answered. "I'm far too old for mischief."

"That's where you're wrong, darling. Mischief is merely a state of mind."

"The state of *your* mind, maybe. My mind is in a state of hunger right now. Yogurt isn't quite going to do it today."

"Well then, you're in luck, Mae, my dear. Sit back, sip your coffee, and prepare to be amazed." He cracked his knuckles and his neck, still grinning all the while.

"Uh-oh," she tutted. "Don't tell me you're going to cook."

"Not only am I going to cook," he said, walking over to the refrigerator and rummaging around, "I'm going to cook you the world-famous Dominic O'Kelley Toast Extraordinaire."

Mae wrinkled her nose. She was trying to bite back her laugh—Lord knows Dominic didn't need the encouragement when he got going like this, with such pep in his step—but she wasn't doing such a good job of keeping her smile hidden from him.

"What makes it so extraordinary?" she asked.

"That is a secret I'll take to my grave," he answered gravely. "Now, shoo. I'm annexing this kitchen into my domain."

She laughed, shook her head, and walked away to fetch the newspaper from the stoop outside. It had been two years since Dominic first walked into her life. Two years of listening to that rolling Irish brogue, and yet she never tired of hearing how words came out of his lips, smooth like mossy pebbles in a riverbed. *Toast* wasn't just crisped-up bread when Dominic said it. It was something new, something special, something different.

But he was a terrible cook, so her expectations for the dish itself were quite low. She'd probably just have another yogurt when he wasn't looking. What he didn't know wouldn't kill him, right?

She chuckled under her breath as she opened the front door and stepped outside into the Nantucket June sun. It wasn't yet hot, but it would be, no doubt. The sun was making its way up the sky like an egg yolk sliding around in the pan. Clear blue sky, not a cloud in sight, and the not-so-distant murmur of waves sliding across the sand. Marvelous.

She eyed the mailbox at the end of the drive and had a quick internal debate about whether she ought to drag her tail down there to see if they'd received anything. She decided on a random whim that, if the bird feeder on the side of the house was empty, it was a sign she should go fetch the mail. Sticking her head around, she saw that it was in fact empty. Not a morsel to be seen.

"Drat!" she said to herself, laughing. Oh well. A little stretch of the legs on such a fine day wasn't exactly cruel and unusual punishment. She had a sneaking suspicion that one of the squirrels who lived in the pine tree in the neighbor's yard was responsible for emptying the bird feeder. Dominic, whose little writing nook upstairs looked out on the tree in question, had named the squirrels. He swore he could tell them all apart, but Mae was doubtful. Pistachio, Cashew, Pecan, Almond, and Walnut (all the members of the Nut family, according to Dominic) looked way too similar for that.

She kept an eye on the tree, looking for any Nuts who looked particularly well-fed, as she waltzed down to the mailbox. When she got there, she saw that it was bursting full. "Oh goodness," she sighed. Dominic's publisher must have forwarded all of his fan mail here. They got bundles of the stuff periodically. It always fell to Mae to force Dominic into a seat so he could respond to the letters. Left to his own devices, Dominic would've used them for wall insulation. *Typical man*, she bemoaned. *No sense of personal touch whatsoever.*

She hefted the bundle under one arm, newspaper under the other, and made her way back inside. The squirrels must be sleeping off their illicit snack. Lucky little critters. They'd catch her wrath if she saw them stealing from her feeder again.

She coughed as soon as she crossed the threshold back into the living room, finding it filled with acrid smoke. The fire alarm was going off, too. She waved a hand in front of her face, still coughing, and ran into the kitchen. Dominic was standing in the middle, flapping a dish towel frantically at the toaster, where all the smoke was coming from. When he saw that she'd returned, he froze and looked at her like a little kid caught doing something naughty.

"'World famous,' my behind!" she laughed. "Get out of my kitchen, you goon, before you burn the whole house down." She took the dish towel from his hand and swatted him on the bottom as he trudged sheepishly past her.

Typical man, she thought again. But he was *her* typical man.

That was marvelous, too.

~

ELIZA

No one had ever told Eliza Benson that wedding planning was so freaking difficult.

Actually, that wasn't true. Lots of people had told her. Just like lots of people had told her that motherhood was hard. She hadn't listened to that, either. Wrong on both counts, as it turned out. Wedding planning was hard. Motherhood was hard. She really ought to start listening to others' advice.

Lord, was she getting stubborn as she approached her mid-thirties! She was becoming more like her sister Sara. And, now that she thought about it, Sara was becoming more like her, too. Like a strange, Freaky Friday-esque switching of bodies and personalities. Sara the business owner? Eliza the headstrong? That was completely backwards.

And yet, it was the state of the world these days. Such is life, she had learned. *We grow, we change, we all turn into our parents.* It was both a blessing and a curse.

Speaking of parents, Mom was thriving these days. It made Eliza's heart sing to see her so happy with Dominic. It was still weird, of course, to see her mother in the arms of a man who wasn't her father. But Dominic was a good man; he loved Mom and he treated her well.

Happiness was by no means limited to Nantucket's Sweet Island Inn, either. Eliza's house was full of joy, full of her daughter's laughter and her fiancé's music.

After their spontaneous, preemptive, quasi-but-not-quite-honeymoon to Bermuda, the burgeoning Patterson family had come home to Nantucket brimming over with love. They were tan and they were all in love with each other. Eliza loved Oliver, Oliver loved Winter, Winter loved Eliza. Winter, coming up on eighteen months, loved lots of things, actually. She loved clapping and the song "Wheels on the Bus" and waddling around the house at breakneck speed. She had a little toy guitar that she played while Oliver made up words to songs, and when he picked her up and raced down the hallway with her, Winter squealed with that little girl laughter that instantly melted Eliza's heart.

As a matter of fact, that was what they were doing right this second. Oliver called the game "Rocket Ship." He made the sound effects to match as he zoomed up and down the hallway in his socks, sliding across the hardwood with Winter held out in front of him so she could feel the wind on her face.

"You know, some of us are trying to work!" Eliza hollered after him with a smile on her face. She was seated at the computer that lived in one corner of the living room, working out the kinks of a new set of Facebook ads for the Sweet Island Inn. Since Dominic's purchase of the inn from Aunt Toni, Eliza had been officially installed as the inn's business manager. Dominic had even ordered her business cards, which was both thoughtful and completely unnecessary. Honestly, the inn did all the work for her. Who could resist the allure of Nantucket in the sunshine? Beaches and lighthouses and quaint shops lining the cobblestone streets—*sign me up, please,* was the standard response. Eliza checked on the set of ads she'd pushed through this morning. There were already a few comments from potential customers.

OMG—how do i get here?? said one.

Heaven on earth, said another.

Eliza grinned. Well, they weren't wrong.

"Work, shmork!" Oliver shouted back as he *vroom-vroom-vroomed* back down towards Eliza. Winter was still cackling like a maniac.

"You better make sure she breathes," Eliza warned. "I can see all the blood rushing to her face already."

"This is literally the greatest moment of her life thus far," Oliver shot back as he got a running start and went skidding down the hallway once more. "Until tomorrow's session of Rocket Ship, that is."

She could only laugh and shake her head. She might be getting more stubborn these days, but she was no match for her fiancé. Oliver did what Oliver wanted, no matter the time or place. Luckily for her, what he usually wanted was to treat her like a queen and make her laugh. Sure, he got on Eliza's nerves every now and then, but what kind of couple lived a perfect life around the clock? She was far from perfect, and so was he. But their cracks lined up nicely.

A ding on the computer drew her attention as Oliver and Winter collapsed onto the living room carpet, giggling. Winter immediately crawled over to the toy bucket in the corner. She picked up her favorite toy—an oversized purple bubble wand—and handed it to Oliver. "Bub-bub!" she cajoled, clapping her hands together. "Bub-bub!"

Oh goodness. As if Eliza's heart hadn't melted enough already. She and Oliver might not be perfect, but Winter was an angel sent from the heavens above. Well, most of the time.

She watched as Oliver pretended to consider Winter's request. He was going to give in, of course—duh; he was a softie for their little girl —but they both held back laughter as Winter's eyes got big. She tugged on his wrist and said it again and again—"Bub-bub! Bub-bub!"—until he cracked a huge smile, unscrewed the wand, and started to fill the living room with huge, iridescent bubbles that drifted around in the lazy draft of the fan overhead. Winter stood stock-still in the middle of it all, reaching out one chubby little finger in wonderment. Every time a bubble popped near her, she jumped a little in surprise and giggled.

Another ding on the computer drew Eliza's attention. Turning back to the monitor, she saw that an email had come in. Oliver must've left his email account open. "Babe, you got an email," she called over.

"Check it for me," he replied. He looked occupied with trying to top his personal record for how many bubbles he could get going at once.

Shrugging, Eliza double-clicked the notification and pulled his email up. She read it, blinked, read it again. "That can't be right ..." she mumbled under her breath.

"Everything okay?" Oliver asked.

"Uh, yeah, all good," she said. "It's, uh ... just check later when you have time."

"Sure thing, babe." Scooping up Winter, he went to scrounge up some snacks in the pantry.

Eliza sagged back in the chair, brow furrowed. It wasn't like Oliver to keep secrets from her, but it seemed like she'd accidentally stumbled across just that. The email that had come in was from a job recruiting site. It said, "Your application has been accepted—please select an interview time below."

Oliver was looking for a job?

That was news to Eliza.

It had been an ongoing topic over the last year. An understandably confusing one. After everything that had happened during their short stint on the Fever Dreams tour the previous summer, Oliver's music career had taken a strange and unexpected twist. He'd done well while he was performing. Better than he'd ever expected, actually. That didn't surprise her. Everyone who had ever heard him sing and play the piano, even back in those days when he was just playing for tips at Nantucket bars, knew he was talented. But there's a difference between "talented" and "making it big." And it was awfully hard to say which side of that line Oliver fell on. Not because he wasn't good enough, but because the difference came down to luck. The guys who made it weren't always better than the guys who didn't. They just happened to be in the right place at the right time.

The question wasn't whether or not Oliver could make it. It was whether he could keep waiting until he did. Sooner or later, his lucky break would come. He knew that; she knew that. But what if it didn't come until a *lot* later? How long could he wait, playing at bars and private parties for the rich folks in 'Sconset, until the right person heard his song and decided to put him in the recording studio or on the radio or whatever? He had a family now—a fiancée and a little girl. They wanted to build a life together. He couldn't be in two places at once.

He had to choose.

And last year, it seemed like he had chosen *them*. He'd wavered, sure. He and Eliza had rehashed that plenty in the days and weeks since then. But every time they talked about it, he answered with firm resolve: he chose them. He chose his family. He chose his girls. He might not get fame, but he'd always be able to have them. Night after night, day after day, he reiterated that decision with every kiss, every wink, every game of Rocket Ship.

That, Eliza was learning, was real love. Waking up each morning and choosing your partner again. That was the hard part, the work of it all. Not a single day could pass without making that choice.

It wasn't easy. Not by any stretch of the imagination. Eliza knew that the cost of his choice still weighed on him, no matter how strong his conviction. He loved Eliza and Winter, yes, but he'd loved music first. He'd loved music since he was a little boy looking for somewhere to belong, and he'd wandered into the music room after school. Eliza adored that story. Every time Oliver told it, she closed her eyes and pictured a miniature Oliver—hair flopping over his face, shrunk down to four foot nothing, but with those green eyes shining exactly the same as they did now—stepping up warily to a piano, pressing a single key and hearing it ring out into the silence. In her mind's eye, she saw his face light up. *This is what I want,* he'd say. *This is the thing for me.*

She never, ever wanted to change him. But the fact remained that opening one door meant closing another. He wrestled with that nightly. And every time another email or call came in from a record label A&R scout, asking what he was working on these days and if he wanted to maybe do a show or two, she saw that it pained her fiancé to say no. To say, "I'm a family man now."

"Whoa!" came a sudden cry from the kitchen. "Liza, get in here!"

The shock interruption of her thoughts sent her heart leaping into her throat. Her brain immediately went to dark places. *Winter fell and got hurt. Oliver sliced his finger off chopping potatoes. There's a gas leak in the house; it's about to explode.* She raced into the kitchen, ready for the sight of blood and gore.

But it was just Oliver bent over the kitchen counter with the newspaper spread out in front of him. Winter was playing contentedly at his feet, babbling to herself. He glanced up at her as she came skidding in. His eyes were wide in surprise. He waved her over urgently.

"You scared me!" she snapped. "Don't do that!"

He chuckled and whistled low in surprise. "Trust me, babe. You're gonna want to see this."

Frowning, she walked around and looked over his shoulder to see the article in the business section he was pointing at.

Prominent Goldman Sachs VP Arrested, read the headline.

She gasped. "No way."

Clay Reeves, the Executive Vice President for Customer Relations of the Goldman Sachs Leveraged Finance Capital Markets group, was arrested today in a joint FBI-SEC sting on charges of embezzlement, wire fraud, and possession of Schedule I narcotics, the article began. *Sources say Reeves acted alone in appropriating several million dollars' worth of firm revenue into private offshore accounts. These illicit gains funded a lavish lifestyle, including the purchase and distribution of cocaine and methamphetamine, according to court documents obtained by investigators.*

Eliza couldn't believe what she was seeing. The article went into further detail describing Clay's crimes. But the gist of it was that her ex-fiancé was almost certainly going to jail for a very, very long time.

She looked up to Oliver, eyes wide. He whistled again. "That puts an end to that mess," he said quietly.

She knew exactly what he meant. "That mess" referred to the ugly underbelly of the last year—Clay's intermittent attempts to seize custody of her daughter. He'd had a lawyer send a nasty, threatening letter demanding visitation and a co-parenting arrangement in which Winter would spend time with both Eliza and her biological father. Eliza, with the help of her brother-in-law Pete, who was a lawyer, had fought off the advances as best as she could. Fortunately, Clay didn't seem to be too consistent with his threats, because he'd follow up one aggressive demand with months of radio silence before resurfacing.

Now, though, that disturbing saga was over. Clay was in jail. That meant no more threatening letters. No more custody battle.

It was over.

She put her arms around Oliver and her head against his chest. She fingered her engagement ring behind her back as she just breathed and relaxed in his embrace.

Things were going to be good from here on out. She just knew it. Her wedding was in seven days. Her soon-to-be-husband loved her and wanted to provide for her and their daughter. Her ex was no longer in the picture.

It was going to be a very good week indeed.

Who cared if wedding planning was hard? Who cared if motherhood was hard? This—this hug, this smell, this warm and beautiful moment—this would always be easy.

Click here to keep reading NO WEDDING LIKE NANTUCKET!

ALSO BY GRACE PALMER

Sweet Island Inn

No Home Like Nantucket (Book 1)

No Beach Like Nantucket (Book 2)

No Wedding Like Nantucket (Book 3)

No Love Like Nantucket (Book 4)

Willow Beach Inn

Just South of Paradise (Book 1)

Just South of Perfect (Book 2)

Just South of Sunrise (Book 3)

JOIN MY MAILING LIST!

Click the link below to join my mailing list and receive updates, freebies, release announcements, and more!

JOIN HERE:

https://readerlinks.com/l/1060002